HIS CURVY NURSE

A SMALL TOWN CURVY GIRL ROMANCE

BOOK BOYFRIENDS WANTED
BOOK SEVEN

MARY E THOMPSON

BluEyed Press

BOOK BOYFRIENDS WANTED

Welcome back, friend! Are you ready for this story? I sure am. I'm so happy you didn't miss it. You must be a subscriber. No? Join now. I'll wait.

Romancing the Curves comes with subscriber exclusive freebies, sneak peeks, and a first look at everything Mary has to offer. Be the first to know about new releases and sales and all the curves ahead!

SUBSCRIBE NOW AT MARYETHOMPSON.COM

Happy reading!

To anyone waiting for that best thing...I hope it's everything you hoped it would be and more.

LAURA

I stared at the man across from me and wondered how long I needed to stay there before I could leave without feeling like a complete bitch. He continued to drone on and on about himself and how smart and funny and wonderful he was. Seriously. Did the man not realize how boring and thoughtless he was being?

I nodded and sipped my wine, trying to give him the benefit of the doubt. Maybe he was nervous. I understood that. Dating sucked. I hated it. The only problem was I really liked men, so I had to suffer through the dating part. Life would be so much easier if I found that one guy who was perfect for me, but...

Nope, I wasn't going there.

I forced a smile as my date paused and waited for me to respond. I added a nod, and he smiled back like that was the only thing he was waiting for and kept talking.

Dear God, there wasn't enough wine in the world for a date like this one.

Our server approached and offered me a sympathetic smile. It was bad when the waitstaff looked like they were trying to come up with ways to extract me. Maybe I should fake an emergency.

Nope. That only spurred them on. I'd been there. One emergency, one uttered word of what I did for a living, and they all thought I was a saint. And they all wanted to bring a saint home to their mothers.

I was too damn old for that crap.

Brutal honesty would do the trick, but I *liked* this guy. I wanted to get along with him. Our chats online were good, great even. He was clever and funny and…not at all like the boring, self-absorbed man opposite me.

"I'm sorry, but are you catfishing me?" I blurted.

"Catfishing?" he asked. He slow-blinked as though trying to place the term.

"Yeah. One person online and another live. Pretending to be someone you're not. You just don't seem like the same guy I've been talking to."

He shook his head. "No, it's me. You've been talking to me."

"Hmm. Okay." I reached for my wine glass, and he jumped right back in where he left off.

Harry. His real name was Harry, not MoneyMan like he called himself online. He was in real estate. I wasn't even sure what that meant because he was not a real estate agent. He actually laughed when I asked. So, I let it go. But I had no idea what he actually did.

I tried to listen to him, but he was just so boring. With his equity and transactions and investments. My eyes could win Gold for all the rolls they did.

"More wine?" the server asked. She had another bottle in her hand. Bless her.

"Yes," I said before Harry could object. I didn't know if he would, but I wasn't taking any chances.

The server filled my glass up, nearly to the top. She winked at me and left the open bottle next to my plate.

"...equity..." I took a drink. "...investments..." Another drink. "...equity..." Hmm, maybe the conversation was interesting.

I snorted, which made Harry pause for two-point-seven seconds. I flashed him a brilliant smile that claimed I was invested—ha!—in whatever he was saying and he jumped back in.

And so did I.

I drank my wine and pretended to listen to Harry while we finished dinner. I offered to pay the check, or at least split it, but he insisted he pay. While Harry reviewed the receipt to make sure they didn't overcharge him for all the wine I drank, I texted Elise for a ride.

Did you make up another drinking game?

She knew me too well.

Yes. Best part of the date.

LOL. And ouch. Sorry. We'll be there soon.

Thanks.

I tucked my phone away as Harry handed over his credit card and the receipt.

"They didn't overcharge me. I wasn't sure since the waitress wasn't super attentive."

"Really? I thought she was great."

He snorted. "She barely asked if we needed anything. She wasn't around much. She would drop things off and leave."

"I don't think she could get a word in," I mumbled.

His head tilted to the side like a dopey dog who couldn't find the ball his owner never threw. Wow.

"So, are you going to follow me home or do you want me to follow you?"

"Why?" I was genuinely baffled that he thought I was up for anything beyond dinner.

"We just had dinner. It was expensive. You drank almost two bottles of wine. I assumed…"

"Wow." I took a minute to collect my thoughts before I laid into him. "Do you know what I do for a living? Do you know where I'm from? Do you know anything about me? You spent the last two hours talking about yourself. Two hours. Maybe if you'd asked even one thing about me I would be open to…No. No, actually, I wouldn't. This is our first date. I don't know you. I'm not sleeping with you."

"Seriously? Why date if you aren't going to have sex?"

I just sat there. He was why dating sucked so much. Men who thought they were entitled to a spot between my legs simply because they paid for dinner. Um, no.

"I'm dating because I'm looking for someone to spend my life with. Someone who cares about what's in my head as much as he cares about what's in my pants. If you're just here for sex, you should have said so and saved us both a few hours."

I stood up and walked out, hoping Elise and Colin got there before the server came back with Harry's card and he left.

I was almost to the door when the server hurried over to me. "Are you okay?"

I stopped and smiled at her. "I am. And I'm really sorry."

"Sorry? Why in the world would you be sorry?"

"He was rude and is probably going to give you a bad tip. Let me—" I reached into my purse.

"No, please. It's not a big deal. I just wanted to make sure you're okay. Do you have a ride?" Her brown eyes were kind and concerned, more than my date's had been all night.

I nodded. "Friends are on the way."

"Are they here yet?"

I glanced at my phone. "I don't think so."

"I'm going to walk out with you. The owner is really big on safety. I'll wait with you until your ride comes and then I'll give him back his card so you don't have to worry about him coming after you."

I sighed. "Thank you. You're awesome. Seriously, Jane, can I give you a tip? He's going to stiff you."

She shook her head. "I've already told my manager, who told the owner. He's agreed to cover what my tip should be if it isn't that. I'm good."

My phone buzzed in my hand. I glanced down at it. "My friends are here."

"Okay, good. Be careful."

"Thank you. I don't think he's violent, but I also didn't think he would expect sex on the first date, so be careful."

"I will. Enjoy the rest of your night."

"You, too." On impulse I hugged her then ran out to find Colin and Elise. Elise took my keys and drove my car home while I told her all about my date with Horrible Harry.

Ugh. Men.

I WAS SO ready to get back to work Monday morning. When I was working, all my focus went into my job. I didn't worry about the world outside the four walls of MacKellar Cove Cancer Care. I was zeroed in on my job and the patients I was treating and I didn't have to think about dating or relationships or the fact that my chance of having kids was shrinking faster than the tumors in our craziest success stories.

I pushed all thoughts about my dating life from my mind when I arrived at work. In the lounge, I put my purse in my locker and swept my unruly blonde waves into a ponytail and smoothed a hand over my scrubs. Dr. Allison didn't require them, but they were comfortable. Plus, the ones I wore had a bunch of cute saying on them and gave me something to talk to the patients about.

"Hey, Laura," Ally said from behind me. "How was your weekend?"

I shrugged. "It was okay."

"That doesn't sound promising. I thought you had a few dates lined up."

I nodded and added lip balm then closed my locker. "I had three, but blah."

"Sorry. You'll find someone."

I smiled at her perfection and asked, "How was your weekend? Did you guys do anything fun?"

Ally married her high school sweetheart two years earlier. They were adorable in a way that made it impossible to hate them even though I wanted to on principle. Her husband worked at the local grocery store, like he had since high school. They were both painfully sweet and the most positive people I'd ever met in my life. They were perfect for each other.

"We went to the movies then had dinner with my sister. I should introduce you two. She's single, too. You can go out together or be each other's wingwomen," Ally said with a nudge.

I smiled and shook my head. "We'll see." Ally was constantly encouraging me to widen my circle. It was funny coming from a woman who spent all her time with her family and didn't seem to have a lot of friends herself.

"I think you both could use it," Ally continued. "My sister is fine, but she's a little…distant. And you're so friendly and outgoing. I think the two of you would compliment each other well. I mean, I guess I don't know either of you all that well, but I think it's important to have people in your life who matter."

"I do," I told her, trying to ease the blow while not asking how she doesn't know her own sister. "I have a group of friends, and they're amazing. I would love to find someone like Spencer is for you, but I just don't have the best of luck with men."

"Ahem."

I looked up at Dr. Allison standing in the door. My cheeks heated under his glare.

"Good morning, Dr. Allison," Ally said brightly. "How was your weekend in Syracuse?"

Syracuse. Where his girlfriend or fling or whoever she was lived. Yes, I was jealous.

"Fine," he said, still glaring at me. "We have a new patient in the waiting room. Are you going to go get her?"

Ally slipped out of the room around him, leaving us alone. I tried not to drink the man in, but he was impossible to ignore, and impossible for me to resist. His dark brown skin glowed in the soft lighting. His near-black eyes blazed into me. The stretch of his suit across his broad shoulders and chest made me want to burrow in and never let go. I'd never seen him in anything other than the suit he wore daily, but I could imagine, and had, what he was hiding beneath those clothes.

"Nurse Kempis," he said louder, breaking my reverie. "The patient?"

"Ah, yes, Dr. Allison. I'm on my way now."

He didn't move as I walked toward him, his eyes locked

on mine until I was standing next to him. He stared at me, that same irritated look he always had lately.

"Excuse me," I said softly. I wasn't tiny like Ally. I was a big woman with a lot of curves. And he was a big man. Standing next to him, the top of my head reached his chin. His stubborn, hard, bearded chin. I wanted to trail my fingertips over it. Lick him. Press him against the wall behind him and run my hands through his dark hair and find out if it was as soft as it looked.

But he just turned and walked out, ignoring me yet again.

I sighed and tried not to take it personally. I was an employee, and that meant I was only there to serve him and his patients. Time to get to it.

"What does this mean, Dr. Allison?" Marie Kaufman had been referred to our clinic by her family physician. She lived 30 minutes north of MacKellar Cove and was young, mid-twenties, and alone.

Dr. Allison wheeled his stool close to Marie. Her legs were crossed and her hands were wrapped around each other. It would all change when he did. Dr. Allison was about to become Nico. Dr. Allison was strong and smart and tough, but Nico overflowed with compassion and understanding and kindness. He had an uncanny way of making the patients feel as though there was nothing he couldn't do, and in the four years I'd been there, I knew it was the truth. The treatments weren't always successful, but we did everything possible to give every single patient the best possible chance at a good outcome. And the man who made that happen wasn't the cold, distant Dr. Allison. It was Nico.

Nico was the reason I moved to MacKellar Cove four years ago. I was drawn to him when I first heard about

MacKellar Cove Cancer Care. The work he was doing amazed and inspired me. The man himself amazed and inspired me.

It wasn't long after I arrived that my infatuation with Dr. Allison's skill set became an infatuation with more than just the work he did. Seeing him become Nico over and over again was what made me fall for him. Dr. Allison could be an ass, but Nico…Nico was everything I wanted a man to be.

"Marie, I know this is terrifying for you. I'm not going to tell you not to worry. Cancer is an ugly beast. It's the kind of thing that fights like hell to destroy you. But we're going to fight, too. Nurse Kempis and I are going to make a plan for you. We're going to look at every option. I'm going to call colleagues and make sure we haven't missed anything. We are not writing you off. We have a very high success rate, and I have every confidence that you will be another one of those successes. This will not be easy. You will need people to help you. But we will be a part of that team."

Marie nodded and chewed her lip. Her hands no longer twisted together.

Nico leaned back in his seat and dug a card out of his pocket. "This is my personal phone number. I don't give this out to everyone, but I want you to have it. You can call me anytime. You are not alone."

She smiled up at him and took the card as tears ran down her cheeks. "Thank you, Dr. Allison."

He nodded and gave her a smile that made it seem like a date instead of a doctor's appointment. "We will do everything in our power to beat this, Marie. This is not the end of your story."

Marie nodded. I struggled to pull myself together, but I stuffed down my emotions so she could have hers. She was more important than me, and I knew it. I also knew if Nico was giving her his personal phone number, it meant things were going to be tough for Marie. She was going to have more bad days than good. She was going to need support. And he was willing to give it to her.

Once Nico left, I went through the next steps with Marie and asked her if there was anything else she needed from us before she left.

"Can I ask you something?" She looked up at me like I had all the answers.

"Of course."

"Does he really give his number to everyone?"

I shook my head. "No. He doesn't. I don't even have his personal number. He's a very private man, and he only gives his number to patients he has a connection with. Patients he knows are special."

"Really?"

I nodded. "Yeah. You're in excellent hands."

"Thank you. All this is a little overwhelming. I thought my family doctor was joking when she said I needed to come here. I never thought..." She sucked in a shaky breath.

I patted her shoulder and squeezed it gently. "No one does. That's one of the things that makes cancer so horrible. It comes out of nowhere. People who seem perfectly healthy, people who think they know why they're sick, and even people who know there's a high chance for it are all shocked. Cancer doesn't care who you are. But Dr. Allison is the best in the area, and he's going to do everything he can to bring you through this."

Marie smiled. "Thank you. I really...thank you."

"You're welcome. We'll see you soon."

I walked Marie to the front and told Tina at reception she needed to come back at the end of the week for her first infusion appointment.

I grabbed a quick lunch then was onto infusion appointments for the afternoon. My first patient was a single father whose parents smoked when he was young. At forty-four, Lucas was fighting lung cancer, a battle I knew all too well.

"You're looking good today, Laura," he said once he was seated in his chair.

"And you're as charming as ever. How are the girls?"

Lucas chuckled the way he always did when I asked about his three daughters. They were everything to him. His oldest was in her first year of college but stayed home to go to a local school so she could help with her sisters in high school and middle school.

"Carly reminds me of her mother every day. She's running the show. She keeps everyone in line and tells us what we need to do. And as the youngest, her sisters don't really love that," Lucas said.

I laughed with him and tied my gown. I adjusted my mask and opened my kit. "We all need someone like that in our lives. Someone to keep us in line."

"She's it for me," Lucas said, turning his head away while I accessed his chemo port. He winced then sucked in a breath and relaxed.

I tested the access and taped the needle in place. "I have a friend like that. She's a doctor, fertility specialist. She runs her business like a commanding officer, and her house is about the same. She's a badass."

Lucas chuckled and nodded. "Sounds like Carly."

"How about the older two? How are they doing?"

I worked while Lucas told me his oldest kicked ass in her first year of college and the middle one was starting to think about what she wanted to do after high school. By the time he was done, he'd taken his pills and his first dose of chemo was running in.

"I can barely keep up with myself. I don't know how you handle three girls."

Lucas chuckled. "Most of the time, they're handling me. The latest is they want me to start dating."

"Oh, no. That's dangerous."

He laughed. "Right? I told them I'm not interested, but I don't know. It's been six years since my wife died. The girls were six, nine, and thirteen. I've been buried in raising them and never thought about anything else. But all this..." He gestured to the room we were in, a room with nine other chairs with people receiving treatment. "Life's too short to let it just pass me by."

"That's very true," I said. I patted his arm. "My friend designed a dating app, Book Boyfriends Wanted. You should check it out. Even if you don't find someone else, dating and meeting new people can be fun. Your girls are getting older, and when they're all moved out, you might want a friend if nothing else."

"A friend with benefits?" He waggled his brows.

I laughed and shook my head. "You are trouble, Lucas."

"But you love me anyway," he said.

I nodded. "You know I do. I need to update your chart and get my next patient. I'll be back to check on you in a few minutes."

Lucas nodded and closed his eyes as I stood. He usually took a nap during part of his treatment. Most patients did. The meds they took were powerful and knocked them out, so we kept the room quiet with soft music on to muffle any conversation that might distract them.

"Nurse Kempis. A word," Dr. Allison said as soon as I turned away from Lucas.

My heart pounded in my chest and my pulse skipped. He was not happy with me, but I had no clue why.

I nodded and said, "Give me just a moment."

He raised an angry brow and crossed his arms, glaring at

me while I trashed my protective gear. I made a quick note to update Lucas's chart, then followed Dr. Allison to his office.

"Close the door."

I did as he asked and stood just inside while he walked around his dark wood desk and sat in the large black leather chair. Bookshelves surrounded him and his degrees hung above his head. His office could have been that of a college professor or a lawyer or anyone professional. There was nothing that said who he was. No pictures, no paintings, no indication of a personality.

"Why were you flirting with that patient?"

"Excuse me?" I blurted.

"The patient," he snarled. "Were you going to give him a lap dance, too? Because we might be a full service clinic here, but I expect you to keep things professional."

I drew back and tried to figure out what I did that was so unprofessional. "I apologize, Dr. Allison, but I wasn't treating him any differently than I do any other patient. And I believe I was being very professional."

"Oh, so you tell all your patients about dating apps and offer to be their friend with benefits?"

"What? I didn't say that!"

"You said you love him."

I drew in a deep breath and slowly let it out before my attitude got me in trouble. How dare he? I was not out of line with my patients. I was respectful and considerate. I asked about their lives and made small talk. I never once crossed a line. I did not give out my personal phone number to any of them. Not since Ms. Georgia. But that was different.

"I love my patients, Dr. Allison. I love working here. I love seeing people get better. And you know a positive mindset is huge when someone is going through what every single one of these patients is going through. I talk to them and laugh with them and ask about their personal lives. I need to know who these people are so they trust me."

"No, you don't. They need to trust you because you're good at your job, but today…"

"What are you saying?" I asked him, flabbergasted.

"Twice today I've had to speak to you about personal matters in the workplace. Twice today I've overheard you speaking to someone about your…relationships. Do not let it happen again."

"Are you telling me I can't ask my patients about their personal lives?"

"No, I'm telling you you can't fuck them!" he bellowed.

I froze. I was paralyzed with fury. I'd never been so pissed off in my life. I wanted to walk across the room and punch him. It took everything in me not to.

Four years I'd worked for that man. Four years I'd killed myself to follow his lead and treat the patients who came from all over to see him. Four years. And he thought I was using the clinic as my own personal brothel.

I shoved down the anger and pain and *fuck you*.

"Yes, sir," I said with a sharp nod. "Is there anything else?"

He shook his head.

I pursed my lips together and turned and left his office. What did I ever see in that asshole?

2

NICO

Fucking hell. I closed my eyes and took a breath for the first time since I walked in and saw her flirting with the patient. A fucking patient. Red. It was all fucking red.

Lighting into her…I couldn't stop myself. As soon as the words were out, I knew I said the wrong thing. What the hell was I thinking exposing that much? I thought for sure she would call me out, but she didn't. She just about crumbled. I wanted to reach for her. To comfort her. To hold her. Thank fuck my desk was between us or I might have done it. But then her face, that beautiful, heart-shaped face that I saw in my every fantasy, it turned again. To anger. Hatred. And that turned me on even more.

Except for the fact that those emotions were directed at me.

I thought about chasing her down, but what was the point? I didn't want her fucking the patients. I didn't want her fucking anyone. And after overhearing about her dates over the weekend, for months, and then listening to her flirt with a patient, I lost it.

I took a deep breath and thought about calling for an emergency session with my therapist, but I could handle it. Usually I talked to her about work, but lately I'd been sharing more and more about Laura. She was becoming more of an issue for me, and it needed to stop.

I turned my thoughts to other things, like another new patient I had coming in shortly, and managed to push Laura from my mind. I took a deep breath and focused on work. I had to compartmentalize. I was an expert at it, and it came in handy now.

The consultation went well. The patient was understandably upset, but she was joking and talking instead of crying. She was ready to fight, and she had the support system in place to do it. She would be one of my success stories.

I spent the rest of my day catching up on paperwork and meeting with the remaining clients. My schedule was getting busier than I could handle and I really needed to put plans in place to hire another doctor. That also meant finally going through with the plans I had to remodel the second floor of the building into a dedicated infusion center.

The Margaret Allison Memorial Clinic.

My mother would have adored Laura. Laura was exactly the kind of woman my mother wanted me to find. Kind, compassionate, tough. She also would have loved that Laura didn't fit the definition of conventional beauty, although I couldn't fathom why. She was stunning. Her curves, her smile, her long blonde hair that begged for my fingers to run through it.

I cleared my throat and adjusted myself. I couldn't let my mind wander when I was still at work.

"I'm heading home, Dr. Allison," Ally said with a knock on my open door. "Is there anything you need before I go?"

I shook my head. "No, Ally. I'm all set. Is everyone else gone?"

She nodded. "I think so. I haven't seen anyone. I was just getting the paperwork ready for tomorrow. It's another busy day."

"Unfortunately, yes. Cancer doesn't stop."

She smiled sadly. "We're all lucky you're willing to fight it. Have a good night."

"You, too. See you tomorrow, Ally."

"Bye."

I waited until I heard the solid metal door swing closed behind Ally to get up from my desk. I walked through the offices and made sure the place was empty, then I turned off the lights and headed upstairs.

The open space echoed with my footsteps. Ceiling panels dangled from the spots they should have filled. Wires snaked across the vinyl flooring. Overturned chairs and broken desks were scattered around haphazardly, as though tossed there in a fight.

The abandoned office space had seen better days. There were times I thought the entire town had. I loved MacKellar Cove, but it was a little rough around the edges. A little worn in, or worn out depending on how you looked at it. I never felt like I fit in, but I couldn't bring myself to leave.

I heard my mother's laugh in my head. She was always laughing, up until the end. She told me I didn't fit in because I never gave others a chance. I told her it was because no one wanted to get to know me. She would have chastised me for the way I treated Laura, for embarrassing her. She would have said it was proving her point. Maybe it was. Maybe I wasn't fair to her. But I couldn't help it.

From the first day she showed up in my clinic, she captivated me. So much so that I could barely speak to her. She was stunning. And the way she treated patients, even before her training was complete, made me wonder who she'd lost that she understood their pain so acutely.

Ally told me more about Laura than Laura ever did. Laura's mom died of lung cancer when she was younger. She knew the pain the patients felt. And she knew the pain their caregivers felt. It was a unique skill set. One I wish didn't exist.

I walked through the space and laid it out in my head. Three times as many beds for infusion. Four private rooms for patients who needed spinal access or couldn't sit upright in a chair. I wanted to add large windows along the west wall so patients could look out over the water while they received treatment. Something beautiful so they weren't left feeling trapped.

I finally had the money to do it all and was putting it into motion. I hadn't told a single person about it except Veronica. She knew everything about me, but that was her job as my therapist. She helped me see things I couldn't see, and one of those things was that not doing this meant I was holding myself back. I needed a new challenge, a new goal. Something to keep my mind off all the things I was missing in my life.

Like a woman to share it with.

I took a deep breath and closed my eyes once more. I could see it, and I held on to that vision as I left the office and went home for the night. Alone, as always.

I'D COME to dread Thursday as much as Monday, but this Thursday was especially painful. Laura wasn't speaking to me, not that I blamed her. She wasn't even speaking around me. When I walked in the room or even near, she closed her mouth. I missed the sound of her voice. The sound of her laugh.

She was working with me for the afternoon. Each nurse

saw patients with me one morning and one afternoon every week. They handled infusion of those same patients so their care was consistent. It worked for me, until I had to spend the time with her. Then it was torture.

My morning went by quickly with a few new patients and a few who were done with treatment. That was the cycle. We had patients at every stage along the way. It was always good to see some move on, but there was never a shortage of more waiting to start.

I ate lunch in my office, grabbing a frozen meal from the mini freezer below my desk. It burned my mouth when I took the first bite, and the second was barely warm enough to not be frozen. I hated the things, but I didn't take time to cook most days so I suffered through them. Another thing my mother would chastise me for if she were around.

The alarm on my phone went off and I used my private bathroom and brushed my teeth, then went to the exam room to see our first patient of the afternoon.

"Good afternoon, Robert," I said as I walked into the room. "How are you today?"

"Feeling good, Dr. Allison. Hoping for some good news."

I nodded and accepted the tablet from Laura. Our fingers brushed when she handed it over. A jolt of awareness burst through me, but she pulled back so quickly we almost dropped the device. I scowled and righted it, clearing my throat before I turned the screen to face Robert.

"This was your last scan. We talked about it a few months ago. We weren't sure what kind of improvement we would see in the first two rounds, but this…" I flipped to the second picture, "is your newest scan."

Robert looked up at me with tears in his eyes. "That's good, right? It looks good, but I don't really know how to read these."

"It's very good, Robert. The treatment is working. Nurse Kempis is taking excellent care of you."

"Thank you, Dr. Allison. And you, Laura. Thank you so much."

"Of course. Now, we'll keep you on the same treatment plan and keep going. We'll do another scan in two more months. I'm very happy with how things are going, though. How have you been feeling?"

"Good. As good as can be expected. I'm tired the day of treatment and I have a rough day on day three, usually. My wife is always trying to make me rest, but I feel the need to move. We go for walks every day just so we can get some fresh air."

"That's always a good thing to do. Jump up here and let me do a quick exam and then we'll get you on your way. Laura will get you set up with your appointments for the next month. I'll see you soon."

Robert laid back on the exam table and followed my instructions. When he was done, Laura picked the tablet up again and held it in front of her chest like armor. She didn't look at me. I wasn't surprised.

The rest of the day went pretty much the same. She handed me the tablet when I needed it, but practically threw it at me so our hands didn't touch again. As the day wore on, so did my patience. By the time our last patient was walking out, I couldn't hold back another second.

"Can I speak to you, please?" I asked, my voice letting her know it was not a request.

She looked up at me, her eyes narrowed and angry. She nodded once, still not speaking.

I walked into my office and stood behind my chair. She closed the door and stayed directly in front of it, barely inside the space I spent most of my time in. She stared at me, waiting for me to speak first.

"I would like to apologize for the way I spoke to you the other day."

She continued to glare at me.

"Are you going to say anything?"

"Was that your apology?" she asked.

"You realize I'm your boss, right? And that I could fire you for insubordination?"

She stiffened and straightened. "I apologize. I will go back to refraining from speaking so I don't say anything inappropriate again."

"Dammit, Laura, that's not what I want!"

She simply stared at me.

"Fuck. I'm screwing this all up. I'm sorry for the way I spoke to you the other day. And I'm sorry for making you feel as though you can't speak freely. That was never my intention."

Again, she just stared.

"Do you have anything to say?"

"No, sir."

I growled. "I'm not a dictator."

"Just the first part," she mumbled, low, but loud enough that I could hear her.

I raised an eyebrow and she had the decency to look ashamed. Her cheeks pinked and the flush sank to her neck and below her scrub top. Her breasts rose with the sharp intake of her breath. My cock rose at the imaginary sight of her nipples pressing against her clothes.

Too bad I couldn't actually see them. And I never would.

"Have a good evening, Nurse Kempis."

She nodded and left my office in a hurry. She probably figured I'd fire her, but then I wouldn't see her anymore. I could handle her hating me better than I could handle her not being in my life.

The only thing I couldn't handle was her with another man.

"HOW MANY DATES do you have this weekend?" Ally asked.

I was on my way past the break room and would have kept going, except I heard Laura's voice. It had been another day without her speaking to me, and I was desperate for anything I could get from her.

"Three, maybe four. I have been talking to this one guy who said something about meeting up, but we haven't set a date yet."

Her casual tone tried to have me believe these dates were no big deal, but this was Laura. My Laura. And she was going out with other men. Men who weren't me.

"Three or four?" Liz said. "Where do you meet all of them? When I was single, I was lucky to find one guy to go out with."

"Book Boyfriends Wanted," Laura said simply, like that explained everything.

"The app? Seriously?" Bonnie asked.

"Yep. There are definitely a lot of duds on there, but I've met some that were sweet enough that I keep trying. It's a numbers game. I'm too old to wait forever for a relationship. I love my work and I love my friends, but I'd love to have an orgasm that involved another person once in a while."

I choked on my breath. I could hear the panic in the break room at being overheard, and I could feel the tension from Laura. I needed to get the hell out of there before someone walked out and saw me standing there like a creep.

I turned the corner and went into an exam room. I had no reason to be in there, but it didn't matter. I could not look Laura in the eye after what I just heard. Not without offering to give her all the orgasms she wanted. She didn't need to try online dating. She just needed to drop her pants for me and I'd make sure she never had to touch herself again.

My head spun with need. My cock was so hard I was sure it was going to split my zipper. Even my lab coat did nothing to hide the bulge tenting my pants. I just needed to wait until everyone was gone so I didn't have to face them for a few days.

Not that it would make the desire go away.

"I don't know where he is. Usually he's in his office by now," Ally said. Her voice was right outside the door. "I always check in with him. There's no way he left already."

I slowed my breathing so they didn't hear me. Maybe they would just leave.

"Let me text him. Make sure everything is okay," Ally said.

I scrambled to dig my phone out of my pocket and made sure it was still on silent. I never turned the ringer on in case I got a call when I was with a patient, but I still checked. It buzzed in my hand a second later.

> I'm heading out for the day. Is there anything else you need before I go?

> I'm good. Thanks. Have a nice weekend.

> You too.

"He said he's good. I still don't know where he is, but he replied so at least we know he's okay. Let's go grab that drink. You can advise us all on how to snag dates," Ally said.

"You don't need a date. You're married," Laura argued.

"Yeah, but it never hurts to have ideas for dates with my husband. After all…"

Their voices faded as they walked away. I stayed hidden

until the back door slammed closed behind them and I knew I was alone.

"Fucking hell," I breathed.

I finally left the exam room and headed back to my office. I spent another hour going over patient records and reading reports of the chemo sessions from the day. My phone buzzed with an alert and I turned it over. An appointment reminder for a call with Veronica. She suggested we try phone calls instead of asking me to drive down to Syracuse when we had a session. I agreed to try it.

I added the meeting to my calendar on my work computer so Ally didn't schedule something else in that time slot and was about to put my phone away when I paused.

"Book Boyfriends Wanted," I said out loud as I typed in the words. I read through the reviews and was surprised by how many of them were positive. They raved about the ease of use, the success of matches, and the creativity of the app.

"Am I really signing up for a dating app?" I grumbled to myself.

I tapped Install and sighed. Yep.

It was official. I'd lost my damn mind. And it was all because of my beautiful, curvy, infuriating nurse.

What were the chances we'd end up matched? High, I hoped.

3

LAURA

"He's just such an ass." I rolled my eyes and groaned to hide the hurt.

"Did you really expect anything different?" Elise asked.

I was complaining to my friends about Nico. It had been on my mind since he spoke to me about the way I was with patients and I thought my friends would be on my side. I was wrong.

"You think I was acting like a whore?" I asked her.

Elise chuckled and shook her head. "No. Of course not. I know you, and I know you are friendly and affectionate and kind. You're the kind of person who puts others at ease. It's a part of why you're such an amazing nurse. But I can also see why Nico would be upset by it. He's not like that from what you've told me. He's stoic and almost rude."

"It's not that he's rude," Karissa broke in. "He's just not as warm as you are, Laura. And for someone like him who is always keeping work and home separate, he doesn't understand being friendly to someone if you aren't getting personal with them."

"All I did was recommend your app to a patient. I didn't give him my name and tell him to look me up," I argued.

"And even if you did, I don't think it would be wrong," Blake said. "I think the point is Nico will never understand who you are and why you do the things you do. Letting it stress you out and upset you will not make it better."

I sighed and leaned back in my seat. I tugged my hair from behind my back and tossed it over the edge of the chair. I looked around at my friends and their kind faces. I didn't know what I would do without them.

"You guys are right. He's an ass, and it's beyond time I move on. I'm too old to waste my time on people who don't want to be a part of my life."

"Aren't we all," Sofia said with a grin. She raised her plastic cup in salute, and I nodded.

"Have you had any dates lately? How are they going?" Trinity asked me.

"I had two this weekend. I was supposed to have three, but one blew me off. I thought another guy I've been talking to wanted to meet up, but it's been radio silence from him, too. Dating is hard," I declared.

Everyone laughed in agreement.

"I'm not open to dating right now," Finley said. "I'm happy to have a few minutes with a guy, but to actually sit down and have a conversation isn't in my plans."

"Is everything okay?" I asked.

Finley shrugged. "Mostly. I'm struggling a little with the store, and I'm not sleeping well. I don't have time to dedicate to dating. I've pulled back from the couple of guys I've been chatting with so I can focus on making sure these doors stay open."

"Why didn't you tell me?" Karissa asked. Karissa and Finley had lived together since before I moved to town. All of them were close, but Finley, Karissa, and Blake had been friends for years and were like sisters.

Finley shrugged. She looked at the floor, her brown hair hiding her face. "I don't want you to worry that I won't keep up my share of things. Or for any of you to feel like you need to do anything for me."

"It's not charity to ask your friends for ideas," Blake argued. She and Finley had been best friends for decades. After Blake married Ian, they actually became sisters. In-law, but close enough. "We all want to help. Maybe we can think of ways to advertise the store. Or you could offer other products. Book things. Not generic stuff, but products that a reader would love."

"I've thought about it, but I don't know. It's overwhelming. And we were talking about Laura's love life, not my work life. There's that balance Nico seems to have a handle on." Finley smiled, but it didn't reach her dark eyes. She was worried.

"I don't mind," I told her. "My love life will always be a disaster. This place is home for us. We need to do whatever we can to save it."

Finley shook her head and forced another smile. "We'll figure it out. How were the two dates you went on?"

I could tell she was trying to change the subject and went with it. "The dates were okay. I've chatted with both guys and they're nice enough, but they didn't inspire any I-need-you-now desire."

"Do we need that?" Sofia asked. "Passion is great, but is it necessary for a relationship?"

"I think so," Blake said. "When I was with William, he was nice enough, but the passion wasn't there. It was blah. Sex was always the same, our routine was always the same. I didn't know how different it could be until Ian and I got together, and then I wondered why in the world I spent so long with William."

"Is there something in between? I don't know if I can handle the emotional upheaval that comes with throw-you-against-the-wall-and-kiss-you passion, but boring sounds... boring. There's nothing in the middle?" Sofia asked.

"I think there are a lot of different degrees of passion, but it depends on what turns you on," Elise said. "I'm not a throw-me-against-the-wall kind of person. If Colin did that, I would walk out, and he knows that. But I love when he gets a look in his eyes and chases me through the house. We end up falling into bed laughing."

"Maybe that's why I don't date," Sofia said. "I don't want highly emotional, all-consuming relationships. I want something simple and predictable."

"Like Sebastian?" I asked her.

Sofia snorted and shook her blonde ponytail. "Not even a little bit. He's like a brother to me. We speak the same language, but I don't think of him that way. Plus, I don't think he's over Zoey. And if she moves here in a couple of months like she's talking about, Sebastian is going to fall apart."

"You care a lot about him," Trinity said with a grin.

Sofia shook her head again. "Not gonna happen, people."

"How do you know if a guy is going to inspire I-need-you-now kind of passion?" Karissa asked. "I've had that, but it built slowly over time. And it's been a while."

The rest of us laughed. Karissa's college boyfriend was almost legendary. We teased her about him not even being real and about her making him up since none of us knew him. Karissa was a quiet person. I couldn't think of the last time she'd dated anyone, even though she was the creator of Book Boyfriends Wanted, the dating app we all used.

"I have to meet a guy to know," I admitted. "I think some

people are really good in text, and some people are better in person, but I need to know both sides before I can decide."

"I agree with that," Sofia said. "I'm a better-in-text person. I need the time to think about what I'm going to say. I'm not quick on my feet."

"I'm the same," Blake said. "I have my moments, but I definitely prefer to think through my words. Ian isn't like that. He can come up with a reply to anything in an instant. I wish I had some of that talent."

Sofia laughed and nodded. "Me, too."

"I think I'm better in person," I admitted. "I can make people laugh and feel comfortable. At least, I think I can." They all nodded. "In writing, I reply too quickly sometimes, without thinking through my answers. Without tone and context, I can come across as mean instead of funny."

"Then they don't get you and aren't for you," Finley said.

"True."

"I think I want the passion you guys are talking about," Finley said. "I just don't have time for it right now. I don't have time for someone to throw me against the wall and make me forget everything else. I'd love for it to happen, but only if he can fit into my schedule."

The rest of us laughed.

"It's not easy being a strong, independent woman," Karissa said.

"I still think I'm independent," Blake said with a pout.

"You are," Karissa said. "I don't think being in a relationship makes you dependent. You and Ian complement each other. You work well together. But you can be apart from each other and still function. We are all strong, independent women."

"Hell, yes, we are," I agreed with her.

"But I still like to be thrown against the wall once in a while. Or chased. Or whatever," Blake said.

We all laughed and nodded.

Maybe one day I'd know what that felt like.

WHEN I GOT HOME that night, I realized I had a new match. It said the guy had only been on Book Boyfriends Wanted for two days and his screen name was a little off-putting, so I hesitated in accepting him, but I decided to say yes to the match.

I sent him a message to say hi, like I did with all my matches and was surprised when he replied right away.

DICTATOR

Hello, NoRegrets. I appreciate that sentiment.

NOREGRETS

Good to know. I'm not sure I can appreciate yours. I don't know if I can find the good in a dictator.

DICTATOR

It was the first thing that came to mind when I signed up. I've been accused of such.

NOREGRETS

And are you?

DICTATOR

I don't believe I am. I try to be kind and fair.

NOREGRETS

But...?

DICTATOR

LOL. You know how to dig. I like things to be a certain way. If they aren't, I tend to get frustrated.

NOREGRETS

I'm not sure online dating is a good idea for you. People usually lie about who they are.

DICTATOR

Are you lying? Your profile says you enjoy helping people and spending time with friends. Also that you know life is too short to not live it fully.

NOREGRETS

Not lies. All very true. But I'm not typical. I'm actually looking for something here. I'm not just here to find a fling.

DICTATOR

Is that what most people do?

NOREGRETS

Have you seriously never tried online dating?

DICTATOR

Nope. Am I in trouble?

NOREGRETS

LOL! You're in for a rude awakening. Unless you're one of the people who's lying. Then you probably know all this and are trying to hook me.

DICTATOR

Trust me. I'm not that smart.

NOREGRETS

I'm not sure I'm going to believe that. But you definitely need to figure out what you're looking for here. That will help you decide if you want someone like me who's going to talk for a while before I'm willing to meet, or someone who's going to meet on day one and never see you again.

DICTATOR

I think I prefer it your way. Sounds much
better to me.

NOREGRETS

Then tell me something you've never told
anyone else.

DICTATOR

Wow. You really do jump right in. Hmm, okay.
Well, most people who meet me don't like
me at first.

NOREGRETS

You really know how to sell yourself.

DICTATOR

Right? Hard to believe no one has snatched
me up yet.

NOREGRETS

Maybe your screen name is a good fit
for you.

DICTATOR

Ouch. And accurate.

NOREGRETS

LOL! Sorry. I'm just joking with you.

DICTATOR

I know. And thanks. I don't feel comfortable
around a lot of people.

NOREGRETS

Sounds like online dating is right for you. Do
you live in your mother's basement? Please
tell me you don't keep bottles of lotion for
people to rub on themselves.

DICTATOR

Ouch! Nope on both counts.

NOREGRETS

Phew. That's good.

DICTATOR

Tell me something about you. Something that makes you unique.

NOREGRETS

I put myself through college as a phone sex operator.

DICTATOR

You're joking, right?

NOREGRETS

Nope. The pay was fantastic and I needed the money. All it meant was sitting in a room and talking to whoever called. Usually they wanted to listen. I started reading a lot of romance novels to get ideas and actually ended up hooked on them. All true.

DICTATOR

That's...crazy smart. I wish I'd thought to do something like that.

NOREGRETS

It was weird at first, but I didn't mind it after a few tries. And they let me study when I wasn't on a call. It was one of the best jobs I've ever had.

DICTATOR

What about your job now? Do you still love it? Are you still a phone sex operator?

NOREGRETS

Not still an operator, but I do love my job. Most of it anyway. No job is perfect.

DICTATOR

That's very true.

NOREGRETS

> Speaking of which, I need to get some sleep.
> I start work early. But it was nice to talk
> to you.

DICTATOR

> You, too. I hope to talk again soon.

NOREGRETS

Definitely.

I signed out of the app with a smile. Maybe I should amend my earlier statements. Maybe it was possible to feel that spark before meeting someone. And maybe I just felt it.

I LET the conversation with Dictator play in my mind on my way to work. If nothing else, it would help me be less annoyed by Dr. Allison. I hoped.

I let myself in and went to the employee lounge. I stashed my things and headed out to review charts and start my day before he came looking for me. Especially since I still wasn't sure how much he overheard Friday before I left work. I expected another conversation with him about that.

"Hey, Laura," Ally said when I walked into the front office. "How was your weekend?"

"It was good. How about yours?"

"It was great. How were your dates?"

I glanced around for Dr. Allison. "They were okay. Nothing too memorable."

Ally scrunched up her nose. "Sorry about that. I'm rooting for you to find someone special."

"Thanks," I said. I tapped the screen on the tablet and went to the waiting room to get my first patient.

The morning went by quickly, which was good. I was

polite and kind with Dr. Allison, but I was not friendly toward him. Normally, I'd smile when he said something, but I wasn't in the mood. Maybe I was finally getting over him.

I ate my lunch quickly and had just enough time to run to the bathroom before my first infusion appointment.

I checked my phone as I walked out of the bathroom, hoping for a message from Dictator. I was not surprised to see he hadn't reached out, but I was a little disappointed. I tucked my phone away and turned to go to the waiting room when I ran smack into Dr. Allison.

"Nurse Kempis," he said firmly.

"Dr. Allison."

"Are you distracted by your phone?"

I shook my head and met his gaze. I would not be afraid of him or worry about what he thought of me. Not anymore. "No, I'm not."

"Are you sure? Because you didn't see me standing here because you were on your phone."

"I was checking for a message. And now, if you'll excuse me, I'm going to do my job."

I sidestepped around him and rolled my eyes as I walked away. I don't know why I never realized how much of an ass he was.

I called Damien back to the infusion center and got everything ready for him. I asked him how he was feeling, like I did with all my patients, before I got started.

"I'm okay, I guess."

"What's wrong? Does something hurt? Your labs were good."

He shook his head. "No. I'm...Do you remember Beth? My girlfriend who came with me to my last appointment?"

I nodded. She did not give me a warm reception when we met. Some women were like that, so I blew it off, but it didn't disappoint me that she wasn't back this time.

"Beth broke up with me yesterday."

"Oh, Damien, I'm so sorry," I said. I put my hand on his arm and smiled. "Are you okay?"

He shrugged. "I will be. I thought I knew her, but I obviously didn't. She said she didn't sign up to be with someone who's sick. She's not interested in being a caregiver."

I drew back and tried not to let my face show what I was thinking. I definitely failed.

Damien chuckled. "Yeah, that's pretty much how I feel. But I love her, you know, so I go back and forth between incensed like you are and wishing she would come back."

I drew a breath and got everything ready to start his infusion. It was the only thing I could do for him, and I needed to be busy so I didn't say something I shouldn't. He was a patient, not a friend.

"I'm sorry," I finally said.

He chuckled. "Thanks. I don't think I am. She showed me who she really is. I hate that I wasted two years with her. I have a ring. I was going to ask her in a few weeks, but then all this happened."

He turned his head while I accessed his port. He drew in a breath and let it out slowly.

"Last night, I found myself wishing I'd never gotten cancer. Not because cancer sucks, but because she'd still be here if I hadn't gotten it. How messed up is that?"

I smiled at him and hung his first bag. "I think it's normal to wish you'd never gotten cancer."

"Yeah, but because of my girlfriend? My ex-girlfriend? She's a selfish person, and I'm an idiot for loving her."

I sighed and sat down next to him. I smiled and grabbed his hand. "You're not an idiot. People show us what they want us to see. She was good at it. I've fallen for men like that. Who fooled me into thinking they were different. We don't always want to see the bad in people. But you're a good man. I wish you'd never gotten cancer, but I think you're better off without Beth."

He smiled and squeezed my hand. "Thank you, Laura. That…I needed to hear that."

I nodded and rubbed his forearm with my other hand. He drew a breath and let it out, then released my hand. I made a note in his chart about the breakup so I could follow up with him and make sure he had a solid support system in place, then documented his first dose.

I turned to get another patient and found Dr. Allison watching me with a furious look on his face. He pointed at me then crooked his finger and turned and walked away.

Son of a bitch.

4

NICO

I sat behind my desk to keep a barrier between us. I needed something to block me from her. To keep that distance. Her eyes said she'd lose it if I got close to her, but the pulse through my body said I needed to. I needed to show her exactly what she did to me.

I wouldn't. I couldn't. She was never going to find out how much I wanted her.

She walked into my office, leaving the door open. I wanted to tell her to close it, but it was her act of defiance. It was a moment for her. A minor victory. A challenge.

"Nurse Kempis, didn't we talk last week about your personal behavior with patients?"

"Yes." One word. I groaned internally.

"And didn't I tell you to stop the highly personal nature of your conversations?"

"Yes."

"Then what the hell did I just witness?"

She tilted her head to the side and sucked in a breath. Her breasts lifted with the move. My eyes were glued to them as they slowly fell again on her extended exhale.

"My patient shared something deeply personal with me. Without provocation. He is having a hard time. My job, Dr. Allison, is to put my patients at ease. To make sure they know they are not alone in their fight. That I'm there by their sides for everything. And that patient needs someone."

"Why?"

"Why what?"

"Why does he need someone? Why you? They all need someone, but you're their nurse, not their friend. What can you do?"

"This patient needs someone to talk to. Someone to let him know that not only can he get through this, but that he's better off without his bitch of an ex-girlfriend who dumped him because she didn't sign on for a life of cancer treatments." Her chest heaved with her anger. Her face and neck flushed a sexy pink color. Her hands clenched at her sides.

I cleared my throat and tried to focus on her words instead of how badly I wanted to kiss her. She cared. It was a beautiful thing. I'd hired far too many nurses who didn't, or who only cared to a point. What I loved about Laura was also what drove me crazy about her. I was jealous, according to Veronica, and it was only getting worse. In the last year, Laura had become different. She was more relaxed around the office, and she was dating. And the two things combined to make me extra crazy when I was near her.

"If all you're doing is talking, it's fine. But if you do anything else—"

"Lap dances are off the table then?" she asked with an angry glint in her gaze.

I drew in a breath. She was goading me. And it was working. "Please keep your actions professional."

"I always do."

I nodded for her dismissal. She hesitated a second, then spun on her heel and walked out of my office. I waited a few extra seconds until I was sure she was gone and released a deep breath. That woman could make me crazy in so many ways all at the same time.

I WORKED HARD to keep my distance from Laura for the rest of the day. I saw patients, and she administered infusions and the day ended without another interaction. Home was quiet and before I knew it, I was back in the office and waiting for a call from Veronica.

"Good morning," Veronica said as her face filled the screen in my office.

"Morning."

She narrowed her gaze and tilted her head. "This is going to be different for me, and probably difficult. You look like you're angry, but I can't see you picking at your nails to know for sure if that's the case."

I stopped the habit I wasn't aware I had and glared at Veronica. Her brown eyes glimmered with delight that she called me out. She loved being able to do that. We met in med school, two people who felt like we didn't belong. She was a good friend almost instantly. We talked about everything off the bat. It wasn't until we had almost finished school that I realized I did most of the talking and she listened. Because she was that good.

Asking Veronica to be my therapist was a no-brainer. She had built a large and successful practice with other psychiatrists working under her. Most of the clients Veronica saw herself were high-powered people, people who valued their privacy above all else.

She'd used the term narcissist a few times.

"What's wrong?" she asked me.

Veronica had a way of making me talk that made me feel like we were just chatting. Like we were back in school in our apartment and sharing beer and pizza.

"Nothing," I said.

She snorted. "What did Laura do now?"

"She's flirting with the damn patients."

"So? She's a beautiful, single woman. Why shouldn't she flirt?"

"Because it's against policy."

"We both know you never enforced that policy until she started working for you and you got jealous. You didn't want to see her with other men."

I grumbled and leaned back in my chair. I crossed my arms and glared at her. I hated when she called me on my shit.

"Don't pout," she said with a laugh. She tossed her long, dark hair behind her shoulders and leaned in. Her red top gaped in the front, but the only reason I noticed was because I didn't want her to show it all off to everyone she spoke to.

I blocked the screen with my hand and shook my head. "Lean back. I don't need to see that."

"Am I popping out?" she asked. She straightened and fixed her shirt. "Dammit. I'm going to need to change before my next call. Thanks. Jeff will lose his shit if I'm sharing too much."

I grinned. Jeff was Veronica's husband and love of her life. They met at a fundraiser years before. She married him after only a few months. I told her it wouldn't last and almost ruined our friendship. I'd never been happier to be wrong. Seeing Veronica happy made me realize how much was missing from my life.

Then I hired Laura.

"Okay, so, Laura is flirting with patients. Are you sure

she's flirting and not just talking to them? Some people seem like they're flirting when they aren't."

"She told one guy she was on a dating app and to join it."

Veronica's brows rose, and I felt victorious. Until she said, "Did she invite him or just relay the information?"

I scowled, and she pursed her lips at me.

"You need to figure out a way to get over this. Either you need to ask her out and find out for sure if there's something between you or you need to move on. This isn't healthy for you. She has every right to date. And she should be dating. No woman, or man, should sit around and be miserable. That includes you."

"I met someone," I blurted.

"You did?" Veronica was more than a little skeptical.

"Online. I joined a dating app—"

"The one Laura told the patient about?"

I shrugged and avoided her gaze.

Veronica laughed. "You are a masterpiece. I love having you for a client because it's guaranteed income forever. You will always find ways to fuck things up."

"Should you really be talking to me that way?"

She laughed and shook her head. "For one, our conversations are private. For two, you and I both know if you had any friends you wouldn't complain to me about Laura. You hired me because losing patients got to you. Because watching someone die brought it all back." Her voice was soft. Her eyes full of emotion I didn't want to think about. "I love you, Nico, but I want you to be whole. Years ago, that meant finding a way to deal with loss over and over again. Now, it means something else. I think you've separated yourself from loss and life so much that you've forgotten how to actually live. How to connect with another person."

"I can connect," I argued.

"Can you? Because we've known each other for a long time. I know we have a connection. I would do anything for you, and I know you would do anything for me. But it's been a while since you've let another person in. I think you want to let Laura in, but it scares you. Love is terrifying, but it's worth it. Especially when it's with the right person."

"You have Jeff. You think everyone else can find that. I don't know if I'm cut out for a relationship."

Veronica smiled. "You are one of the most amazing people I've ever met in my life. You are kind and caring and you're so funny and gentle and passionate. You are an amazing human, but you don't show that side to people. You hold back. You bark and scare them off. I'd be willing to bet you've barked at Laura a little more than usual lately."

I grumbled again, which made her laugh again.

"Okay. Let's talk about this new person you met. Tell me about the dating app."

I sighed. I wasn't sure if she was mocking me or not, but we were there to talk, so I was going to talk.

"The app is designed by someone local, a former patient's daughter actually. It doesn't allow pictures, so there's no way to really know who you're talking to. I matched with three women over the weekend and started chatting with one of them. She's funny and smart and it was fun."

"This is good," Veronica said. "You need someone to talk to besides Laura. Someone to think about. Keep talking to this woman. But I want you to do something else."

"What?" I asked with dread. She was always giving me assignments that pushed me out of my comfort zone. I liked my comfort zone.

"Talk to a friend. It doesn't have to be someone you hang out with, but have a conversation with someone you could consider a friend."

My mind went blank. I worked and I read papers about cancer research and I worked some more. I didn't socialize. I kept to myself.

"You don't have one person there to talk to?" Veronica asked when I said nothing.

"I…"

"You're a workaholic. Go out for a beer. Sit in a bar and strike up a conversation with someone. Ooh, no. What about the boat guy? Didn't you say you two got along?"

"I will not go talk to the guy who built my boat and ask him to be my friend," I said.

Veronica shook her head. "I didn't say he had to be your friend. I want you to have people. You've been living up there for years. I know why you moved there, but you haven't built a life. You've built a practice, but you need a life. Talk to the boat guy. Or go to a bar. Do something that gets you talking to a person who doesn't work for you and doesn't talk to you through chat in a dating app."

I grimaced at how pathetic she made me sound. I couldn't argue, though. She was right. I had no one in my life. No one to socialize with. At all. And I hadn't since I moved away from her. It had been a long time since I'd had a friend.

"Fine," I finally agreed.

Veronica grinned and said, "Okay, good. We'll talk again in a week, but you know we'll talk before then. I love you."

"I love you, too. I think."

She blew me a kiss and signed off. Smart woman. She knew if she stayed on, I'd try to talk us both out of the assignment.

Dammit.

I PUT off going to see Ian Jameson for two more days. All that did was prolong the inevitable. And make me more anxious. It was like asking a girl out in high school. I knew she was going to say no, but I did it anyway. Every single one of them said no.

I tried to tell myself it wasn't the same with Ian. He was a good guy from what I knew. He was talented as hell, and he was always friendly. I still felt like an ass walking over to his shop when I'd never done it before.

The large garage door at the end was open. Music blared from inside the space. Someone sang along, their voice mixing with the sound of a sander or grinder or something. Tools were not my thing.

I walked in and looked around. I didn't see anyone, but I followed the singing until it brought me around the edge of a large boat. Feet stuck out from underneath, toes moving along with the beat of the music.

I waited. Just like surgery, it wasn't smart to startle a person when they had a tool in their hands.

It wasn't long before Ian rolled himself out from under the boat and met my gaze. He drew back, obviously surprised I was his visitor. He set the tool down and stood, reaching to shake my hand.

"Dr. Nico Allison. What brings you by?"

I made up a story, a good one. Because dropping in on a man I'd never been friends with was weird. "I was thinking about doing a few upgrades to my boat. I wanted to get your thoughts. Maybe toss around a few ideas."

Ian rubbed his chin and nodded. "Yeah, sure. Your boat could probably do with a few upgrades by now. It's what? Seven years old?"

I nodded, surprised he remembered.

"The cabin is small, but I don't think you need much since it's mostly for going back and forth to Doc Rock."

"Doc Rock?"

Ian grinned. "Yeah. You've never heard that?"

I shook my head.

Ian shrugged. "Most people in town call your island Doc Rock since you live there and the island is basically all rocks. I think it's also because we're totally jealous of you and love rhyming."

I chuckled with Ian. I bought a condo when I first moved to the area, but I found it didn't afford me enough privacy. Especially when I started to struggle to separate my patients' health and my own life. Living in the Thousand Islands meant there were plenty of islands that offered all the privacy I could ask for. One came up for sale, and I jumped on it. I held onto my condo for the winter months and for when I worked late, but I went to my island on the weekends and whenever I could. It was the only place I felt truly comfortable.

"Anyway, the boat. So, what are you looking to do?" He glanced at his phone then back up at me.

"Am I keeping you from something?" I asked.

Ian shook his head. "No, it's fine." He stopped and examined me for a long moment. I wasn't sure what he was looking for, but I wanted to pass whatever test I didn't know I was facing. "Actually, what are you doing right now?"

"Uh, nothing?"

"Why don't you come with me to get a beer and some dinner? I'm meeting up with some friends at O'Kelley's."

"Oh, no, I didn't come here to intrude."

"Nope, I insist. You work too hard, and I've never seen you there. And since I feel like I live there sometimes, it means you don't relax nearly enough. One beer. Maybe a burger. Fries. They have a dart board. And friends. They can all help figure out what to do to your boat. Come on. Let's go."

I resisted everything he said, but I heard Veronica's voice in my head telling me to have a conversation with a friend. Or go to a bar and get a beer. Maybe if I did both, she would leave me alone. It was already Thursday. One more day in town and then I could disappear to Doc Rock and no one would bother me for a few days.

I could do it. I could sit and talk to other men, have a beer. Veronica would be proud.

I nodded. "Okay, let's go."

Ian grinned. "Awesome. This will be fun. And hey, there are always some pretty women there. Not sure your type, but maybe you'll meet someone since you're going out."

I snorted. "Not likely. Besides, I'm already…Um…"

Ian's brows rose as he pressed a button to lower the massive door. "You're seeing someone?"

"No. I mean, not really. I just started talking to someone the other day."

"Yeah? What's she like?"

"She's funny and smart. She made me laugh."

"Nice. Where did you meet?"

"Oh, um, well…Online." I muttered the last word like it was a dirty word. Like I should be ashamed.

Ian laughed. "No shit? I met Blake online."

"I thought you knew Blake forever."

He shrugged and nodded. "I did, but she wasn't interested in me. We were paired on Book Boyfriends Wanted and got to know each other in a whole new way. I don't think we would have gotten married if it weren't for that app. What one are you using?"

I stared at him, wondering if he was messing with me. "The same one."

Ian chuckled. "Be careful. I think Karissa has magical powers. Almost all the guys we're meeting have found someone on that app. This one you're talking to might end up your future Mrs. Doc."

"You do realize I have a last name, right?"

Ian laughed and opened the door to O'Kelley's. "I do, but it's kind of fun to watch you squirm a little."

I raised an eyebrow at him and shook my head. I couldn't help but laugh. Maybe Veronica was right about talking to a friend. If nothing else, I could tell her I tried.

5

———————

I honestly couldn't remember the last time I'd set foot in a bar. I typically preferred my drinks on my patio overlooking the water with silence around me. Not drunk people shouting and a bartender to tip.

But I was trying.

Ian led me to the bar and sat down. He nodded to the stool next to him when I hesitated.

"Guys, this is Doctor Allison. He treated Ms. Georgia, if you haven't met him." Ian could have swallowed a canary with that wide grin. Smart ass.

"You can call me Nico," I told the others. "Ian thinks he's being funny."

"He always thinks that. It's rarely true," Ramsey Holland said.

"But that is true," Hudson Grant added with a nod to Ramsey. "What can I get you to drink?"

"Just a beer is great."

Hudson eyed me for a long moment and asked, "Are you sure? You don't seem like a beer man."

I raised my brows at him. Wasn't he the bartender?

Wasn't his job to pour drinks for customers? How did he make money if he was arguing with them all the time?

"Hudson considers himself an amateur psychologist. And he thinks he knows what people drink, without them telling him," Ian explained for the silent man across the bar.

I looked at Hudson. I didn't really know him. I'd seen him around town, same with Ramsey and the others. Living in a town as small as MacKellar Cove made it easy to find out who people were, but I wasn't friends with them. I wasn't friends with Ian either, but I'd had a few conversations with him. The others? Never. So, why did Hudson think he knew what I'd drink?

"Okay, what do you think my drink is?" I asked, meeting Hudson's assessing gaze. I tried not to smirk.

Hudson leaned back and scanned me. He took in my expensive suit, how straight I sat on the barstool, and the confident look I aimed his way. I waited. I wasn't going to give him any clues. I also was fairly certain he wouldn't ever be able to come up with my preferred drink.

"You drink beer, Scotch, or maybe a rum and Coke because you think it's what people expect from you, but in reality, you'd rather have something sweeter. Blended. Peach margarita." Hudson leaned back and waited for me to say something.

I wasn't sure I could. How the hell did he know that?

"I'm right, aren't I?"

"Um…how the hell did you come up with that?"

Hudson shrugged. "It's a gift. Do you want one or are you going to choke down a beer because it's what the rest of them are drinking?"

I chuckled and shook my head. "Well, since you've already told everyone, I guess I might as well have one."

Hudson nodded. "Anyone else?"

"I'll try it," Colin Jones said. "Elise likes peaches."

"Make mine strawberry," Ramsey said.

"Yeah, mine, too," Ian agreed.

"I'll stick with the beer," James Rucker said.

"Peaches," Gavin Holbrook said.

"What the hell. I'll try strawberry," Rowan Masterson said.

"Sure you don't want one?" Hudson asked James.

"Nope. Sweet stuff gives me a headache."

I looked at the group of them and laughed. I expected harassment, not agreement.

"What's going on?" Sebastian Parks asked as he took a seat next to Ramsey. "Can I get a beer?"

"Do you know Nico?" Ramsey asked with a nod in my direction. "We're all drinking margaritas tonight. Peach or strawberry."

Sebastian shook his head. "Beer for me. It's cheap. I don't need to get a taste for something expensive."

"My treat," I told him. I met Hudson's gaze. "All of it tonight."

Hudson nodded. The other guys laughed and thanked me. Not Ian, though.

"You don't have to do that," Ian said low enough that the others couldn't hear.

I shrugged. "It's no big deal."

"It might not be, but that's not why I invited you out with us."

I held his gaze. We weren't friends, but I was also a fairly good judge of character. He wasn't looking to screw me over. "I know."

"I hope so."

I nodded and turned back to Hudson while he made the drinks.

"Nico's looking at making some upgrades to his boat. It's

beautiful already, if I do say so myself, but it's been a few years. Any suggestions?" Ian asked the others.

"A bar," Gavin said.

"You can't get back and forth to an island without a drink?" James asked him. "It's a good thing you live on the shore."

"You live on an island?" Gavin asked me.

I nodded, but the other guys answered for me.

"Doc Rock."

"No shit?" Gavin said.

I chuckled and nodded. "Although I don't call it that. Ian told me that name today."

"That's awesome. What do you do in the winter?" Gavin asked.

"I have a condo I stay in. Sometimes I can still get back and forth, but once it starts to get cold, I don't bother trying. The ride over is painful."

"Tell me about it," Sebastian said. "I dread trips out to the lighthouse in the winter, but I have no choice."

I was an ass. I was complaining about having to drive a boat to my private island in the winter, and the men I was talking to were ordinary men with jobs they needed to survive.

"Don't feel bad," Ian said quietly. "We all have different struggles."

I nodded, not sure how I was supposed to feel like less of an ass after I complained about the advantages of my life. Maybe going to a bar wasn't such a great idea.

"Nico's on Karissa's app," Ian said, dragging my mind away from my charmed life.

"It's no big deal," I told them as Hudson set my drink in front of me. I nodded my thanks to him.

"Good luck," Ramsey said. "I was almost divorced and met my wife on the app. Best thing to ever happen to us."

"Trinity and I met there."

"We all did. Met them in real life, but the app gave us that push we needed to change things. Who are you paired with?" Colin asked.

"Her name is NoRegrets. She's easy to talk to," I told him.

Colin shook his head. "I wasn't ever paired with her. Can't offer insight." He looked around and the others shook their heads. "Any idea who she is?"

I shook my head and wondered about her. Her phone sex operator confession made me curious, but I didn't know anyone who'd ever done that. These guys might, but I didn't really want to share that part of her with them. It felt too personal. Like something secret between us.

"Eventually, you'll meet her. If it keeps working out. A bunch of the women meet their dates here. It's safe for them," Ian said with a nod toward the corner of the bar.

I turned to see what he was nodding at and found Laura at a table with two other women. Her head was tipped back in laughter, her blonde curls wild around her face. Her brown eyes sparkled with amusement at what the other woman said. She lifted her glass and drank, her gaze never leaving the woman she was talking to.

I didn't see her relaxed very often. She was buttoned up and stiff at work. She didn't laugh, not like that, and she kept her hair tied up. It made me want to walk over and run my fingers through it. To look into her eyes. To—

"Earth to Nico. Want something to eat?" Hudson said.

I turned back to the bar abruptly and cleared my throat. I ignored the smiles and looks around me and focused on Hudson. "Yeah, a burger?"

"We have those. What do you want on it?" Hudson asked.

"Bacon, cheddar, and ketchup."

"Fries, tots, or onion rings?"

"Fries. Thanks."

Hudson nodded, his smile saying he understood it was for more than just taking my order.

I sipped my margarita and tried to pretend nothing had happened even though I knew the men around me were exchanging private glances and would likely talk about me once I was gone.

As I drank, the weight of the evening pressed on me. I shouldn't have come out with them. I should have just called Ian instead of going to his shop. That would have still meant having a conversation, but I wouldn't have gotten dragged into a bar where I was exposed.

I suffered through mockery my entire childhood. I never fit in anywhere. I learned to be my own person, to stop trying to fit and to stand out if I needed to. I kept to myself because others never got me. They never wanted to. I thought Ian was different, but maybe I was wrong. Maybe he just invited me because I was there, and I was an easy target.

I shifted in my seat and made a move for my wallet.

"Don't," Ian cautioned. "Please stay."

I looked at him, angry he'd chosen me to be his entertainment for the night and frustrated that he knew I was getting ready to leave. "Why?"

"Because we're not laughing at you for the reasons you think. We all recognize the look in your eyes. We've been there."

"I don't know what you're talking about." I tugged my sleeves down and straightened.

Ian breathed a laugh. "I said the same thing about my wife. I pretended I wasn't in love with her for years. I knew I wasn't good enough for her, so I convinced myself and everyone around me that I didn't love her. It was easier than taking a chance and ending up alone because I was right and she didn't want to be with me."

"But you're married."

"Yeah, now. It wasn't easy to get there. I saw the same look you just had in my mirror for a long time. Why don't you just ask her out?"

I snorted. "No. She works for me. And she thinks I'm an asshole."

"So prove to her you aren't."

"It isn't that easy."

"Why not?" Colin asked.

I turned and realized all of them were listening.

"None of this is easy. Relationships suck. But waking up in the morning to the woman you love is better than anything else on earth," Gavin said.

"Am I here for your amusement?" The words jumped out before I could stop them.

They all shook their heads.

"I didn't know you were coming until you were here," James said. "But we wouldn't do that. We all adored Ms. Georgia, and she loved you. Even if you weren't a well-respected doctor who works to save lives, we wouldn't sit here and make fun of you just because of Ms. Georgia."

"That doesn't mean we aren't going to harass you a little, though," Ian said. "It's what friends do."

I looked at the men and saw the same open expression on all their faces. I'd learned to read people over time. I had to in my profession. I needed to know if my patients were telling me the truth about their pain or their habits. I knew the signs of someone lying. I wasn't seeing any of them in the faces of the men around me.

"If it makes you feel better, Masterson can buy dinner and drinks tonight to prove we aren't taking advantage of you," James said.

"Hey! What the hell?" Rowan shouted.

James shrugged. "You're the new guy."

"I've been here longer than Gavin," Rowan argued.

"Doesn't matter. I outrank you," James said.

"All right, gentlemen. Let's stop the pissing contest," Hudson said.

Rowan scowled at James who grinned back at him. Ramsey shook his head at their antics, not surprised. After a minute, I just chuckled and settled back into my seat.

"I wouldn't have done that," Ian stressed. "You just looked like a night out might be a nice change."

I met his gaze and nodded. "Thanks. It's just what the doctor ordered."

Ian grinned. He didn't have to know I meant that literally.

THE REST of the evening passed without incident. I forced myself not to watch Laura all night and talked to the men. When we all left, they invited me back the following week to join them again.

"Masterson's going to pay," James said with a nod toward the other man.

"I'm not going to make it next week," Rowan said without missing a beat.

"Hudson can put it on your tab. You can settle when you come in again," James said.

Rowan flipped him off.

"Are you making lewd gestures at an officer of the law?" James asked, getting in Rowan's face.

Rowan snorted a laugh. "Would you rather I use my words?"

James chuckled and stepped back. "See you tomorrow." James walked away with a wave, the others dispersing with him. Except for Ian.

"Listen, I'm sorry you felt like we were laughing at you. It really wasn't my intention. We've all been there. We want to help."

I nodded. "Thanks, but there's nothing to do."

"I think you could be wrong, but I won't get in the middle of your personal life. I know people have to be ready to make that leap."

"What leap?"

"From wherever they start to something more. I will say one thing, though. If you like her as much as you look like you do, don't sit back and let her find someone else. I did that with Blake and wasted years, for both of us. She almost married another man."

"I'm not...I have a tendency to piss her off. She's barely spoken to me in a week."

"Have you apologized?"

"I tried."

"She might be less angry after a week. If not, you need to make her see that whatever you did that made her so mad isn't a big deal now. That you're over it."

"And what if I'm not?"

Ian raised a brow. "What happened?"

"She was flirting with a patient."

Ian shrugged. "That's how Laura talks to everyone. She flirts with me, but it means nothing. She knows I'm married."

"I don't like it," I spat.

Ian's lips curled up on the edges. He shook his head. "Sorry, but if you like her, you need to accept who she is. If she flirts when she talks, you're going to need to get over that. I can't imagine who Laura would be if she wasn't friendly and chatty and flirty. She'd be a different person. Then she's not Laura."

"I..." I thought about the woman I knew. The smart, friendly, talkative woman I first hired. I loved that she was kind and compassionate, but I was drawn to her as a person for the same reasons. And Ian was right. I'd been so wrapped up in not wanting her to flirt with the patients that I lost sight of the fact that she'd changed at the office over the last few weeks. She wasn't that same woman. And I made that happen.

"I need to go," I blurted. "Thanks for inviting me tonight. I enjoyed it. Thank you."

Ian nodded and let me walk away. His words rang in my head as I walked the short distance to my vehicle. I went to my condo since I needed to be back at the clinic in far too few hours. It was time to make some changes at work. And the first one was scheduled to start bright and early.

"I didn't know this was even here," Eddie said as he walked around.

I hadn't seen him much in the almost two-and-a-half years since we lost Ms. Georgia. Eddie was her world at the end. Eddie and her daughter. The two of them were at every appointment with her, every treatment, everything. They were there for her. We all tried to save her.

"It was part of why I bought the building. I wanted the option to expand eventually. I rented it out for a while, but I stopped that a few years ago when it got to be more than I could handle," I told him.

"Well, it looks like a beautiful spot. Georgia would have loved it up here."

"Morning," another voice said from the elevator.

I turned and greeted Peter. Eddie recommended him as someone who could do a job like the one I had in mind. The size of him said he could probably do it without any equipment.

"Peter. Thanks for coming," Eddie said, walking over to

the other man. They exchanged a hug that said they were close. Eddie clapped Peter on the back and guided him toward me.

"This is Nico. He was Georgia's doctor. And he's going to help more people by expanding this beautiful place he has," Eddie explained.

"Nice to meet you," I told Peter. I extended my hand to shake his.

"You, too. Ms. Georgia and Eddie have always spoken highly of you. This is a great place." Peter looked around, taking it all in.

"Thanks. It definitely needs a lot of work in order to make it functional, but I want it done right. It sounds like you're the man for that job."

Peter nodded. "I can do it. I just need to know your time-line and budget. Once I have that, we can start talking about plans. I'll do a few different layout options for you. I'm assuming the staff downstairs is going to be a part of this. I always recommend bringing in at least one person who will work in the space. They might have suggestions you didn't think about."

"Dr. Allison?" Laura said from the direction of the elevator.

I didn't even hear the elevator, but when I looked up, she was standing there with a confused look on her face.

"What's going on?"

"I guess we have our volunteer," Peter said.

6

LAURA

"Eddie? Are you all right?" I asked. My voice shook. My hands shook. My entire body shook. Eddie couldn't be sick. He just couldn't be. We already lost Ms. Georgia. We couldn't lose Eddie, too.

"No, sweetheart. I'm not sick. I'm just here with Peter," Eddie said with a smile. He reached out his hands and I took them. Smiling back at him as his words sank in.

"Peter? What's going on? Why are you guys up here instead of in the clinic? I'll take you on as my patient. Let me help you," Laura insisted.

"I'm not sick either," Peter said. He chuckled.

My head was spinning. I saw sick patients every day. Dying patients. Patients who were losing their will to fight. Patients who would not last much longer. But I kept my distance from them as I did everything possible to save them. They were patients, and there would always be more. But these two men, men I knew and loved and had to see healthy, I couldn't handle it.

"Come here, sweetheart," Eddie said. "We're fine."

I stepped into his arms and let his calming presence soothe me. He rubbed my back as I tried to control my breathing so I could step back and look at the three men around me without shaking.

"Peter is going to help Dr. Allison with his expansion plans," Eddie said.

I drew back. My eyes narrowed and I asked, "Expansion plans?"

Dr. Allison cleared his throat. "Yeah, I, um, haven't told anyone yet."

Eddie looked at him with regret. "Sorry, Dr. Allison. I assumed…"

"It's fine, Eddie. Everyone will know soon enough." Dr. Allison drew a breath and faced me. "I'm expanding. This entire floor is going to be for infusions. I want to have space for more patients so we can help more people. Peter and Eddie are up here to help me get started."

"Wow," I breathed. I had no idea he had plans to expand. Or the available space for it. I assumed the upstairs was vacant, but I didn't realize it was a blank canvas. Or that he was going to do something with it. "This will be amazing."

Dr. Allison nodded. "I hope so. Was there something you needed?"

I looked around and imagined the space. We could treat at least three times as many patients with this much space. And we could help patients who needed a different kind of treatment, patients in need of a spinal tap. I—

"Nurse Kempis?" Dr. Allison's voice broke through my mind and I remembered why I was up there.

"Yes, I need to speak to you about a patient."

Dr. Allison nodded to Eddie and Peter. "Excuse me, gentlemen."

"We're all set actually," Peter said. "I can work up those

estimates and have them back to you by the end of the day for you both to review."

"Both? No. This is not my clinic," I told him, wondering why he thought I had a say in anything.

"Yeah, but we told Dr. Allison it would be smart to bring in someone who would work in this area, one of you nurses makes the most sense, to help review things to make sure it's how you would like it all to be. Since you're the only one who knows, now, you're the best choice," Peter explained.

I shook my head. "No. I'm sure someone else would be better."

Peter shrugged. "Well, I guess it's up to you guys. We'll head out. I'll get you those plans, Doc." Peter shook Dr. Allison's hand, then clapped Eddie on the back. "I think I owe you some breakfast."

Eddie grinned. "I'm always up for a free breakfast. Good to see you both." He hugged me and shook Dr. Allison's hand, then they walked out.

I couldn't move. I wanted to ask him about the whole thing, but we hadn't been on the best of terms. We hadn't been alone in weeks without him yelling at me to stop flirting with patients. Standing there made me uncomfortable, but I still couldn't move.

"I would appreciate your help, if you're willing. I know I haven't given you any reason to want to help me, but this is for the patients."

He was good. Very good. I was ready to say no. To tell him to go to hell. To walk out if I had to. Then he said it was for the patients.

"Fine," I breathed.

"Will you meet me up here this afternoon to review the plans?" he asked.

He asked. He actually asked me. He wasn't ordering me around. He asked me.

I looked up at him and found him staring out the window. He looked…wounded. Maybe scared. Like there was more going on.

"Yes," I whispered.

His gaze snapped to mine. He stepped closer to me. He paused, but the air between us sparked with something I'd never felt from him before. I drew in a breath, giving my lungs much needed air, and the spell snapped.

He took a step back and cleared his throat. "You said you needed to speak to me about a patient?"

I cleared my throat. "Yes. Um, Marie Kaufman is in for an infusion appointment today. She's complaining of being run down and extremely tired. Her port looks good, and her labs are on the edge but acceptable. I'd like to give her fluids today with her infusion and schedule her to come back early next week for more fluids and labs. I think we need to keep a close eye on her."

Dr. Allison nodded. "I'm fine with that plan. I agree we need to keep an eye on her. That's why I gave her my number. She doesn't seem to have much of a support system."

I shook my head. "She doesn't. Her parents are a few hours away and both work full time. She has friends, but they're all working. She lives alone and so far has shown up alone for her appointments."

Dr. Allison blew out a breath and nodded slowly. "Monitor her closely. Tell her to call me or the office any time if she has any issues. Thank you."

I nodded and turned to walk away. I stopped at the elevator, looking back at the space before I stepped on. "This place is going to be amazing. You're going to help a lot of people."

He pressed his lips together in a smile that reached down inside me and grabbed a hold of my heart. "Thank you."

I pressed the button to go back downstairs and held his

gaze until the doors closed between us. When the elevator started moving, I blew out a deep breath and sank against the metal wall. "What the hell was that?"

MARIE WAS RESTING while I felt like a ping-pong ball on a concrete floor. I didn't know what to do with Dr. Allison. There was a moment. A moment filled with something that shouldn't be there. A moment where he looked at me like he wanted...me.

I had to be crazy. It was all in my head. I'd worked for him for years and he'd never looked at me like that. It was just...I didn't know what it was, but I was wrong.

While Marie rested, I went through patient files to get prepared for the rest of my day. Seeing Eddie and Peter threw me off almost as much as my imagined moment with Dr. Allison. Every single one of my patients was important to someone. They were all special. They all deserved the best. Working with Peyton in her fertility clinic taught me to go that extra mile to ensure each patient knew they mattered, but the last few weeks with Dr. Allison...

Something was going on with him. I wanted to figure it out and help, but it wasn't my place. He was my boss, and his personal life was none of my business.

I checked in with Marie and went to get my next patient. All the chairs were full once he sat down and my mind drifted to the second floor.

We did our best to take in as many patients as possible, but there were always more. Each infusion nurse had two or three patients at a time, staggered so we could keep up with their care. I assumed we could double our intake with the second floor. But it would mean hiring another oncologist and more staff to do scans and blood work. Dr. Allison would probably need to hire more nurses also. And more office staff. And—

"You okay?" Gregory asked.

I looked at him and smiled. "Sorry. My mind is racing."

He shrugged. "I get that way, too. Especially lately. I don't know how you handle being around sick people all the time."

I smiled and patted his arm. He was one of the success stories. He was almost at the end of his treatment. He was doing so well that Dr. Allison considered ending his treatment early. He consulted with another oncologist who said not to but agreed that Gregory was textbook.

"It gives me hope," I told him. "I had a patient tell me once that getting cancer was like winning the lottery but without the big check. She said people come out of the woodwork to tell you how much you mean to them. I get to see that every day. This job isn't always easy, but it shows me the good side of people a lot of the time."

"I imagine you see some bad, too," Gregory said.

I nodded, thinking about Damien. "There's definitely some of that."

Gregory wrinkled his nose. "That's what I struggle with. It's not like this"—he held up his arm—"makes me a bad person. I didn't ask for it. I wouldn't wish it on my worst enemy. Why judge someone for it?"

"I think it's a way out," Marie said. "A way for people to escape what they wanted out of anyway."

"That could be," Gregory said. "What would you escape if you could? Besides the obvious."

Marie smiled faintly. "I don't know. I love my job, and I have great friends and family. I'm single, so maybe that, but who wants to be with a radioactive woman?"

Gregory chuckled. "I know what you mean. I keep telling

my husband I'm going to go to the airport just to see if I set off any sensors. He gets mad at me."

Marie laughed. "That's hilarious. I think we need to find the humor in all this. It's hard enough."

Gregory nodded. "I'm Gregory, by the way."

"Marie."

"Nice to meet you. Do we have the same sentence? Every Friday?"

Marie nodded. "It appears that way." Marie shifted in her chair to look at him more. "It would have been much nicer to meet you anywhere else, though." She looked at me. "No offense."

I smiled. "Trust me, no offense taken. I would gladly be out of a job if it meant not having to meet anyone like this."

"I was just telling Laura that I don't know how she does this," Gregory said. "I think wishing your job didn't exist is tough."

I shrugged. "It's more wishing cancer didn't exist. I'd still have a job as a nurse doing something. Coming here to work was an extension of that. A new challenge in a way."

"What did you do before this?" Marie asked.

"I worked at a fertility clinic."

"Seriously? You went from starting life to ending life? With all the same heartbreak? Are you a glutton for punishment?" Gregory asked.

I laughed with them. "I never thought of it that way, but I might be. I guess I like being there for people when they're going through the worst possible things. It's not easy to sit in those chairs. It wasn't easy for those couples to sit in their chairs. But in both jobs, I wanted to help."

"I don't think I have that gene. The one that says I should give back. I go to work, do my job, and spend time with my friends. I don't volunteer or donate money or do anything to help others. I'm not a very good person," Marie said.

"Do you smile at strangers? Or treat servers with respect when you go out? Are you there for your friends?" Gregory asked her.

Marie nodded.

"Then you're a good person. You don't have to give away everything you have in order to be a good person. Saying hello to a stranger can have a huge impact. It has on me. I hate sitting here. I like to be moving. If I could pace this room, I would, but talking to you, because you were willing to say something to me, has made me a lot less restless."

Marie smiled at him like he gave her something she'd been missing. Seeing that reminded me of why I did what I did. So people like Gregory and Marie could live their lives. So they didn't have to stay tied to these chairs forever.

"Tell me something juicy," Gregory said. "What's the first thing you're going to do when you're done with this?"

"Have a drink," Marie said with a laugh.

Gregory chuckled. "I'm going on vacation. I've always wanted to see Italy, and this has reminded me that life's too short to do it tomorrow. We need to grab it by the balls and live it."

Marie grinned, the brightest and most genuine smile I'd seen from her yet. "I'm so happy I met you today."

"Me, too."

MARIE AND GREGORY talked through the rest of their treatments. It made me think about Damien. He needed someone to talk to. Another patient who could bring him out of his funk and make him see he was better off without Beth in his life.

My friends were trying to get me to see the same thing about Dr. Allison. I hated that I was starting to agree with them. When I started dating, I mostly did it to give myself a little confidence. I wasn't hoping any of the dates would turn into something more serious. But I was hoping I would start to see other men as options.

Dr. Allison…Nico…he was an amazing man, but he wasn't mine. And it was time to let go of the fantasy that one day he might be. It had been long enough.

I had a date scheduled for that night, and I was going to give him a real shot. It might not work out, but I didn't open up to the others. I held them back. It never worked out because I didn't want it to.

It was time to change that.

I finished up my work for the day and went to the lounge. I said goodnight to everyone and checked my phone. I had a text from Nico asking me to meet him on the second floor to go over some of the options from Peter. I took my stuff and headed up there. Time to let go of my fantasy.

Or not.

Holy. Fucking. Shit.

Nico was standing in front of the window when the elevator doors opened. The late afternoon sun was shining through, highlighting him and ensuring my eyes didn't drift from his form. His dark suit fit perfectly to him, draped across his shoulders like it was actually made just for him. His dark hair sparkled in the sunlight and his beard glowed. He stared at the water outside the windows, either unaware I was there or disinterested.

I drew a breath and told myself it didn't matter. We weren't going to be together. We were Romeo and Juliet if their parents had gotten their way. A missed opportunity.

"Dr. Allison?" I said quietly so I didn't startle him.

"This view is amazing. I can't believe how beautiful it is sometimes." He turned around and looked at me. I swore his eyes darkened. He swallowed roughly. He held my gaze for a long moment then gestured to the table on the far side.

I followed him over and set my things on a chair. He stood close enough to me that I could feel the heat of his body. Was it getting hot?

"I want to capitalize on the view," Nico said. "To give the patients something good when they're here. At least something peaceful. I want them to forget for a few minutes that their lives are on hold until we find out if they are going to live or not. They deserve that."

The conviction in his voice said there was more to this whole thing than I knew. He cared, but that wasn't a surprise. He was dedicated. Committed. It was personal.

"Since the building is wide and not deep, I was thinking of putting some rooms back here. A way to access spines or give patients who need to lie down some privacy. That's what this first plan has. Chairs up front with dividers for the patients who want that. Room in the middle of the space for the nurses. Storage, desks, whatever. What do you think of this?"

I looked at the plans and shrugged. It looked nice. It wasn't fancy, but it didn't need to be. It was peaceful and accessible. That was what mattered the most.

"I think it's fine. I have a hard time imagining it. I've never read blueprints before, but I think I get the point."

Nico looked up at me then down at the papers in front of us. He smiled then moved to the center of the room and threw up his arms. "This would be for you, Laura. Your space. However you want it." He walked toward the windows. "And here would be chairs. We need to decide how we want them set up, but we could have semi-circles or straight lines. Anything you think so the patients are comfortable. Maybe a snack area over here since it's a blank wall. Coffee, water, healthy snack options in and out of the fridge. Things that we know help." He walked to the back. "And here are the rooms. The most privacy. Extra equipment. Make it comfortable for the patients who need this."

I laughed and shook my head. "You really thought of everything didn't you?"

He stared at me for a long moment then said, "Not even close. I need you, Laura."

7

―――

NICO

She sucked in a breath at my words. I wanted to move across the room toward her, to take her in my arms and kiss her. But she was my employee. She worked for me. If that wasn't wrong, I didn't know what was.

When she laughed, I almost lost it. She wasn't laughing at me. She was entertained. She'd never seen this side of me. I kept it bottled up at work. I wanted to be professional. I was the boss. I couldn't laugh and joke. I needed everyone to know I was in charge.

It was a lie. She was in charge. If she said to do something, I'd make it happen. I was subtle about it, but I always did what she said. My plans to move forward with the expansion were because of her. She mentioned a month ago a patient needed to use an exam room for treatment because we didn't have a bed for him. She advocated for her patient and worked it out with the rest of the staff to shift others around to give her patient what he needed.

She was right, but it took her push to make me get off my ass and start thinking about construction. And again, she was the one calling the shots.

"So, what do you think of the first option?"

She smiled. "I think it'll work."

"But not great. Okay. Let's see the others."

We went through the other three layouts Peter came up with. For each of them, Laura didn't appear to be sold. She bobbed her head side-to-side and wrinkled up her nose. Nothing said yes, that's the one.

"What is your vision for this place?" she asked.

"My vision?"

She nodded. "I know you want to help people, but what is your plan. What do you want it to look like or feel like or be like?"

I thought about it and knew she was right. There was something missing. The design wasn't there yet. Even though I knew what I wanted, we could have been setting up any business in the space. It lacked personality, and that was what I needed. It was also the last thing I showed to most people.

"Come home with me," I blurted.

"Excuse me?" She took a quick step back. Her eyes widened as she gawked at me. Way wrong move. I didn't mean it to sound how it did, but her reaction said she took it the wrong way and was not okay with it.

Retreat. RETREAT!

"I meant come to my house for dinner tonight. We can talk through everything. I know what I want and what I'm thinking, but I'm not articulating it correctly. I was hoping you'd help me. Have dinner with me so we can talk about work. Just for work."

"I, um, I...I can't. I have plans tonight."

Plans meant a date. Plans meant she was seeing someone else. Plans meant she had zero interest in spending time with her boss because she had another man.

And it meant I'd opened myself up to a lawsuit because I was inappropriate with an employee.

"Understood. I apologize if I made you feel uncomfortable. Maybe we can discuss this next week?"

I rolled up the blueprints as I spoke, getting ready to make my escape. I couldn't stand there and ask her about her date or pretend I was a friend. I was her boss and I was about to cross a line I couldn't uncross. I could not do that.

"Yeah, of course," Laura said. "I, um, I guess I'll see you Monday. Have a good weekend."

"You, too," I said without looking up. She let herself out, leaving me to my stupidity. It was better that way. Alone I wouldn't make a fool of myself. Alone I wouldn't screw up. Alone I could be myself.

Once I was sure Laura had left, I packed up the plans and went down to my office. I finished the work I needed to do and got ready to head home for the weekend. I was looking forward to the solitude of my island. Doc Rock. I smiled to myself at that one.

I didn't expect to enjoy my evening out with Ian and his friends, but Veronica was right. It was good to see people who didn't report to me, and it was good to have a conversation about something normal.

The ride out to Doc Rock was peaceful. Most people were already eating dinner, so the water was calm and quiet. I took my time, slowly crossing the channel and enjoying the feel of the breeze on my face without the splash of water if I'd gone faster. I tied the boat to my dock and headed inside, past the one tree required to make my island one of the Thousand Islands.

The home was built decades ago and hadn't been updated in almost as long when I bought it. I'd slowly made improvements, but getting contractors out to an island wasn't always easy. The kitchen and master were complete. One day I'd work on the rest of the house, but the clinic was going to come first.

Once I changed out of my suit into sweats, I grabbed a peach margarita pouch and dumped the frozen drink into a glass. I went out to the deck and sat down. The grill I bought the summer before was still shiny and new looking, a testament to how little time I spent using it.

As I enjoyed my drink, I thought about the clinic. I wanted it to be peaceful and calming, but I didn't want it to feel clinical. I wanted the patients to be in a living room. Not a loud room with TVs or anything, but cozy and welcoming.

I wanted it to feel like I did at that moment on my deck. Relaxed. At ease. Safe.

As ideas hit me, I went inside and started writing them down. I could take one of Peter's plans and add to it. Make it personal. Make it perfect.

I let my mind wander as I fired up the grill and fixed myself dinner. When I sat to eat, I wondered if Laura was enjoying her date.

I grumbled to myself. I didn't want her to enjoy her date. I wanted her sitting beside me. Talking to me. Getting to know me.

I pulled out my phone and opened the Book Boyfriends Wanted app. I hadn't spoken to NoRegrets much during the week, but it was the weekend. I wondered about her. She was easy to talk to. And she made me laugh. That hadn't happened in a while. And if I couldn't talk to Laura, at least I could talk to NoRegrets.

DICTATOR

Are you off for the weekend and able to enjoy it?

I assumed she'd be busy on a Friday night, but she replied only a few minutes later.

NOREGRETS

I am. Thankfully. It was a long week.

DICTATOR

Mine, too. This drink in my hand is hard earned.

NOREGRETS

I hear you. I'm ready to put my feet up and watch a movie.

DICTATOR

What movie are you watching?

NOREGRETS

I haven't decided yet. I'm torn between a rom-com that will give me hope and a comedy that will make me laugh.

DICTATOR

So, super dark movies. Got it.

NOREGRETS

LOL. Yep, I'm a very dark person.

DICTATOR

You sound like it.

NOREGRETS

What movies do you watch?

DICTATOR

I don't watch a lot of TV. I read more.

NOREGRETS

Books are the same as TV, you know. But with a book, the movie plays in your mind.

DICTATOR

That's a unique way of looking at it.

NOREGRETS

I love to read. TV is easier after a long week because I can zone out and not think, but normally I'd prefer to read.

DICTATOR

I usually only watch movies or shows that are based on books I've read.

NOREGRETS

Like what?

DICTATOR

Fantasy and sci-fi.

NOREGRETS

So you like lots of action, a little bit of romance, limited magic, but crazy smart people who've figured out how to create things that seem magical?

I laughed and nodded. She nailed it.

DICTATOR

I'm impressed.

NOREGRETS

I've seen GOT. Although that has magic in it.

DICTATOR

You might be my dream woman. Tell me something that will make me not like you.

NOREGRETS

That's a good question. I need to think about that one.

DICTATOR

Do you make fun of people? Or steal candy from children? Or hate strangers for no reason?

NOREGRETS

No, no, and no. I always have a reason.

DICTATOR

LOL!

NOREGRETS

Just kidding. I like people. I'm pretty friendly. I think my biggest negative is that I'm kind of blunt at times. I'm not going to sugarcoat something if I think someone needs to hear it. That and I flirt too much it seems.

DICTATOR

Blunt isn't a bad thing in my world. People need to know the truth so they can figure out what to do. And flirting can be a lot of fun.

NOREGRETS

Not everyone agrees with those things, but thank you. And yes, flirting is fun. My job is hard enough and I don't think I flirt a lot but I've been told the way I talk to people is flirting. I think I'm just being friendly.

DICTATOR

What do you do? For a job, I mean.

NOREGRETS

I don't think I should tell you that. It would probably make it easy to find out who I am.

DICTATOR

Good point. Sorry.

NOREGRETS

No reason to be sorry. I'm careful about who I share my personal info with. Have you met anyone from here? In person?

DICTATOR

No. Have you?

NOREGRETS

Yeah. I decided it's time for me to start dating again, so I'm putting myself out there.

DICTATOR

Bad breakup?

NOREGRETS

No, just getting lost in my work.

DICTATOR

I completely understand that. My work is my life. I don't have much else.

NOREGRETS

No family or friends?

DICTATOR

Nope. I'm working to change that, I guess, but it's not easy.

NOREGRETS

Very true. I moved a few years ago and getting to know new people was a challenge. Now, I feel like I've known them forever, but it took a while.

DICTATOR

I think people just don't like me. Like I mentioned before, people tend to think I'm an ass.

NOREGRETS

So, maybe don't be an ass.

DICTATOR

Why didn't I think of that?

NOREGRETS

LOL. See, that's why we met. So I can help you be a better person.

DICTATOR

I think you're right.

NOREGRETS

I found a movie to watch. Want to join me?

I stared at my phone and wondered what she was asking. I didn't know her, so how…

NOREGRETS

Not come over, obviously, but if you're interested in watching we can text still. If that's dumb, you can tell me no.

DICTATOR

No, it sounds great. Let me get my TV on and I'll see if I can find the movie.

I smiled as I sat and cued up the movie. It was almost like being on a date. Almost.

I CHATTED with NoRegrets on and off through the weekend. I started to ask to meet her more than once, but I wasn't sure the protocol for that. I didn't want to rush into it. Maybe Ian could help.

It was strange to me to think of Ian as a friend, or at least as an acquaintance. He was someone I hired years ago, and in that time, we hadn't spoken much. But he was the only person I'd shared a meal with besides Veronica and Jeff in longer than I'd care to admit.

Late Sunday afternoon, I was getting ready to fix dinner when my phone rang. Few people called me so when a number I didn't recognize showed on the screen, every inch of my body coiled up like a spring.

"This is Dr. Allison."

"Hi, Dr. Allison. I'm…I'm so sorry to call you. This is Marie Kaufman. I'm a patient of yours…"

"Hi, Marie. How are you? Is everything okay?" The tension did not dissipate. If she was calling, there was an issue. I started closing up the house so I could leave as soon as we were off the phone.

"Um, not really. I don't feel well at all. I have some—" she groaned "—pain and I feel a little lightheaded."

"Is anyone with you, Marie?"

"No. I live alone."

"Okay. Marie, I need you to listen to me. Call for a ride. Do not drive yourself. Call someone. If it's a friend, fine. If it's a car service, whatever. Just call someone and get a ride to my office. I'll meet you there. Can you do that, Marie?"

"I'm sorry, Dr. Allison. Maybe I shouldn't have called you. I didn't want you to come in."

"Marie, this is my job. I want to make sure you get better. Call for a ride right now. If you can't get someone, call me back and I'll come pick you up if I have to."

"No, I'm sure I can find someone."

"Okay. Let me know, Marie. Call now. I'm on my way to the office. I'll see you there."

"Thank you, Dr. Allison."

Marie hung up. I finished packing up the things I would need for the week and made sure the house was secure while I called my answering service and notified them to get in touch with the nurse on call so I had help with Marie. I set the alarm and got onto my boat for the quick trip to the mainland.

The wind whipped at my face on the quick ride back to the mainland. Water sprayed all around me, a layer settling on my overnight bag as I raced across the water instead of taking my time. I drove on autopilot, running through every possibility for Marie in my head. Laura said Marie was dehydrated and tired when she was in the office a few days ago.

Maybe it was worse than she let on. Or maybe something else was going on.

I liked Marie. Her treatment was going to be a challenge, but I gave her my number because she reminded me of my mother. She should have come in months ago, but her primary care doctor missed all the signs that she was having trouble. It was common, and I knew it was, but it still made me furious.

The clinic loomed in the impending darkness, taking up nearly a full block on the edge of the cove. I turned on the exterior lights and left the front door locked so no one else wandered in. I knew the on-call nurse would have keys to let herself in through the back door, but I turned those lights on so she wasn't walking in to a dark space.

I pulled up Marie's file and went over Laura's notes from Friday. I listened for someone at the door and kept my phone on my desk so I didn't miss Marie.

I'd just finished reading through Marie's file when I heard someone come in the back door. Footsteps led to the lounge where whoever it was stopped briefly before continuing down the hall to my office.

"Hi, Dr. Allison," Laura said from my doorway. "Who's the patient?"

I had to stop myself from groaning. She was pulling her wild waves into a ponytail. Her shirt lifted with the movement and exposed a strip of pale skin. My mouth went dry at the sight and I had to look away before my restraint failed.

"Marie Kaufman."

"Crap. I was afraid you were going to say that. Have you reviewed her file? I think I was the last one to see her. Is there anything new since Friday?"

"Nothing new. You were the last one," I said. Thank God she finished fixing her hair and dropped her hands. She tugged her shirt down and smoothed it over her jeans. She usually wore scrubs, but seeing her in normal clothes was… fucking torture.

"Do you want to change? I'm guessing she'll need labs and fluids."

Laura shook her head as someone knocked on the front door. "I'll be fine. And it looks like we're out of time anyway."

Laura rushed to the front door and opened it for Marie and her friend. Laura gave both women a kind smile and led Marie straight back to a seat in infusion.

"What's going on, Marie?" she asked as she opened a kit to draw her blood.

"I've been really run down. I felt better Friday, but I was sick some yesterday and today I could barely get out of bed. Thankfully, Janice was off and could bring me down here." Marie smiled up at her friend.

"I wish she'd called me earlier. I keep telling you I'll stay with you or move you into my place if you need help." Janice looked up at me. "Does she need help?"

"Let's see how she's doing. Nurse Kempis is going to run some labs and find out. While we're waiting for those, we're going to give you some fluids. That will help with the dehydration. We'll go from there," I told them.

The women nodded. Laura kept working, but the way her face pinched when Marie and Janice weren't watching her said she was worried. She glanced up at me, and I knew it was going to be a long night.

Laura finished drawing Marie's blood from the port in her chest and hung a bag of saline. She shook the vials and nodded toward the other room for me to follow her.

"We'll be right back," I told Marie and Janice.

They smiled, sitting close together. Marie was pale, and Janice clearly worried. I was, too.

Laura put the vials into the hematology analyzer and glanced behind me.

"What's wrong?"

Laura shook her head. "I'm not sure, but it's not good. If she didn't have a port, I don't think I could have gotten an IV in. She looks really run down, more than two days ago. I'm worried. Hopefully something shows up in her blood work, but if not, I don't know what we're going to do."

I drew a breath and nodded. We had to make her better.

8

---

*L*aura went to check on Marie while we waited for the analyzer to do its job. I stared at the machine and asked my mother to help. I always turned to her when something felt insurmountable. She was my rock, forever. She'd always been the one to tell me things would be okay.

I was wondering how it would all be okay when Laura walked back in with a thoughtful smile on her face.

"What?" I asked.

She shook her head. "Marie's spirits are good. I always go by that. If she's happy, then she has a good chance. Right now, she's happy."

I nodded. It was definitely a good sign that she was happy. "Is she feeling better?"

"Yeah, I think so. She has a little more color. People don't realize how worn out they get, how much this takes out of them. I try to tell them, but people are so accustomed to being tired that they don't know how exhausted they are until they can barely function."

"You're a very talented nurse. And very thoughtful."

Her gaze slammed into mine, and I wondered if I'd ever complimented her before. The surprise on her face made me realize I hadn't. That needed to change.

"Have you figured out which plan for the clinic you're going to move forward with?" she asked.

I didn't like that she changed the subject, but I went along with it. "None of them."

"What? Why not?"

"Because you were right. There was something missing. The whole point of the new clinic was to make patients feel comfortable. To give them a relaxing place to heal. And it was still a clinic. It was stiff and uncomfortable. When I was home, I realized I want it to feel like my house does. I want people to put their feet up and take a deep breath and feel good."

"That sounds pretty amazing." She stared at the analyzer for a moment. "Can I ask you a personal question?"

I nodded but she wasn't looking at me. "Yes, of course."

"Why did you become an oncologist?" She still didn't look up, letting her focus stay on anything other than me.

"You haven't read my bio?" I knew she had. On day one she mentioned something from it.

She shrugged. "Well, yeah, but there's always more to it than someone puts in their bio. It's like a resume. You stretch the truth a little."

I raised a brow as she finally lifted her eyes to mine. "As your boss, I don't love that statement."

A laugh popped out. Fucking hell, I loved that sound. "I don't mean lie. I just mean polish. Massage. Instead of saying receptionist say customer service specialist. Instead of babysitter say managed the care and wellbeing of others. Things like that."

She was clever and full of surprises. "You make things interesting."

"It's part of my charm. And you're dodging the question."

I sighed and leaned against the counter. She wasn't going to let up, and it wasn't like no one knew my story. I didn't make it public, but it wasn't secret either.

"I grew up in a rough neighborhood outside of Atlanta. My mother was Black and my dad's Puerto Rican, so I didn't blend in or fit in anywhere. I was picked on constantly from elementary school on, so I was a loner. I didn't have a lot of friends."

"I'm so sorry," Laura said. Her face pinched like she actually felt my pain.

I shrugged as though it didn't bother me. "Thanks, but I think it was good for me in some ways. I got into trouble and got into fights, but I also studied a lot. I learned that it's easier to defeat a bully when you're smarter than they are. I read about martial arts and philosophy. I taught myself about science and math and read biographies of amazing historical figures. I got scholarships to college and took out loans because my parents both worked two jobs."

"Wow," Laura breathed.

I nodded. "They were amazing parents. They gave me everything they could give."

"They inspired you to go to med school?"

I shook my head. "Unfortunately, no. Not like you think. When I was in my second year of college, my mom got sick. She went to doctors and tried to get help, but none of them believed her or trusted her or something. For a year, she was so sick she couldn't work. When she went back to her doctor, she'd lost almost thirty percent of her body weight and could barely walk unassisted. They finally ran some tests."

"What was wrong?"

I drew in a loaded breath. "Pancreatic cancer. She was

gone the next month, and the day after her funeral I changed my major to premed."

"Like Marie. I'm so sorry, Dr. Allison," Laura murmured.

"Thanks. It wasn't easy, but losing her taught me that women are dismissed too easily by doctors, especially Black women. Pancreatic cancer is hard to diagnose until it's in later stages anyway, but cancer in Black women goes misdiagnosed or undiagnosed much more often. It's avoidable if doctors are willing to listen."

"You're a fantastic doctor," Laura said. "Your mom would be proud of you."

I smiled. "Thank you."

"Can I ask you another personal question?"

I nodded.

"Why did you go to O'Kelley's the other night?"

"Excuse me?"

"With Ian Jameson. I've never seen you there before. I didn't even know you and Ian knew each other."

"He built my boat a few years ago. He's a good guy."

"I know he is. He's married to one of my good friends. I just didn't know you knew him."

"Does it bother you?" I asked, wondering where she was going.

She shook her head. "I just...we all get together sometimes. If you're going to be spending time with Ian and the other guys, I want you to know that I might be there. That I'm friends with him."

"I have no problem with that. Why? Did Ian say something to you?"

"About what?" She immediately pulled back. Her eyes narrowed and darted around the room. She thought I was badmouthing her. She thought...

It didn't matter. I had to make sure she knew I thought very highly of her.

"I would never say anything negative about you, Laura. You're very talented and great with the patients. I assure you."

"If that's true, then what would Ian have said to me?"

I sighed. "I saw you there and was watching you. I couldn't remember seeing you outside the office. Laughing and in something other than scrubs. I was…It was nice to see you happy."

"Why? Why would you care?"

I looked up at her and let her see me. Let her really see me. Let her see all the things I couldn't say but wanted her to know.

The ragged intake of her next breath sucked all the air from the room. Her eyes went wide then narrowed. Her gaze slipped to where I held onto the counter, keeping myself from crossing to room to her. She scanned my body, taking in every restrained muscle.

"Dr. Allison?" Her voice trembled.

I couldn't move other than to nod for her to continue.

"I need to ask you another personal question."

My stare didn't waver from her face.

"Does Ian think you…that we…Did you tell him you're interested in me?"

I shook my head and her shoulders slumped almost imperceptibly. "I didn't have to tell him. It was fairly obvious to him and the others." That got her attention again. "But Laura, I'm not ever going to do anything. I'm over here so you know you can leave the room whenever you want. I would never force you into anything. I would never ask you for anything. I would never do anything. Nothing is going to happen between us unless you ask for it. Your job will always be secure here."

She turned to leave and my entire body deflated. She reached for the door and slowly closed it then turned back to me. Her eyes were bright and expectant, and I froze as I waited for her to explain. "I have another personal question."

I nodded for her to continue.

"Can I kiss you?"

I was hard. Everywhere. Instantly. "Laura, you don't have to do anything. I know you hate me."

She chuckled to herself like she had a secret and moved toward me. "No, I don't. I like you, Dr. Allison. But you make me crazy."

"You can't kiss me, Laura…" I paused. I needed to know she was listening to me, deciding based on what she wanted, not on what she thought she was supposed to do. "Not until you call me by my name. It feels like I'm pressuring you. I don't want you to feel—"

"Nico?"

"Yeah?"

"Shut up."

She looked up at me. Fire licked across my body. I needed her. I wanted her. I had never been so close to her. I kept my distance so I didn't cross any lines. I stayed away from her. But she was right there. Close enough that if we both took a deep breath, our bodies would brush against each other.

I still didn't move. I couldn't. I liked her too much to risk making her feel uncomfortable. I didn't matter how uncomfortable I was, she was the one who mattered.

"Nico?"

"Yes?"

"Kiss me."

I shook my head. "I can't, Laura. I won't unless I know it's what you want."

"Trust me, it's what I want."

She went up on her toes and pressed her lips to mine. A groan tore through me. My hands were on her hips, bringing her body into contact with mine before the next second passed. My tongue requested entrance into her mouth, and she eagerly granted it. I took a step toward her then spun and pressed her back to the counter I was just leaning against.

Her hands slid up my chest and wrapped around my neck, drawing me closer to her. The kiss was sloppy and passionate. Like two people who'd waited too long to let go. Who couldn't control themselves. Who didn't want to control themselves.

I lifted the edge of her shirt and spread my hand over her bare skin. She moaned and scraped her nails across my scalp. I pressed my hard length to her core. I wanted her. Right then and there, I wanted her. I wasn't sure if I was going to be able to stop myself.

She shoved against my chest, pushing me away. I wasn't sure I had the strength, but I took a step back, giving her space. She was done. It was done. We were done.

She moved around me and went to the hematology analyzer. The beeping should have drawn my attention, but I didn't notice it over the pull of Laura in my arms.

Laura in my arms.

Dear God, what did I do?

I held on to the counter again, unsure how she felt about what just happened. She reviewed the results of Marie's blood work then turned to me.

"Um…she's, uh, do you want to see this?"

I nodded and released the counter. I reviewed the results, noting that Laura put distance between us as I did. I wouldn't press. I promised myself I wouldn't. I had no interest in losing her. Maybe one kiss was all I needed to get her out of my system.

I almost laughed out loud at the thought. I was so hard I could barely walk, and my fingers tingled from the feel of her soft skin. My lips and tongue were on fire from kissing her. I wanted more. I needed more. I couldn't live without more.

But I'd lock it all back up and throw away the key because Laura was done.

I cleared my throat and kept my gaze on the numbers on the screen in front of me. "She's still borderline with a lot of her numbers. Her white count is low, but not outside of where we want to see it. We definitely need to watch that. Her CA19-9 is stable, which isn't great but it isn't going up. If the fluids are helping, we can bring her in more often. Encourage her to get more on her own. You know what to do."

I set the tablet down and moved back to my spot across the room. Far away from Laura and her sweet scent that had seeped inside of me and was making me crazy.

"Nico?"

"Yes?"

"I really enjoyed that."

My gaze snapped to hers. A shy smile teased her lips. "So did I."

She licked her lips and drew one in between her teeth. "I've wanted to kiss you for a long time."

"You have?"

She nodded.

"Nice to know I'm not in this alone."

She shook her head. "Definitely not."

She smiled at me then walked out of the room to see Marie. I took a long minute to calm myself down then followed her to the infusion center. She was already explaining everything to Marie and Janice.

"She needs to pay attention to her body," Janice said.

Laura nodded. "She does. I know it isn't always easy, but chemo will zap you. It sucks you dry, literally, so you have to drink more water than you normally would. Eat foods that have water in them, like fruits and vegetables. Patients can struggle with certain foods, so if you can't eat those, try other things, but get that water. We will bring you in once or twice a week for fluids until you feel better."

"And that'll help?"

"It should. Pancreatic cancer is ugly. It's not an easy fight. We don't see anything wrong in her blood work right now. There are a few things that concern us, but nothing that's unexpected. We'll do blood work whenever you come in. If you need anything, call us. We're always happy to help, but we want you to feel well. At least, as much as possible."

The three women laughed. Laura put her hand on Marie's and smiled at her. I realized what Ian was telling me the other night. Laura flirted, but she did it with everyone. She wasn't trying to flirt, it was just the way she spoke to people. And if I wasn't okay with that, I needed to take a step back and let her find someone else.

I needed to be okay with that. Because I didn't think I could stand by and watch her be with someone else.

Laura sat and talked to Marie and Janice while the rest of Marie's IV bag emptied. When it was finished, she walked them to the door and said she'd see them both soon. Then she came back to my office.

"Is there anything else you need from me?"

I nodded. "I need to know you aren't upset with me."

"Why would I be upset with you?"

"I'm your boss, Laura. I've put you in a tough position. I don't want that. I never want you to feel like you can't say no to me."

"It feels like you're pushing me away right now. Like you regret kissing me and are trying to find a way out." She crossed her arms over her chest.

I couldn't let her think I regretted a single moment of what happened. "That's not true."

"Well, maybe you need to figure out what is. I know

where I stand on this. I don't need an escape. But it definitely seems like you do." Her voice dripped with frustration.

"I don't. I don't want that. But I don't want you to feel like you can't say no to me."

"Dr. Allison, I've worked for you for more than four years. In that time, have you felt like I've held back from telling you the truth? Or that I've bowed down to everything you wanted?"

"No, but—"

"Then why would you think I can't say no to you now?"

"This is different. I know women have to protect themselves. If I say the wrong thing, you could think your job is at risk. If I do the wrong thing, you could think your job is at risk. If I act the wrong way, you could think your job is at risk. I never want you to worry about that."

"Then don't say or do or act wrong."

"I don't know if I'll know."

"I'll give you a hint. This right here? Kissing me, telling me how you feel, then asking me if I want out, telling me I can leave whenever I want, pushing me away, this is the wrong thing."

"I'm trying to protect you."

She took a step forward and pointed at me. "You're trying to protect you, Dr. Allison. I get it. You're the one in charge. You're the owner, you're the doctor, you're the one with the power. But don't tell me I have power when I don't. We both know I don't."

I got up and walked around my desk. I didn't stop until I was right in front of her. She didn't move. Didn't take a single step backward.

"I have no power here, Laura. None." My voice barely restrained my weakness at being close to her again.

"That's not how it feels."

I dragged her into my arms and sealed my lips over hers. I

pried her lips apart and licked my way inside her mouth. She sighed happily and grabbed the back of my shirt. Her soft moans filled the air as we kissed like frenzied teenagers.

"How does that feel?" I whispered against her lips.

"Amazing," she breathed.

"Go out with me. On a date. Let me take you out. Please."

She drew a breath and took a step back. She looked up at me. "Are you sure?"

"I want to see you in a dress. I want to hold your hand and share a meal with you. I want to make you laugh and see you with your hair down. Say yes, Laura. Please."

She smiled up at me. She reached up and pulled her hair out of the ponytail she had it in and shook, letting her waves tumble around her shoulders. "I don't wear a lot of dresses."

"I don't care. I just want to take you on a date."

"I don't know if that's a good idea, Dr. Allison."

I growled. "My tongue was in your mouth, Laura. The least you can do is call me Nico."

"It's kind of fun to piss you off, Dr. Allison."

I snarled at her and moved into her space again. I slid my hands into her hair and ran my fingers through her waves. Her hair was like silk, soft and fine. I could stand there all night touching it. Touching her.

Her hands went to my chest, sliding under my jacket and caressing me. She pushed my jacket off my shoulders, trapping my arms. I shrugged it off and wrapped my arms around her waist, bringing her close to me again.

"I want you, Laura. I know I shouldn't tell you this, but I do."

"Why shouldn't you tell me?"

"I suck at dating. I am awkward and uncomfortable. I usually let a friend set me up with someone if I need a date. I don't know how to talk to women. And you have all the power, Laura. I will follow your lead."

"I don't think I have any power, but I do have plans tonight."

I nodded and took a step back. She had a date. She was in my arms, kissing me, and instead of staying there, she was going out with someone else. "I'm sorry I kept you."

She smiled. "It's not a problem, Dr. Allison. My friends will understand. And besides, tonight was my pleasure."

I groaned as she walked away laughing. If nothing else, she was going to make life interesting. For as long as she let me have her.

9

LAURA

I was still floating when I made it to Book Boyfriends Unlimited for book club. Nico kissed me. He actually kissed me. And he told me he wants me. What the hell was I supposed to do with all that?

No. I wasn't going to worry about it. He said he wanted me. He kissed me. He was taking me on a date. Everything else was going to figure itself out. Or it wouldn't. Either way, I would finally know if this could be something.

Finley opened the door and let me in with a questioning look. "You okay? You look weird. And you're late."

"I got called into work."

"Is everything okay?" Finley asked as we joined the others.

"What's wrong?" Blake asked.

I shook my head. "A patient wasn't feeling well. She called Dr. Allison and I was on call so I had to meet him there." I couldn't help my grin.

"Um, that's a really messed up thing to be so happy about," Elise said. She wrinkled her nose and leaned back with her cake.

I breathed a laugh. "I'm not laughing about the patient."

"Then what are you laughing about?" Piper asked.

"Dr. Allison kissed me," I confessed, feeling more like a teenage girl and less like a thirty-eight year old woman. I wasn't even embarrassed by that.

"Holy shit."

"Are you serious?"

"Good for you."

"About damn time."

I nodded at all their comments. "It was amazing. He said he wants me. That he's wanted me for a long time. He was afraid to kiss me because he's my boss. He refused. Even tonight."

"I thought you said he kissed you," Melody clarified.

I nodded. "He did, but only after I kissed him and told him I'd wanted to kiss him for a long time."

My friend's smiles froze and they exchanged Stepford Wife glances. Wide eyes, empty smiles, and secrets I wasn't a part of.

"What?" I demanded. "What are you all thinking?"

They dropped the act and looked around for a spokesperson. Someone who was going to tell me what they were all thinking. Who was going to admit what I couldn't see myself.

All eyes landed on Willow. I glared at her and crossed my arms. She huffed and shot daggers at the others. "Why me?"

"Because you won't sugarcoat it. And you don't care what people think," Elise said. Usually she was the one who was blunt with everyone.

Willow sighed heavily and met my angry gaze. "Fine. We're all worried he's telling you what you want to hear. That he's saying back to you what you're saying to him."

"That's not how it happened," I argued.

"Really? Because you said he told you he wanted you for a long time, but it sounds like that was only after you told him you wanted him for a long time. Maybe it's true, but maybe he's mirroring."

"He is not." I still felt like that teenager but for a very different reason. "You guys weren't there. You didn't see the look in his eyes. You didn't hear our conversation. You have no idea what you're talking about."

"We want to be wrong," Finley said. "We want you and Dr. Allison to be together. We want to see you happy. But you're still calling him Dr. Allison. You only do that when you're mad at him or feel distanced. You came in telling us he kissed you. Why isn't he Nico?"

I chuckled, thinking of him telling me to call him Nico. I wanted to share it all with my friends. I wanted to tell them everything that happened. But I wasn't sure they were going to be supportive. They weren't cheering for things to work out.

"You have adored him forever," Karissa said. "I adore him. I want you to be happy, but it hasn't been that long since you said you were going to date other men and forget about him."

"You guys know why I did that," I said.

Karissa and the others nodded. "We do. We also know part of that was because he was seeing someone else. Do you know things are over with the woman in Syracuse? You were worried about that," she said.

"I don't know. I didn't ask him. But if he's kissing me, doesn't that mean things are over with her?"

"I'd love to say yes, but I think we all know some men are cheating assholes," Finley said. "We don't want that to be true with Nico, but you've also said Ally is the one who mentioned Veronica, so Nico might think you don't know anything about her."

"That's why we're worried. This isn't us not being supportive. It's us not wanting to see him hurt you. Again," Elise said.

"Then why aren't you telling me this is a great thing. I don't know about Veronica, but I know Nico. I've liked him for years. Do you have any idea how hard that is? To like a man that I see every single day for years, and then to finally kiss him and have him ask me out and the people I'm closest to think he's playing me?"

"You're right," Trinity said. She met the gazes of our friends. "You're right. We should be asking how great it was. We should be begging you for every detail. If things go badly, then it wasn't meant to be, but we don't want it to go badly, so we need to be supportive. Like the friar in Romeo and Juliet. We'll marry you in secret if we have to."

I breathed a laugh. "Hopefully it won't be like that, and hopefully I don't have to kill myself in order to be with him."

Trinity nodded. "I hope not. But for some kisses, it's worth it."

I groaned. "This was definitely that kind of kiss. All the kisses were."

"All the kisses? How many kisses were there?" Trinity asked.

Willow handed me a piece of cake and I finally told them everything. The tension was still there in the room with us, threatening to ruin my good mood, but I did my best to ignore it. I knew my friends were still worried, but they were trying. They wanted everything to work out. I hoped it would. I really hoped it would.

I ADMITTED to myself that I needed to find a way to ask Nico about Veronica. Even if I wasn't really supposed to know about her, I had to mention it. I hated the idea of accusing him of cheating on his girlfriend, with me, but I hated the idea of breaking up a relationship even more.

I was seeing patients the next morning with Dr. Allison. I brought our first patient back to the exam room and recorded his vitals and made notes on how he said he was doing. When I finished, I noted on the chart that he was ready for Dr. Allison to come in.

We chatted while we waited for Dr. Allison to arrive. Roger was a nice man in his sixties who'd been a patient of Dr. Allison's since before I started working there. He came in annually for a survivorship appointment, my favorite kind because it showed me that people got past the horrible illness I saw every day.

"Good morning, Roger," Dr. Allison said as he walked into the exam room. "How are you feeling today?"

"Doing well, Doc. Ms. Laura said things look good, so I just need you to agree with her."

He smiled. "I'll see what I can do." He turned to me for the tablet and gave me a brief smile. I wasn't sure what to do with that, but we were working. If he'd kissed me in front of a patient, I would have been upset. Treating me like he always had was definitely what I wanted.

Dr. Allison reviewed Roger's chart and did a quick physical exam. "It looks like Ms. Laura was right. You're doing well. How's Lisa? The kids and grandkids?"

"Everyone is doing well. Lisa's watching the youngest grandkids right now. We keep them three days a week so Mom and Dad can work."

"That sounds like a fun way to spend your retirement."

Roger laughed. "They definitely keep us moving. You should have a couple rugrats, Doc. Why haven't you found some pretty young thing and snapped her up yet?"

Dr. Allison chuckled. "Kids and marriage might not be in the cards for me, Roger. Not many women understand that I'm married to my work."

"Ms. Laura here gets it. She is, too."

Dr. Allison shot me a heated look that burned my cheeks. I bit the inside of my mouth to keep from smiling. Or moaning. Jeez, the man was dangerous to be around.

"I'm happy to be single, Roger," I told him.

Dr. Allison cleared his throat and changed the subject. "Well, I think we can let you get back to those grandkids, Roger. Give Lisa a hand."

He got off the exam table and laughed. "I think she considers me another child she has to watch over. I get down on the floor and make as much of a ruckus as they do."

"Like you said, they keep you young," Dr. Allison said.

Roger laughed and nodded. "That they do. See you next year, Doc."

"Stay out of trouble." Dr. Allison nodded at me and left the room, propping the door open.

"I've put it in for you to come back in a year. Tina will get it set up for you."

"Thank you, Ms. Laura. Don't you two work too hard."

"We'll try," I said. I followed him to the front and grabbed my next patient.

The morning was over before I had a chance to take a breath. I had two new patients, one more survivor, and eight patients there for mid-treatment exams. One patient was trying to get into a clinical trial because the chemo and radiation weren't working. Those were the hardest ones for me. The ones who seemed to be losing hope.

Ally and Tina were in the break room when I walked in for lunch. They smiled and invited me to sit with them.

"How's your morning?" Tina asked.

"Tough. One clinical trial applicant," I told them.

"I hate those," Ally said. "It has to be so scary."

I nodded. "Sitting there while Dr. Allison tells them it's their best hope is painful. I want everyone to be cured. I want all of them to feel better. I know the clinical trials work sometimes, but sometimes they don't."

"The hardest ones for me are the ones who don't get in," Ally admitted. "The ones who have hope when they come to me to sign all the paperwork and then have none when they aren't accepted."

"Why would they do that?" Tina asked.

"It depends on the trial. Sometimes it's staging or location or just simply that the trial is full. They set guidelines and have to stick to them," Ally said.

"This is not an easy job," I admitted.

"I just have to sign them in and schedule their next appointment. I don't have to do the hard work," Tina said.

"You're the one who gives them a smile and makes them feel like everything is going to be okay," I told her. "You're the one who sets the tone for the entire office."

"Well, thank you. I guess I need to make sure my smile is firmly in place then." Tina grinned broadly.

"Maybe get the lettuce from your teeth first," Ally said.

Tina clamped her mouth shut and covered it with her hand. "Whoops."

"Happens to all of us," I told her. "Besides, we're eating lunch."

"What do you have today?"

"No cake. Sorry, ladies. We demolished the cake last night. Karissa made a lemon buttercream frosted pound cake. It was so good," I told them.

"I really need to go with you one of these weeks," Tina said.

"You should. Everyone is really welcoming."

"It's been a long time since I've seen Karissa," Ally said. "How's she doing?"

I nodded and unwrapped the turkey sandwich I made that morning. It wasn't glamorous, but it was food. "She's doing well. She said she's trying to work fewer hours. She spends all day working and sometimes doesn't notice the sun."

"Sounds like a lot of people," Tina said. "My husband has been working longer and longer hours lately. It's hard. Even if Karissa isn't involved with anyone, it's hard on your body and mind to work that much."

"Willow is trying to talk her into yoga class. She's trying to talk all of us into it," I said.

"Ooh, I could definitely get behind that," Ally said. "I used to love yoga."

"We should all go," Tina said. "When does Willow teach?"

I shook my head. "I'm not sure. I'll ask her."

"Good. Let me know. I should probably get back to the front." Tina stood and threw away her trash then zipped her lunch bag. "Any good dates lately? Andrew and I need something new to do. Any tips?"

Ally looked at me, letting me answer. Being the single one, they always thought I knew the best things to do on a date. Most of my dates were dinner with little else. "I don't know. I have a date tomorrow night, but I don't know what we're doing. Usually my dates are at O'Kelley's. Sometimes something different, but dinner is it."

"Let me know about your date tomorrow night. I want to get Andrew out this weekend. Something to get away from home and spend some time together. I even have a babysitter lined up."

"Wow, an actual date," Ally said with a chuckle. "We're such homebodies we don't go out much."

"It's good to mix things up. I just hope I don't end up pregnant again. Wouldn't be the first time we got carried away on a date night," Tina said with a wink. "Not that I want to pass up that part of it."

Ally and I laughed as Tina walked out of the break room.

Ally turned to me. "I don't know how you keep dating. I've been with Spencer forever and can't imagine actually dating again."

"If I had someone in my life like that, I'd feel the same. I've never been in a long-term relationship. Nothing that I thought would last."

"I know I'm lucky. My sister got divorced a few years ago. We aren't close, but it still seemed really tough on her. More on her son, though."

"Sorry to hear that," I said. I still hadn't figured out Ally's relationship with her sister.

"Relationships are funny. Sometimes they come out of nowhere and surprise you, but sometimes they seem to grow and change over time."

I nodded. The way Ally was looking at me made me wonder if she knew something about Nico and me. I couldn't imagine how she could, but she was giving me a look that said she was waiting for me to tell her something.

"Is that how you and Spencer are?"

Ally laughed. "Oh, God, no. We've known each other forever. A part of me feels like we're the same people we've always been, but I know we've changed. Together, thankfully."

"That's definitely good."

"Yeah. Hopefully your date tomorrow night goes well. Maybe he'll be the one for you and you won't have to worry about more dates after that." She definitely knew something.

"Yeah, maybe. I guess we'll see. Um, I need to get back to work."

"Let me know how it goes after tomorrow."

I nodded as I threw away my trash. "Yeah, sure. Sounds good."

Ally smiled and waved as I walked out. What the hell was that about?

10

"You doing okay?" I asked Thomas as I took the seat next to him.

Thomas was a newer patient in for his second infusion appointment. I hadn't gotten to know him well yet, but he seemed like a nice enough guy.

He nodded. "About as good as can be expected."

I smiled. "I know. It's not easy. What would you be doing if you weren't here? Aside from anything else."

Thomas chuckled. He had a friendly smile. His hair was long, almost to his shoulders. It shined with softness. I couldn't help but wonder how long it would last. I knew losing their hair was often the hardest part for the women, but men with longer hair said it changed them, too. That piece was when it felt real. When they couldn't pretend any longer that everything was fine.

"Anything else is definitely a good answer. I would probably be at work."

"What do you do?"

"I own a restaurant in Alexandria Bay. My parents started

it when they got married and they retired a year ago and turned it over to my brother and me."

"Very cool. That sounds like a big job."

Thomas nodded. "It is, but I love it. I grew up in the restaurant and I've always wanted to take it over. We both have. I met my wife there, and we're raising our kids to work in the restaurant."

"A family affair, huh?"

"Yep. It's great. I just need to kick this cancer so I can get back there full time."

"We're working on it. Are you feeling okay?"

"Actually, yeah. I expected things to be much worse, but the first one went well. I was exhausted afterward and pretty much slept the rest of the day, but then I was fine."

"Good. That seems to be common. The anti-nausea meds we give you make you tired, which is why you sleep, but if the chemo isn't bothering you too much, you're lucky. That's not the case for everyone."

He nodded. "Yeah. My mother-in-law went through chemo a few years ago. It about put her out for days after each session."

"Ouch. That's rough. You guys are strong. I don't think I could handle it as well as my patients. I'm kind of a wimp."

Thomas laughed. "I find that hard to believe. You seem pretty tough."

"Well, thank you for that. I try, but I've never faced anything like this. Every single patient who comes through here is determined. It's literally a fight for your life. That's a challenge no one should have to deal with."

Thomas nodded. "Better me than my kids. I tell myself that every day. I hate it, but I'd hate it that much more if I had to watch my kids go through this."

"I can understand that. And that's not a bad perspective."

He smiled. "I understand what's happening to me. My

kids wouldn't. So far we haven't told them much. I think when my hair starts falling out they're going to ask more questions."

"Your hair is beautiful."

"Thanks. A gift from my mom."

I laughed with him.

"I thought about cutting it, but I'm not ready to let go yet."

"I'm not sure what I would do either. I've had some patients use chemo caps that are supposed to reduce hair loss. Have you looked into those?"

He shook his head. "I haven't even heard of them."

"Check it out. It might be an option. Then you can keep all this beautiful hair."

I started the drip on his next infusion as he dug out his phone. "Looking it up right now. Anything is worth a shot to feel normal. As normal as possible."

"Absolutely. I'll be back shortly to check on you. Do you need a snack or anything?"

"A water would be great."

I nodded. "Coming right up."

I took off my protective equipment and trashed it then washed my hands. On my way to get Thomas a water, I saw Nico watching me. His arms were crossed and the look in his eyes said he was trying to figure something out.

He walked toward me as I headed for the fridge. I stopped and waited for him to reach me. "Is everything okay?"

"No. Please come to my office."

I nodded. "Can I give my patient a water first?"

He hesitated then nodded and turned and walked away.

I rolled my eyes to myself and took the water back to Thomas. I wasn't sure what pissed Nico off this time, but I was not looking forward to whatever he was going to say. After the argument we got into last week, I was on edge, even after everything he admitted the day before.

"Close the door," he said when I walked into his office.

Every inch of me said to run. He was going to say something I was going to get mad about. I could feel it.

"What was going on with that patient?" he asked.

"What patient? Thomas?"

He nodded.

"I'm giving him his treatments. Why?"

"I'm trying very hard to accept that the way you speak to patients makes it seem like you're flirting with them."

I rolled my eyes and sighed heavily. "This again? Are you serious? That's how I talk. I will not apologize again for being friendly with patients. He's a married man with kids."

"I said I'm trying."

"Dr. Allison, I've worked here for years. I've always spoken to patients the same way. I've always been friendly and asked about their personal lives and flirted, as you claim. I don't know why it's only been a problem lately. Have there been complaints about me?"

"No," he snarled. He looked away.

"Has someone said I'm making them uncomfortable?"

"No."

"Then what is wrong with how I'm treating patients? I'd really like to know."

"I don't enjoy watching you flirt with other men, okay? It makes me…" He cut himself off. "I don't like it."

I breathed deeply and walked toward him. He was jealous. The son of a bitch was jealous of the way I spoke to patients. "I'm not flirting with these men. I'm not flirting with the women. I'm talking to them. I'm trying to put them at ease. I want them to know they can talk to me if they need to. This is the hardest thing most of them have ever been through and possibly will ever go through. It's lonely. Even the patients who have a support person with them are lonely. No one else knows how it feels. I don't, but I've seen enough to understand it. I can sympathize without being emotionally involved because I'm not family or friend. I'm the nurse. I'm not someone they're going to feel awkward around for years. I'm neutral."

"I get it."

"No, I don't think you do. I'm not going to change who I am. I'm not going to sit back and ignore my patients. I'm going to talk to them. I'm going to get to know them. I'm going to listen to them and put my hand on their arm and laugh with them. I'm going to try to make them feel as close to normal as possible. If you can't handle that about me, then I need to start looking for another job."

"I don't want that. You're great at what you do."

"Then you need to let me do it. One of the reasons I'm good is because I don't treat them like they're damaged goods or like they are untouchable. I treat them like people. Because they are."

Nico came around his desk and moved toward me. He stopped a few feet from me. "This isn't easy for me."

"What?"

"Wanting you like I do."

"So because you are attracted to me it means I can't talk to other men?"

"No, but it makes me crazy to see you talking to other men the way you do. To know you don't speak to me that way."

"You want me to flirt with you?" I asked. I couldn't avoid the way my lips turned up.

"Hell, yes. I want you to want me."

I smirked. "You have to give me a reason."

"A reason?"

I shrugged. "I talk to my patients to put them at ease. You're always in control. You're calling the shots. You're not unsure about anything." My breath came out wispy. I sounded turned on to my own ears. I wondered if he could hear it.

He moved closer. "I'm not sure about anything with you, Laura. I told you I want you. I told you I've wanted you for a very long time. You're the one with the control."

I drew in a breath and my chest rubbed against his. He leaned closer and all thoughts scattered, fragments of things I was going to say spread across my mind. I reached up the same moment Nico leaned down. Our lips crashed together, both of us fighting for control. I nipped at his tongue and he sucked mine hard into his mouth. He pressed my back to the door and devoured me, rubbing his bearded chin against my neck as he licked his way up my jaw to capture my lips again.

His erection throbbed between us, my body on high alert. I wanted him. I needed him. But he was still my boss, and I had work to do. And I wasn't in the mood to make him think being jealous was okay.

I pushed him back and heaved for breath. His short hair was spiked up from my hands running through it. His dark eyes were black with desire. His hands twitched at his sides. His cock tried to push through his zipper.

"I have a patient," I said.

"Are you kidding me?"

I shook my head and smoothed down my scrub top. "I have work to do. I would assume my boss wants me to do my job." I lifted an eyebrow, challenging him.

He growled. "Fine."

"I'm not going to change the way I treat my patients, Dr. Allison."

"Fine."

I drank him in, enjoying the barely restrained power in him. "I'm also not going to change my mind about whatever this is."

He rubbed his jaw but not before I saw his smile.

I ducked out of the office, closing the door behind me. I stopped in the bathroom on my way back to infusion to fix my ponytail and make sure I looked okay. I couldn't stop the smile in the mirror. Or the one on my face for the rest of the day.

Nico left me alone for the afternoon and all the following day. I wanted to be happy about that because it meant I could do my job, but in the end, it made me more anxious about our date.

Especially since every time I was around him I forgot all about the girlfriend I thought he had.

I rushed home after work and took a quick shower. I needed to wash the day off and feel good for my first date with him. I was confident it wouldn't be my last, assuming his ex really was an ex, and I wanted it to go well.

We never talked about where we were going, but he made a comment about wanting to see me in a dress, so I rifled through my closet until I found a few options. I finally decided on a knee-length black dress with subtle gray designs. The cotton fabric hugged my breasts and flared out at my waist, accentuating my curves in all the right places. The capped sleeves and loose skirt toned it down so it was fun enough for a casual dinner, but sexy enough for a date.

I just hoped Nico liked it.

I dried and fluffed my hair then added makeup. I wanted him unable to stop staring at my lips so I went with a bold red lipstick I rarely had the guts to wear and subtle eyeshadow. I moved all my things to a red purse and added a pair of red heels and drew in a breath.

I looked damn good. If Nico could resist me, he was a better man than I thought.

I was ready.

When he knocked on the door, my heart beat out of my chest. I jumped and had to force myself to take a deep breath before I could open it.

Then I lost my breath all over again.

"Wow," he whispered.

I nodded, trying to see him all at once. His dark hair was neat, his beard the same. His black suit hugged his body. He wore a gray shirt underneath, one that hinted at a casualness I rarely saw in him. A pocket square said the suit was not casual at all, and neither was the man wearing it.

He leaned in and kissed my cheek. "You look amazing."

"Thank you. So do you."

A grin tilted his lips. His dark brown eyes sparkled at me. His barely restrained desire hovered right there, ready to be let out if I was willing.

I was more than willing, but I was also hungry. And I wanted to know him on a different level. We'd kissed, and he was my boss, but I didn't know Nico. Not really.

"Are you going to tell me where we're going?" I asked, moving out the door to meet him on the porch. I locked the door with his heat close enough that I could feel him.

"Dinner first. After that, we can decide. I don't want to overstep and keep you up too late."

My pulse skipped and heat spread through my body. I was hoping he'd keep me up all night, but I wasn't going to tell him that.

"Sounds good," I said instead.

He put his hand on my lower back and guided me to his SUV. It was big, like him. The inside was plush and comfortable. The leather seats still smelled like leather but blended with the unmistakable scent of Nico. A scent I could drown in.

He didn't say anything as he backed out of my driveway

and turned south. It wasn't until we got on St. Lawrence Parkway that I asked, "Where are we going?"

"There's a great Italian place in A-Bay. Sits right on the water. Beautiful views and best wines in the area. I figured we could celebrate and have a night without a ton of people we know watching our every move."

I nodded. He said the right things, but it also felt like he was hiding the fact that we were going on a date. Like he didn't want anyone to know.

I tried to tell myself I was being silly, but I couldn't shake the feeling that something wasn't right.

He pulled into a parking lot with an attendant at the front. He stopped and got out of the car then walked around to my door. "Are you ready?"

I accepted his arm and smiled at the attendant as he slid into the driver's seat. I smoothed a hand down my dress, feeling very underdressed. Most places in the Thousand Islands were casual. Family owned and run, small and simple. People were laidback and relaxed. But this place...I had never been to a place like it.

Another man opened the door as we approached, and Nico nodded at him. I tried to smile, but I felt stiff and uncomfortable. Nico, on the other hand, seemed completely at ease with the opulence of the place.

One thing I couldn't disagree with was the view. He was right. The hostess led us to a table right next to the window. We could see Boldt Castle from our seats, and the glittering St. Lawrence River as it flowed past us.

"It's beautiful here," I said, forcing a smile and trying to act normal. As normal as possible.

Nico nodded. "It is. This is one of my favorite restaurants."

A young female server walked over with a smile and a

bottle of wine. "Good evening, sir. Madam. How are you both tonight?"

"Very well, Crystal. How are you?"

"Doing well, sir. Is this okay for this evening?" She presented him with the bottle of wine.

"Wonderful. Thank you."

Crystal nodded. "I'll give you two a few moments."

Nico nodded again. Crystal opened the bottle and poured a splash of wine into his glass. He sipped it, swirling it around in his mouth before swallowing, then nodded his approval.

Crystal turned and poured wine into my glass then poured a glass for him before setting the bottle in a bucket of ice just behind Nico.

I looked up at him, but he was looking out the window. I wasn't sure what I was supposed to do, so I opened my menu and studied it.

There were no prices. I'd never been to a place without prices on the menu. I'd heard about it, but I wasn't that kind of person. Not that I didn't want to try it, but I wasn't prepared. I should have worn a nicer dress. Maybe I should have pulled my hair back in some complicated updo kind of thing. Or put on some expensive jewelry. I didn't wear any jewelry.

I lifted the wine glass and tipped it up, needing a drink to calm my nerves. It was good wine. Very good. I set the glass down as I realized if the food didn't have prices, the wine was likely the most expensive wine I'd ever had in my life. And I was guzzling it.

I drew my lip between my teeth and tried to stop the panic I felt. I had no idea what to do. I was out of place. I really didn't like that feeling.

Nico looked at me and lifted his wine glass. When I met

his gaze, he nodded to mine. I set my menu to the side and picked up my glass.

"To starting something new."

I smiled. That made me feel better. He was toasting us.

"I signed the contract today for work to begin on the clinic. It'll be done within six weeks. Tonight, we celebrate."

"Oh," I said. He wasn't talking about us. He was talking about work. I pressed my lips together in a smile and clinked my glass against his. I sipped the wine again, letting the sweet, fruity flavor wash over my tongue.

Crystal set a basket on the table between us and stepped back. She clasped her hands behind her and focused on Nico. "Let me know when you'd like the first course to come out. Chef Andre has been preparing all day for your arrival."

Nico nodded. "Thank you, Crystal. I think it would be good for us to have a few moments to relax and enjoy the beautiful scenery. Please thank Chef Andre for us."

Crystal smiled. "Of course, sir. He'll be out to see you at some point this evening. I'll take these out of your way. The hostess didn't realize you wouldn't need them." She reached for our menus as I reached for my wine.

When Crystal walked away, I asked Nico, "Why didn't we order?"

"I know the owner. And the chef. I asked them to create a special menu just for us tonight. We're getting items that aren't available to anyone else."

My eyebrows spiked and I nodded. Wow. I wasn't sure how I felt about that, but it wasn't great.

11

NICO

Chef Andre outdid himself with our meal. Every bite was sensational, and the wine he paired the food with was the perfect compliment. I couldn't remember the last time I'd enjoyed a meal so much.

Until I looked at Laura's face.

"Do you not like it?" I asked.

She forced a smile and shook her head. "It's good. Everything is good."

I smiled. Something was wrong. She wasn't enjoying herself. I had no clue why, but she was not happy.

"So, um…" I tried to think of something to talk to her about. I knew how her day went because I saw her every day and read through the notes she wrote about patients every night. I didn't know her friends, but I wasn't interested in their personal lives. I wanted to know her. "Why did you move to MacKellar Cove?"

She looked up at me, a bite of pasta halfway to her mouth. She drew a breath and set her fork down. She put her hands in her lap and looked just past my head so she was looking at me but not. "I came for the job."

"Just the job?"

She nodded. "Basically. I was looking for something new. Partly a new challenge, but also something different. I'd considered going into oncology when I was in nursing school, but I fell in love with fertility before I had a chance to try oncology."

"Really?"

She nodded again. "Yep."

Getting her to talk was nearly painful. She didn't want to be there. I'd been on enough dates when I knew she wasn't interested. This was the worst because I cared. If it were any other woman, I would have gotten the check and left, but it was Laura.

"Do you like it here?"

She finally looked at me. "Yes, I do."

"Tell me about your friends," I said. I hated it, but she usually grew animated and talkative when asked about her friends. Ally wasn't a part of Laura's circle, but she knew enough of the women in it to ask about them. I'd overheard more than a few conversations between them to know Laura adored her friends.

"You want to know about my friends?"

Her tone said I shouldn't agree, but I didn't know what else to talk to her about. I assumed conversation would be easy with her. She wasn't a stranger. But everything was awkward. "Yeah. I know they're important to you."

Finally, I said something right. Her eyes softened and her lips curled up on the ends. That red lipstick was making me crazy. I wanted to kiss it off her. She parted her lips and started talking, mesmerizing me with the soft words.

"I don't know if I would have survived the last few years without them," Laura said. "Being somewhere without people isn't easy. Especially when—" She cut herself off.

"When what?" I asked as her cheeks pinked. She avoided

looking at me, wiping her mouth on her napkin and staring at her plate.

"More wine, madam?" Crystal asked, interrupting us at the worst moment. Or maybe the best. I wondered if the servers had training in when to notice if something was off so they could step in and avoid a scene.

Laura nodded and gratefully lifted her gaze to Crystal. "Thank you."

Crystal nodded then offered more to me. I declined. Crystal stepped away, leaving us to our conversation once more, but lingered close by. We were the only table she had for the evening. A favor from the owner.

"What were we talking about?" I asked even though I knew exactly what we were talking about.

"You asked about my friends," she said, still avoiding my gaze. "They're funny and sweet and amazing women. We get together every Sunday night and usually at least a few people get together during the week. They're like a family to me."

"You're lucky to have them," I said, not pressing the issue. I wanted to know what she was going to say, but she wasn't my employee hiding something from me. She was my date.

"I am. Do you have people like that in your life?"

I thought about it and realized I didn't. Not the same. I had Veronica and Jeff, but no one else. No one I saw regularly. "Not like that. I have a few close friends, but they aren't local so I don't see them often."

"Why did you start your clinic in MacKellar Cove?"

"It reminded me of summers with my grandmother. In Puerto Rico. Small, peaceful, with water, of course. My parents came up here once before I was born, and I moved to Syracuse for med school. I felt at peace here."

"It is very peaceful," Laura agreed. She smiled at me for the first time since she opened her door.

"Nico," Andre said as he stopped by our table.

I stood and hugged the other man, a man I considered a friend until Laura talked about hers. My friends were more like acquaintances. "Andre. Delicious as always. Please meet Laura. Laura, this is the chef, Andre."

Andre reached for her hand and clasped it in both of his. "A pleasure, Ms. Laura."

"The pleasure is mine, Chef. Everything was amazing. I've never had food this good."

"Ah, well, then you'll have to come back so I can amaze you all over again."

Laura smiled, her cheeks staining pink. I did not like that. At all.

"Yes, well, I'm sure we will be back soon," I said, emphasizing the *we* for my so-called friend.

Andre turned to me, his eyes sparkling. "I look forward to it. I apologize but I must return to my kitchen. It was wonderful to see you, Nico, and to meet you, Laura. I look forward to next time."

Laura waved as Andre worked his way through tables, stopping every so often to check with the other customers. I just wanted to pummel him for flirting with my date.

"Sit down," Laura hissed. "Stop glaring at him."

I cleared my throat and resumed my seat. I hadn't realized I was doing what she said until she brought it to my attention.

Laura finished her wine and declared herself finished. I handed my card to Crystal to pay for dinner and waited for her to return. Laura stared out the window, watching the darkened sky grow darker. The lights from the castle glittered against the deep navy of the water as ships silently sailed past.

Crystal returned with my card and a receipt to sign. I

made sure she got a monster tip since she was dedicated to our table for most of the evening then thanked her. I pulled Laura's chair out for her and followed her out of the restaurant.

The valet brought my SUV around quickly and nodded his thanks when I handed him cash. "Have a good evening."

Silently, I turned toward MacKellar Cove, wondering if there was going to be a second part of our date.

Laura was quiet on the drive. She mostly stared out the window. I glanced at her every so often, but she wasn't looking at me. I cleared my throat as we grew close to MacKellar Cove and asked, "What would you like to do now?"

She yawned and stretched then covered her mouth with a chuckle. "Honestly, I'm a little tired. I think maybe I should just go home."

It hurt. It shouldn't, but it hurt. She was blowing me off. Done.

I nodded sharply and silently drove to her house. I parked in her driveway and shut off the vehicle and started to get out.

"You don't have to walk me up."

"This is a date. I'm going to walk you to the door, Laura."

She nodded and met me in front of the SUV. She glanced up at me and gave me a sad smile. I followed her to the door and waited while she unlocked it. She turned back to me.

"Thank you for dinner."

"You're welcome. I, uh, I guess I'll see you tomorrow," I said.

She nodded and smiled once more then ducked inside. No kiss. No request for another date. Nothing.

So much for that.

I AVOIDED Laura as much as possible the next day. Thursday she was with me seeing patients so I was forced to see her, but I kept things professional and distant. Just like before I kissed her and admitted how badly I wanted her.

She behaved the same, staying away from me and barely speaking. I wanted to grab her and drag her into my office and kiss her until she stopped acting like we were strangers, but that would definitely cross the line.

When I first kissed Laura, I told Ally about it. As my business manager, I wanted her aware of the change in our relationship. I saw it as a way to protect Laura and make sure she knew nothing would happen to her job. I wasn't sure if Ally told Laura that she knew about us, but the sympathetic looks Ally kept shooting at me said she knew something that was not good for me.

What was I supposed to do?

I had three choices. I could ask Ally, ask Laura, or go to guys' night and see if they had any ideas. I completely chickened out and hid in my office until Ally and Laura left. I needed help from men who'd figured out how to have successful relationships.

O'Kelley's was busy, but not so crowded I couldn't make my way to the bar. There was an empty stool on the end next to Ramsey. I asked if I could join them before claiming the stool as my own. They were Laura's friends, and if I screwed up badly enough, I didn't want to make them uncomfortable.

"Of course. How're you doing?" Ramsey asked.

I shook my head. "I've been better."

Hudson set a blue drink in front of me. "Try it."

I lifted the glass and took a sip. "Damn." It was good. Sweet but not overpowering with a definite hit of liquor. "What's in this?"

"Secret recipe. Good?"

"Very. Glad I'm walking so I can have another."

Hudson nodded and grinned. He was a big man like me, but there was a definite soft side to him. It was in his eyes. He took care of people. I recognized it in others because I had it, too. For Hudson, it was pouring drinks and hiding behind the tough guy exterior. For me, it was healing them and hiding behind the white coat.

"Why was your week bad?" Ian asked.

I glanced past Ramsey to where he sat. Curiosity, not judgement, was in his gaze. The other men were the same. They weren't there to tell me I was wrong. They wanted to help. It was why I went there.

"I had a date with Laura Tuesday night."

The men exchanged surprised glances.

"You move fast," Gavin said. "Impressive, Doc."

"Too fast, I guess. We…I thought she was in the same place I was, but the date…she hasn't spoken to me since."

"What did you do?" Hudson asked, his voice laced with threat and danger. The protective man who was watching out for me a moment earlier was ready to rip my head off.

"I have no idea," I told him honestly. "I kissed her cheek, but didn't touch her otherwise before you go there."

Hudson relaxed enough to not look like he was going to tear me to pieces with his bare hands, even though I had no doubt he absolutely could. "Why isn't she speaking to you?"

I shook my head. "I don't know. I'm not speaking to her, but only because I have no idea what was so bad."

"Tell us about the date," James said. "We can break it down."

"Okay. I made reservations at The Starlight Overlook. The owner and chef are friends of mine. I picked her up and kissed her cheek only, then we drove to the restaurant. We had a table near the water so we could see Boldt Castle and watch the sunset. The owner gave us a dedicated server for the night so we wouldn't have to wait for anything. I preordered our entire meal with a special menu the chef made just for us, including wine. We talked, some, but she was not relaxed or enjoying herself. By the end of dinner, she said she was tired and wanted to go home, so I drove her home, walked her to the door, and she went inside without a chance for me to kiss her or say anything."

I looked at the men sitting around me and studied their varying degrees of amusement and astonishment.

"What?" I asked. They obviously knew what the problem was.

Ramsey looked at the others. "I've been with Melody for half my life. I need one of you to explain this to him."

Ian leaned forward. "Women don't want a man who thinks for them."

"Excuse me?"

"Or a man who tells them what to do," James added.

"Or one who won't let her make her own choices," Rowan added.

"And some don't want a man who makes them happy, but I don't think that's your problem," Sebastian Parks said.

I gawked at them and shook my head. "What the hell are you talking about?"

"Do you go on a lot of dates?" Colin asked.

I shrugged. "Some, I guess. Why?"

"Do you always take your dates to fancy restaurants and order for them?" Gavin asked.

I shrugged again. "Sometimes." My cheeks warmed as the others went wide-eyed. "What?"

"Why?" Ian asked.

"Excuse me?"

"I said why. Why do you go to expensive restaurants and

order a special menu? Why don't you let her order? Or grab a burger and sit by the water?" Ian said.

"I…why is it wrong to want to impress a woman? To give her things she doesn't have? To throw my money around since I have plenty?" I countered. Why were they judging me? I thought they were supposed to be friends or something.

"All right, listen. These guys aren't willing to come out and say it," Ramsey said. He turned to face me. "Having money is awesome. Sharing it with people you care about is awesome. Impressing her is awesome. There are a few problems. One is that Laura isn't going to be impressed by your money. She knows you have it, and I have to ask, if she was impressed by your money, would you really want her? You don't have to answer that, just think about it."

"Second," Hudson said, "if you're throwing your money around, you're telling her that's all you are. I see it all the time. Guys, and some women, come in here and drop some major cash to impress their date. All it tells the date is that money is all they have to offer. It makes you look like you don't have much of a personality."

"That's not true."

"Which is when we come to the third reason this blew up in your face," James said. "Why did you ask her out? Was it to show yourself off or to show her off? Trinity hates when she doesn't know where we're going. She wants to be able to dress the right way. Laura probably felt out of place, but more than that, you were trying to show off. You weren't looking to get to know her or trying to find out if you worked well together. You just wanted her to think you have cash, which she already knows because you pay her damn salary."

"So, this is because I'm her boss?" I asked.

They all chuckled and shook their heads. I had no idea what the hell was going on.

"Listen, we all know Laura. She's funny and flirtatious and kind and generous. Money doesn't impress her. She's here a few nights a week and eats a burger or a sandwich. She's not fancy. But she is smart. Ordering for her and throwing your money around probably made her feel like you don't care about who she is or what she thinks. You didn't even let her choose her own food," Hudson said.

"And that's a big deal?"

They all nodded.

"My dad used to order for my mom all the time when we went out," I told them.

"Did he do it after they'd been together a while or on a first date? Because unless you know what she likes and it's a place you've been to a ton and you know she's not looking to try something new, never, ever order for a woman," Ian said.

"I've never ordered for Melody, and we've been together forever," Ramsey said.

"Seriously?"

They all nodded again.

"Shit," I said, rubbing my hands over my face. "So, everything I did on the date pissed her off?"

"Pretty much," James said.

"How do I fix it?"

They all winced.

"You can apologize. Try to explain what you were thinking," Colin said.

"Whatever you do, don't blame her," Gavin said.

"And compliment her. A lot," Ramsey added.

I looked at the men sitting there and shook my head. "Dating sucks."

They all laughed.

"Yep, but when you find the right one, it's worth it," Ian said.

"Absolutely," Colin agreed with a shit-eating grin.

"Then I guess I better do whatever it takes to fix it. Just in case," I said.

They all gave me knowing smiles. I was full of shit. I was already sunk. Which meant I had no choice but to make it right with Laura. No matter what.

12

LAURA

"You haven't spoken to him at all?" Karissa asked.

I shook my head. Karissa and Sofia came over for dinner after work. We were still getting to know Sofia, but when I realized Piper worked every Thursday night at O'Kelley's and Sofia was usually alone, I invited her over instead of risking seeing Nico at the bar again.

"I don't blame you," Sofia said. She twisted her blonde hair into a ponytail and tied it up. "I wouldn't be happy about that either, and I don't date."

Karissa nodded. "I don't know what he was thinking, but he's always been a little odd. I don't know if he understands social norms. I guess Veronica didn't teach him how to be a good date."

It still hurt to think about him with Veronica, even if I knew he wasn't right for me. "Well, she can have him all to herself. It just felt like he wasn't interested in me at all. He wanted to show off for everyone around that he has money. That's just not me."

"Definitely not me either. Money doesn't fix everything and definitely doesn't erase a crappy personality," Sofia said.

"You sound like you're speaking from experience," Karissa said.

Sofia's cheeks pinked and she forced a small smile. "Unfortunately, yes."

Karissa and I exchanged a glance while Sofia sipped her water. We hadn't gotten to know much about her, but it didn't really matter. She was close friends with Piper and she was kind and funny. It took her a while to start to be comfortable with us, which was understandable. She could have her secrets.

"At least now you know," Karissa said. "You can stop wondering what things will be like and stop hoping he'll notice you. It sounds like he's not going to notice anyone other than himself."

I nodded sadly. I didn't want things to be over and done with Nico, but I wasn't willing to trade who I was to be with him. If he wasn't interested in me, then we weren't right, no matter how much I liked him.

"Sebastian says men are mostly clueless. Do you think maybe Nico didn't know he was acting like an idiot?" Sofia asked.

"We're going to circle back to Sebastian in a minute, but I don't know. Is it possible a guy really thinks ordering for you is sexy?" Karissa asked.

I shrugged. "Yes, he technically ordered for me, but it wasn't like he looked at the menu and decided I couldn't do it myself. He ordered a custom menu. It was amazing, but I didn't get to think for myself at all."

"I would be annoyed by it, by all of it, but I also would have been completely uncomfortable in a place like that," Sofia said.

"I was," I admitted. "I couldn't enjoy it because I felt like everyone was looking at me when we walked in because of the way I was dressed. Then all night everyone was watching us because we had different food and our own server. It was just weird. And he was weird. The whole thing was weird."

"If he wanted to go out again, what would you say?" Karissa asked.

I shook my head. "He doesn't, so it doesn't matter."

"How do you know?" Sofia asked.

"He hasn't spoken to me. It's been two days. This isn't like a guy who didn't call after a date, it's my boss, who I spent half the day with today, who hasn't said a word to me. I don't even know if I'm going to still have a job after all this."

"I'm sure you have nothing to worry about," Karissa said.

Sofia and Karissa smiled and patted my hands like I was senile and incapable of taking care of myself. I tried to laugh it off, but it kind of hurt. I'd built Nico up too much over the years. The reality was painful.

The oven timer dinged and we got our personal pizzas out. We set them on the counter to cool for a few minutes while the scents made our stomachs rumble. We all laughed.

"Okay, so you and Sebastian," Karissa said to Sofia. "What's going on?"

"Absolutely nothing, like I keep saying. And that's how I want it. How we both want it," Sofia said.

"Really?" Karissa asked. "You two seem really close."

"I guess we are, but like I said before, there's nothing there. When Piper and Gavin started making plans and fixing up the Inn, Piper brought me in. Sebastian has been there for so long that he knows every inch of that place. We've been working together a lot, but that's it."

"It doesn't seem that easy," I told her.

She shrugged. "It is. We talk and we have things in common, but he's like a brother to me. I have zero interest in him. He's still in love with Zoey, but even if he wasn't, we're just friends."

"Maybe I should do that. Just be friends with men instead of view all of them as potential dates," I said.

Karissa chuckled. "I'm neither. I don't date and I don't have male friends. Not ones who aren't with one of my female friends. I can't remember the last date I went on. Even a bad one would be something."

"You're too picky," I told her.

She nodded. "I am. Especially after all the research for the app. I just don't know. I want to find someone, but not just for the hell of it. I want someone I can actually build a life with. Someone I can love the way my mom and dad were or the way my mom and Eddie were."

"Did I tell you I saw Eddie last week? He was at the clinic," I said.

"Eddie was at the clinic?" Karissa asked. Her face paled and she reached for her phone.

"Sorry, he's fine. I shouldn't have said it like that. I had the same thought. He was there with Peter. Peter's going to do the expansion for Nico. Upstairs."

"I don't think I knew there was an upstairs," Karissa said.

I shook my head. "I didn't either. At least not one that he planned to use. It's a big, open space that he's going to convert into an infusion clinic. More spots so we can help more people."

"Can you? Things always seem pretty busy over there."

"They are. He's going to hire more staff to help."

"Wow. See, that's why it's hard to give up on a man like him. Because at the end of the day, he's a good man," Karissa said.

"Just with zero understanding of how to treat a woman," Sofia added.

I chuckled and nodded, agreeing with both of them. It sucked, but it was true.

AFTER WE STUFFED ourselves with pizza and watched a movie, Karissa and Sofia headed home. I curled up on my couch and thought about Nico and our date. Was it wrong for me to want to reach out to my latest match after such a disaster? I felt like I needed a boost, and a reminder that not all men were complete morons. Not that I actually knew how Dictator would be, but I had hope.

Before I could second guess myself, I sent him a message.

NOREGRETS

What's the last show you binged?

I cringed when the message went through. I was so bad at flirting. Hell, I didn't even know if I was flirting. I just needed something new to watch.

DICTATOR

Are you inviting me to Netflix and chill?

My cheeks warmed at his message. I wouldn't pass it up, but I didn't know the guy.

NOREGRETS

Um, not what I meant, but maybe one day. If I decide to keep you around long enough.

DICTATOR

There seems to be a lot of that going around.

NOREGRETS

A lot of what?

DICTATOR

Nothing, sorry. And I don't watch much TV so I can't even recommend a good show.

NOREGRETS

That's right. I forgot. Sci-fi and fantasy for you. Movies?

DICTATOR

I saw a good one last weekend. I've been watching older movies lately. From when I was younger. I watched Weird Science recently. Have you ever seen it?

NOREGRETS

I have. It was good, but it's been years since I watched it. But good idea to look for something older. I always go through the new releases and end up not finding anything. Maybe I should look back.

DICTATOR

Did you work today?

NOREGRETS

Yeah. It's been a tough week.

DICTATOR

Want to talk about it?

NOREGRETS

Not really. I kind of have a rule I won't talk to matches about other people I'm talking to or seeing. I don't think it's fair.

DICTATOR

Ah, so a bad date. Got it. Sorry. That sucks.

NOREGRETS

It does, but it happens. How was your week?

DICTATOR

About the same as yours.

NOREGRETS

LOL! I guess that's why you're home tonight, too.

DICTATOR

I just got home actually. I met a friend out.

NOREGRETS

If friend is a codeword for hookup, you can just tell me that. I don't think of us as exclusive. You know, since we've never met.

DICTATOR

No, not a codeword. Good to know about the exclusive thing.

NOREGRETS

Drive Me Crazy!

DICTATOR

Um, what?

NOREGRETS

The movie. I just found it. Have you ever seen it?

DICTATOR

Never even heard of it.

NOREGRETS

It's great. It's like Can't Buy Me Love, but 10 or so years later.

DICTATOR

I don't know that one either. I guess I need to expand my interests.

NOREGRETS

You totally do. Cheesy romance movies will totally help you with dating. Most women love these.

DICTATOR

I need all the help I can get.

NOREGRETS

Are you watching?

DICTATOR

Well, you did ask me to Netflix and chill…

NOREGRETS

You make me want to keep trying.

DICTATOR

Keep trying?

NOREGRETS

After my disaster of a date I wasn't sure I wanted to try again. You make me think I should.

DICTATOR

You just need to pick the right person.

NOREGRETS

I thought I did. Maybe I built it up too much in my mind.

DICTATOR

He probably lied about who he was. You said everyone does. It sucks to be lied to. I'm sorry it happened to you.

NOREGRETS

Thanks but I don't think he lied. I think I just saw something that wasn't there.

DICTATOR

No getting upset. I'm going to tell you a story. So there was this woman. She was beautiful and smart and incredibly funny. She had it all. Every man wanted her. But she had no interest in dating any of them. Because she could read their minds, and she knew they all only wanted her for one thing.

NOREGRETS

I bet I can guess what.

DICTATOR

Exactly. So she avoided men and eventually stopped going out in public because she could hear everyone's thoughts. One day, she decided to try again, but she disguised herself. She hid her hair under a scarf and she wore odd clothes and clumpy boots. No one recognized her. She wasn't approached by anyone. She was at peace. She could walk around and she could still hear people's thoughts, but she felt free.

NOREGRETS

Sounds pretty good.

DICTATOR

It was. While she was walking, she smiled to herself and heard the desires of the people around her. She wanted to help and was thinking about ways she could do so when she heard someone wondering where she was. A man. He liked to see her smile and missed it and wondered what happened to her. She looked around and thought she saw him on the other side of the street. She started walking to say hello to him, stepped out in front of a car, and died.

I stared at my phone. I wanted to throw it across the room.

NOREGRETS

WTF? That was horrible!

DICTATOR

No, that's life. Your name is NoRegrets. That woman had tons of them. She was fearful. Instead of telling everyone to back the hell off, she hid herself away. When she finally found someone who wanted her for a different reason, she died. She could have looked for him before, but she waited. She let everyone else tell her who she was and stopped listening to her own desires. She lived and died with regrets. It happens all the time.

NOREGRETS

Okay, but seriously? That story was cruel. I'm over here almost in tears.

DICTATOR

You are not the woman, NoRegrets. You are living your life. You are not hiding from the next date or match or experience. You're strong.

NOREGRETS

Thank you.

DICTATOR

You're welcome. Thank you for chatting with me. It makes my days much better.

NOREGRETS

Mine too.

We chatted on and off through the movie, but I was thinking about his story instead. I didn't want to go through my whole life wondering if things could have been different. I tried with Nico. I gave it a shot. I wanted it to go well. We just didn't work, and I couldn't regret that forever.

I also couldn't wish it were different forever. I couldn't change who I was so I was okay with him taking over all the time. When we were at work, he needed to call the shots. He was the one with the knowledge of how to treat our patients. He was the expert. But outside of work, we had to be equals. If he couldn't handle that, I wasn't willing to keep trying.

When the movie ended, I said goodnight to Dictator. I wanted to keep talking to him, but that wouldn't be any better for me than hoping things would change with Nico. I needed to focus on what I wanted and needed from a relationship.

The next morning I went into work with my head held high and a decision to let go of my attitude toward Nico. Our date didn't work out, but he was still my boss and I still loved my job.

I put my things in my locker and tied my hair up. I was gathering my supplies to go to the office and review my files for the day when Dr. Allison cleared his throat.

"Good morning," he said.

I turned and forced a smile. God, I still wanted him. I didn't want to, but I couldn't stop myself from imagining his hands on me.

I choked down my desire and said, "Good morning, Dr. Allison."

He flinched, the move barely perceptible. "I was wondering if we could speak for a moment."

I tilted my head. It didn't sound like work or he'd just come out and say whatever was on his mind. Which meant... "Of course."

"Thank you. Do you mind coming to my office? So we can speak privately?"

I nodded, my throat unable to loosen so I could force words out. I followed him down the hallway to his office. He waited until I was inside then closed the door behind me. He moved away from the door, putting space between us. Much needed space.

"I, uh…I wanted to apologize for our date the other night."

"Um, okay?"

He sighed and ran a hand over his beard. "I know you didn't enjoy yourself, and I know now that it was all my fault. I was looking forward to our date and overstepped. I admire your mind, Laura. I am drawn to all of you. I wanted to impress you, but I ended up coming off like a jackass. I wanted to tell you I'm sorry."

I'd never seen that side of Nico. The humble side. He was confident and never faltered. Seeing him unsure and apologetic was different.

"Um, thank you." I didn't know what else to say. I turned to go, but he stopped me.

"I…I know I don't deserve another chance, but I wondered if you might want to go out again."

I paused and faced him. He was watching me. His eyes never wandered from my face. His arms hung at his sides. His suit hugged his shoulders. For all my insistence that I was done, I had a hard time forcing the words out.

"I'm really not sure we should. It was…"

"I know. And it's all my fault. I should never have taken you somewhere without telling you where we were going. I shouldn't have ordered for us without giving you a chance to decide for yourself. I shouldn't have controlled the night. I want to get to know you. If you're willing to try again, we can go to O'Kelley's for dinner and darts. Or you can come out to my island and I can cook for us. Or we can drive down to Syracuse and go to this great little Cuban place I know— I'm doing it again. I'm sorry. Most of the women I've dated have want to date the doctor."

I smiled. "I work with the doctor…for the doctor. I don't want to date him."

He sucked in a breath and nodded. "I understand."

"I wanted to date Nico. I wanted to know you."

He nodded again.

"Dinner and darts at O'Kelley's might not be bad," I said.

His gaze snapped to mine. Those dark, rich eyes of his lit up. "Are you saying you'll give me another chance?"

I nodded. "One more chance."

"Thank you. I won't mess it up this time."

I grinned. "I guess we'll see."

His expression changed from the humble man to the predator I knew him to be. He took a step toward me, but I shook my head.

"Nope. I can't think straight when you do that."

He chuckled and stopped. "I know the feeling. Does tomorrow night work for you?"

"It does. Seven?"

"I'll see you then."

I nodded.

"Laura?"

"Yeah?"

"That dress you wore the other night looked amazing on you."

My cheeks warmed. "Thank you."

He held my gaze until I left his office. Damn.

13

Fresh air was good for me. I needed it to clear my head. It brought me clarity. Or something. All I knew was it opened my mouth as I walked around Jones Family Maple Farm with Elise and Willow. Ramsey, Melody, and Amber were up ahead of us.

"Should I have said no?" I asked them.

"No," Willow said firmly. "It was one date. You'd regret it if you didn't give him another chance."

"I'm with her. If he keeps acting like that, you aren't obligated to give him unlimited chances, but it sounds like he wants to be a decent guy. He just doesn't know how to be," Elise said with a smirk.

I rolled my eyes at her. "I don't want to date a jerk."

"I've dated plenty of those," Willow said. "Not worth it."

"I think he's just misguided," Elise said. "You've always spoken highly of him, so does Karissa. He's very good at what he does, but he's careful. He doesn't seem to have people in his life. Colin said he's been coming to O'Kelley's, but he's almost walked out both times. His social skills kind of suck."

"Not everyone has good social skills. Maybe he's just used

to having to be Dr. Allison and isn't sure how to be Nico," Willow said.

"I'm not sure I can handle always having to manage both sides of him. I don't want to date someone who can't be himself. Or who I have to figure out who he is every time we speak," I said.

"You shouldn't have to," Willow said. "Rowan has the cop side, but when he's not at work, he's different. Yeah, he's still badass and alpha, but he's not watching me for bad things. He knows he has to calm down. It might take Nico a little while to figure out the same thing. Especially if all the other women he's dated have wanted him for his title."

"That's shitty," Elise said. "I know there are people like that, but it's a tough spot for him to be in. For people to only care about his money or status or whatever. I didn't think people around here cared about stuff like that."

"How many women hit on Colin when he first moved here? Because he owns this place?" I asked her.

Elise groaned and nodded. "True. Of course, I lived in a trailer most of my adult life. I was much more concerned with feeling safe and standing on my own than money."

"Your trailer was awesome. I'm still proud of you for selling it and moving in with Colin," I told her.

She smiled and her cheeks pinked. "He's unlike anyone I've ever known. I never thought I'd find someone like him."

"I'm right there with you," Willow said. "Rowan is different than the other men I've dated. I'd about given up on finding someone."

"I'm pretty much there," I admitted. "I've been dating lately because I want to believe I can find someone, but I've about given up."

"What about your latest match? I thought you were enjoying talking to him," Elise said.

I nodded. "I am. I think he has potential, but—"

"You're not willing to give up on Nico yet," Willow said for me.

"Yeah."

"That's understandable. You've been in love with Nico since you moved here," Elise teased.

My cheeks heated and I shook my head. "Maybe not quite that long."

Elise chuckled. "Then you're doing the right thing giving him another chance. You owe it to yourself to find out if he's the man you always thought he might be. If he's worth loving."

I drew in a breath and nodded. "You're right."

"When the hell did you get so wise?" Willow asked.

"Probably about the same time you pulled your head out of your ass and realized you needed to change," Elise said.

I shook my head. Elise and Willow had become friends over the last few months, mostly because Elise refused to tiptoe around Willow. Willow respected that Elise was willing to call her out on her past mistakes. I was just happy to see both of them smiling.

We walked a little longer then made our way back to the barn. Things had calmed down and most of the guests were gone for the day. I bought some maple butter and a pancake mix kit then said goodbye to my friends and left to get ready for my date.

I debated what to wear after I got out of the shower. I was buffed and scrubbed and feeling shiny and good in my skin. I lotioned myself up and stared into my closet, still unsure what I wanted to put on.

Nico said he liked my dress, but we were going to O'Kelley's. Wearing a dress there felt like I was trying too hard. Way too hard. He was the one who had to work for it this time. I was going to be comfortable.

I finally settled on a pair of jeans that hugged my curves

and a long top that was soft and cozy and made me feel good. I added a light jacket since spring was still a suggestion to the fickle weather and headed out the door.

I didn't see Nico when I got to O'Kelley's so I grabbed a seat at the bar and smiled at Hudson.

"You look nice. Are you meeting someone?" he asked as he fixed me a drink and set it in front of me.

"I am."

"A date?"

"Yes, but don't worry. He's not from the app."

"Really? Good for you. Anyone I know?"

I smiled at him. "You're good, you know that?"

"I have no idea what you mean," he said with a smirk that told me he knew exactly what was going on.

He started making me another drink and I was about to tell him I didn't need a second one yet when Nico slid onto the stool next to me.

"Hi," he said, adding a nod toward Hudson.

Hudson slid the drink he was making in front of Nico. "Good to see you, Doc."

Nico grinned and shook his head. "Thanks. You, too."

I eyed both of them but knew I wouldn't get answers from either of them.

"Are you two going to order food?" Hudson asked.

"Yes. Do you want to order now or wait a minute?" Nico asked me.

I caught the satisfied smirk on Hudson's face before he ducked. "Let's wait a little bit."

Nico nodded and took a sip of his drink. He caught me looking at it and said, "Hudson figured out that I like sweet drinks. I don't know what this one is, but it's good."

"Sweet drinks?" I asked.

Nico nodded. "One of my many secrets. I ordered a beer

and he called me out. I make blended or mixed drinks at home, but I rarely drink beer unless I'm out."

"Sweet drinks?" I asked again.

He chuckled and nodded. "Yes. I like my women like I like my drinks. Extra sweet."

I snorted and made a move to get up. "Guess this date is over."

He laughed and set his hand on my thigh to hold me in place. I looked down at it and licked my lips. He pulled back but I settled into my seat once more.

"I'm sorry," he said. "I should ask before I put my hands on you."

"I didn't mind," I admitted.

His gaze locked on mine as he nodded slowly. "Good to know." He sucked in a breath, his chest rising with the move. "Darts? Or do you want to stay here? Maybe get a table?"

I nodded. "Let's get a table. We'll go from there."

Nico nodded to Hudson and grabbed his drink. The bar was crowded since it was Saturday night. In a town like MacKellar Cove, there wasn't much to do besides drink, so O'Kelley's was always busy.

On the far side of the makeshift dance floor, there was a cozy table for two. I was hoping to find something bigger, maybe a four top, but that was the only table open as far as I could see.

"How's that one?" Nico asked, his voice in my ear. My neck tingled from his breath.

I nodded and moved toward the table. Sitting down it felt even more isolated and remote than it appeared. We were tucked into a corner, so hidden I wasn't sure we'd get served.

"Do you come here with your friends often?" he asked.

"Again with the questions about my friends?"

He smiled. "I know you, but I don't really know you. I know what you do for a living, and where you live. I don't know where you grew up or anything about your family. I see you five days a week, but we're practically strangers. I want to know you, Laura, so yes, I'm going to ask about your friends, and your family, and your past, and you're going to have to tell me when I'm getting too personal because I want to know everything there is to know about you."

I swallowed roughly, my mouth suddenly dry. He was staring at me expectantly, like he was waiting for me to open my mouth and vomit the answers to all his questions all over him. I wasn't sure what I should do or say. I wanted to know him, too, but he was right. I'd built up this fantasy of who he was in my head, but I didn't know if he was anything like the man I thought he was. I didn't know if the Nico I loved when he showed how much he cared for patients was real or if he was just a show.

"I told you before, my friends are amazing people. They're family to me. We're there for each other through everything."

"Do you have family besides them? I don't remember you taking time off for holidays."

I shook my head. "No, I don't have family."

"I'm sorry."

I smiled. "Thanks. My mom died a long time ago, and my dad followed her after a little while. They were crazy in love. Losing her was the hardest thing for my dad and I think he just couldn't stand to live without her. He had to go."

"That's both sad and beautiful."

"Yep. I miss them, but I'm happy they're together. They showed me what love really looks like. I see it with my friends, too, but growing up with it made me believe that love is possible."

"Have you ever been in love?"

I grinned. "You're not holding back, are you?"

He smiled and sipped his drink.

"In love. No. I don't think so. I feel like that kind of love is one you know is right. There's no going back."

"I have seen that kind of love. So full of trust and commitment that nothing can tear them apart."

"Your parents?"

He shook his head. "My closest friends."

"Are they local?"

"No, unfortunately, they aren't. But I see them whenever I go to Syracuse."

"Oh, yeah. Of course." Syracuse was where his ex lived. Hopefully his ex. I still hadn't asked him.

"I try to get down there about once a month to see them. It's been a couple of weeks."

I nodded, feeling uncomfortable. It was the perfect opening to ask him about her. I should take it. I needed to take it. I totally didn't take it.

"Should we order?" I asked abruptly. I needed to stop talking about Veronica and Syracuse.

"Um, sure," he said. He looked around for a server and caught the eye of someone not far from us. He nodded to her, and she approached our table.

"Hello. Can I get you two some refills?"

"Yes, and we'd like to order food. Is that something we can do with you?" Nico asked.

"Absolutely. Do you know what you want or do you need me to grab a few menus?"

"I'll have the turkey club with cheese curds," I told her.

"Those are my favorite," she said as she wrote my order down.

"They're so good. I can't get enough of them."

"Did Hudson make your drinks?" she asked.

"He did."

"Okay, I'll get refills from him. For you?" She turned to Nico with a smile and a tilt of her head.

"I'll have a grilled chicken sandwich with Swiss and mushrooms. And I'll try the cheese curds. I haven't had those yet."

"You won't regret it. Trust me. I'll have all that out to you shortly. And I'm Megan, by the way."

"Thank you," we told her.

When Megan left, Nico took another sip of his drink. He seemed nervous, like he wasn't sure what to say or do.

"Tell me something you regret," I said.

"Not asking you out years ago," he said without hesitation.

"Years?"

"Okay, now I'm regretting admitting that."

I chuckled. "I wish you'd have asked me out, too, but I also believe everything happens for a reason. I'm not going to question why it took so long for us to get to know each other better."

"What do you regret?"

I took my time thinking about the question. There were plenty of things I wished hadn't happened, but regrets...

"I don't have any. Especially after the work we do. Too many of our patients die still wanting to do something. Losing my parents taught me the same thing our patients do. It's not worth it to regret life. Even the shitty days are better above ground than below."

"That's pretty powerful," he said.

I shrugged. "Life isn't meant to be half-lived. We have to enjoy it. Go crazy, let it all out, and be wild. Yeah, I'm responsible and have a job and a stable place to call home, but I've been getting lost in work lately and I don't want to do that anymore. Tomorrow I'm going to Canada with a friend. We're going to drive across the bridges and hang out for a few hours. We're talking about going to Montreal this summer and New York City sometime. Maybe some longer trips one day, but life's too short."

"I need a little of that in my life."

"A little of what?" I asked.

"A little wild and crazy. A little on a whim. A little not worrying about what everyone else thinks of me."

I smiled. "I think we could all use some of that. I definitely try to see the bright side of things. It's not always easy, but I have to believe everything happens for a reason."

"Dance with me."

"Excuse me?"

"Dance with me. I want to hold you close and spin you around this dance floor until you forget about the mess I made of our first date and agree to keep giving me this chance."

"And you think dancing will help with that?"

He stood and held out his hand. I looked from it up his sky blue button down. He rolled up the sleeves and unbuttoned the top button, but he still looked like the pressed and polished doctor from work. His black pants were creased and perfect. His beard was neatly trimmed, surrounding two perfectly plump lips that tipped up on the ends as he waited for me to take his hand.

I finally gave in and put my hand in his. He yanked me up from my seat and pulled my body flush with his. He held me close with his free hand while he wrapped his fingers around mine.

"If nothing else, dancing means I get to hold you in my arms in a perfectly acceptable way in public. Because truth be told, I wasn't sure how much longer I was going to be able to wait."

All thoughts flew from my mind. His gaze dipped to my lips as I pulled the lower one between my teeth. He groaned and spun me, guiding me to the dance floor without taking his hands off me.

"I'm going to warn you, I studied dance growing up, too. My grandmother taught me."

"Does that mean you're good?"

He shrugged then spun me away and yanked me back into his arms so quickly I was dizzy. "I can hold my own."

"I might regret agreeing to dance with you," I said softly.

"Don't worry, I'll take things very, very slow."

My pulse skittered in anticipation. My entire body heated with desire. I wasn't sure I was going to survive dancing with him. This was definitely a side of Nico I didn't know existed.

We moved together, Nico seamlessly leading me around the small dance floor. He kept his gaze locked on mine, making me wonder how he was avoiding the other people.

"I like seeing you with your hair down. Literally and figu-ratively."

I laughed. "I feel the same way."

A faster song came on and Nico released me so we could dance to the beat. He slid a hand around my waist and pulled my body close to his. I threw my head back and lifted my arms and enjoyed the feel of him against me.

Every inch of me vibrated with energy. I'd always loved dancing, but dancing with him was a new experience. Dancing with Nico was foreplay. I went into the date wondering if it was going to be a disaster. An hour in and I was wondering if we could skip dinner and go straight to dessert.

NICO

*L*aura laughed. It didn't matter what she was laughing at, she was laughing. She was enjoying herself. She talked and laughed and teased me. God, how she teased me. Not just with her words, but with her body and her smiles and her eyes.

I was not going to push for more after our date, but I wasn't going to say no if she asked. I'd been hard since the moment I took her into my arms on that dance floor. I was sure I would blow at some point, but I just kept getting harder. Fucking hell, the woman was intoxicating. Better than any drink. Better than anything.

"I think you should show this side to the rest of the staff," Laura said. "They'd love to see you relaxed."

"I'm not feeling very relaxed right now," I admitted.

"You know what I mean. You're always tense and barking at us. I know you're our boss, but it's good to know you have a fun side, too. I never thought you did."

"Why did you agree to a date? If you didn't think I was fun, why were you at all interested?"

She shrugged. "I admire you. I always have. Before I

moved here, I looked you up. I knew the work you were doing was impressive, and I wanted to be a part of it. But when I got here, I saw the way you treated your patients. The way you would talk to them and reassure them and give every last piece of yourself to help them. It was hard not to find that attractive."

I nodded slowly and studied her. Her cheeks were flushed from the dancing and the drinks and the laughing, but there was something in her eyes. A vulnerability that said she wasn't sure she should have admitted all that to me.

"I'm sorry I've never given that same thing to you."

She shrugged and waved her hand as though it wasn't a big deal, but it was. It was a huge deal. She was taking a chance on me. She was betting that there was something inside me worth discovering.

"I love what I do, what we do. It's not easy, but it's worthwhile to know we tried everything possible to save as many people as possible. And in this area, there aren't enough doctors treating cancer patients. But it's made me...distant a lot of the time. My therapist, Veronica, says—"

"Wait, Veronica? She's your therapist?" Laura asked. Her brows tugged together.

"And a friend, but yes. We went to med school together. Why?"

"I thought she was your...stand-in or something."

"Stand-in?"

Laura shrugged uncomfortably. She avoided my gaze and fidgeted with her straw wrapper. "The woman you took to events and whatever."

"She is. Since we're both doctors, we go to a lot of events together. Her husband isn't a doctor and hates going. He thinks they're painfully boring."

"She's married?"

"Yeah. For a few years now. He's in politics. She's a

psychiatrist for powerful people. Doctors who deal with things like we do, death and illness, but also scandals or slander or things like that. Lots of pain."

Laura's head tilted to the side. Her brows furrowed. She looked past me, searching for an explanation that wasn't there. "Wait, I'm confused. She's your stand-in, but she's married? You sleep with your married friend from med school?"

"What? No! I've never slept with her. She's married!" I shouted the words then glanced around at the people nearby who were staring at me with curious expressions.

"That's what I meant by stand-in. You go to events and when you're lonely you sleep together," she hissed like a snake getting ready to attack.

"No. No. No. Not ever. She's amazing and smart and funny, but she's my best friend. Nothing has ever happened between us. We were roommates in college and have always been there for each other, but nothing more than friendship. I'm good friends with both her and her husband now."

"All the times you went to Syracuse for the weekend... That was just to visit?" Her expression said she thought I was full of shit.

"Yes. I don't have a lot of people here, so I would go and see Veronica and Jeff. You thought I was sleeping with her?"

She nodded. Slowly. Her gaze was in her lap, her cheeks pink. When she finally lifted her eyes to mine, there was a pain I never expected. "For a long time."

I reached for her hand and squeezed it. "It's been a while since I've been involved with anyone. I've had this beautiful nurse on my mind. She's made it impossible for me to think about anyone else."

She sucked in a breath and drew her lip between her teeth. "Do you want to get out of here?"

"I do."

"I live close."

I wanted to tell her we didn't have to do anything, but I didn't want her to think I was trying to back out. I was following her lead. For as long as she was willing to lead me.

I paid the bill and led the way through the crowd with her hand in mine. When we were outside in the cool spring night, we paused. I looked at her closely, making sure she wasn't second guessing herself.

She threw herself at me. Her arms came around my neck and I caught her, our lips colliding as our bodies did. I groaned and pulled her closer, needing to feel as much of her as possible. She pushed her tongue between my lips and moaned when it brushed mine. I leaned back against the wall, protecting her from the rough surface. She was in charge. She was in control. She was…going to make me lose it on the street in front of a busy bar.

"We need to go," I growled, needing to get moving before I embarrassed myself.

She grabbed my hand and took off toward Catherine Park without a word. She crossed over and kept going down one of the side streets. She turned up the driveway of her small bungalow with a light on above the solid wood front door. She unlocked the door and had us inside and back in each other's arms in seconds.

I pressed her against the door and covered her with my body. I let her feel how desperately I wanted her, needing her to know I was in this. She moaned and rubbed herself against me, tugging at my shirt before splaying her hands wide across my back.

"Laura," I groaned.

We pulled back and stared at each other. A lamp on a nearby table gave me enough light to see her, to see the desire in her gaze. I wanted her, but I'd walk away if she wasn't as interested as I was. If she was having any second thoughts.

But her gaze was clear. Her lips were red from our kisses and her cheeks were pink with desire. Her breath rushed out of her in impatient pants.

"I want you, Nico. I know you need to hear the words because you're my boss, but right now you're just a man. I am baring myself right now, telling you this, but I want you. If you don't feel the same, I—"

"Trust me, that isn't something you have to even guess at. I want to touch every inch of your body. I want to taste you while you come on my lips. I want to hold you in my arms while I fill you. I want to kiss you and make love to you and be with you until you get sick of me and throw me out. But don't ever think I don't feel the same. It's killing me to stand here and not peel back every single layer that's covering your beautiful body so I can see you. I've dreamed about you for far too long, and I want you so badly that my hands are shaking. I hope your friend is driving to Canada tomorrow because I plan to keep you up all night long."

"Oh, God," she breathed.

"Come here," I said, crooking my finger for her to step closer to me again. "Then show me where your bed is. We're going to need it."

A sultry smile curled her lips after a few seconds. She smirked then turned and walked away, leaving me to follow. When we made it to her bedroom, she turned on the lights and moved to her bed.

"Lights on?" I asked.

She nodded. "I want to see you."

I grinned. "Good."

I took a step toward her, but she put her hand up. "Shirt."

I smiled and unbuttoned my shirt. I considered wearing something I wouldn't normally wear to work, but I wanted her to know I was trying. As I stood in front of her and slowly worked the buttons loose and watched the desire pool in her gaze, I knew the shirt was the right call.

When the buttons were free, I shrugged out of my shirt. She licked her lips and made me feel like all those years I missed going to the gym wouldn't have made a difference. I didn't have a six-pack, never had. I wasn't model material. But Laura looked at me like there wasn't a thing she would change. And damn if that wasn't a boost to my ego. And my cock.

"Now yours," I told her.

Her gaze snapped to mine. She grabbed the hem of her shirt and pulled it over her head. Underneath she wore a blue bra with lace on the top edge. A small silver necklace nestled between her breasts. Her wild curls flowed toward her breasts and around her back, giving her a relaxed and care-free look.

"You're beautiful," I breathed, unable to stop the words. I clenched my fists to keep from rushing across the room and putting my hands all over her. In time. We had all night.

"So are you," she panted. "Don't stop."

I smirked, hoping that wouldn't be the last time she said those words tonight.

I unbuttoned my pants and let them slide to the floor. I toed off my shoes and kicked my shoes and pants to the side before balancing to remove my socks. Socks were not sexy. Except on Laura. Everything was sexy on her.

I stood before her in my black boxer briefs and tried not to suck in anything as she looked her fill. I throbbed against the soft cotton that barely covered me. I wanted out.

Condom. I almost forgot. I grabbed my pants and pulled out three condoms. I stuck them in my wallet before our first date. Not because I thought I would get to use them, but because I hoped that maybe one day I would. I tossed them on the bed and watched her as her eyes registered all three of them.

"Are we going to need all of those?"

"If I had more, I'd use more. I told you, Laura. All night. If you'll have me."

She sucked in a shaky breath and hooked her thumbs in the sides of her jeans. She drew them down and kicked them to the side with the short heels she was wearing. Her panties matched her bra.

Dear.

Fucking.

God.

Her panties matched her bra.

I wouldn't have cared what she had on under her clothes, but seeing that told me she hoped for this moment as much as I did. She wasn't going into this on a whim. She wanted me to see the blue. She wanted me to see her. She wanted this.

I growled and crossed the room in three large steps. I yanked her against my body and kissed her, catching her surprised gasp and plunging my tongue between those beautiful lips of hers. She wrapped her arms around my neck and kissed me right back. Our tongues fought, licking and sliding together. I didn't care who won because we both won. Laura was in my arms, almost naked. We were standing next to her bed. She was going to be mine.

I was already hers.

We moved onto the bed together, half falling, once again laughing as we seemed to be of one mind. Laura moved up the bed and laid on her back. I positioned myself over her and brushed the hair from her face.

"I am honored you want me. Truly. Thank you."

She smiled, her eyes shiny. She bit the inside of her cheek and nodded. "Thank you."

I kissed her softly, holding my weight off her as much as possible. I wanted to prolong this as long as I could. To stretch out our night until she was begging me. Partly because I wanted her to feel good and partly because if I went too fast, it'd all be over too fast.

The happy little whimpers she made as we kissed told me she wasn't going to be as patient as I was. Her hands slid down my back and up again. She wiggled herself beneath me, trying to position our bodies just right. I laughed against her lips and drew back to kiss her neck.

"What are you doing?" I asked.

"I don't do slow very well."

"I do slow very, very well. You're going to have to wait."

"I don't want to wait. I've been waiting long enough."

"Trust me, it'll be worth the wait."

She groaned and dragged her nails down my back. I hissed and nipped at her collarbone. She moaned softly. I licked the bite then slid my tongue down between her breasts and teased the edges of the lace.

She tried to shift to take her bra off, but I pressed my weight against her so she couldn't. She groaned again. "Why?"

I smiled against her flesh. "Because I like you like this."

"Frustrated and horny?"

"Hell yes," I said. "I want you so wet and ready for me that you lose your mind as quickly as I do when I finally sink into you. I want you writhing and begging me. I want you desperate for an orgasm so that when I fill you up, you can't help but come all over me."

"Please, Nico."

"I like that."

"Like what?"

"My name on your lips," I told her, looking up from her

breasts to catch her eye. "I'm always Dr. Allison at work, but hearing you say my name makes me harder."

"Nico," she breathed. "Nico. Nico."

I groaned. "You're not going to get me to hurry." I went back to licking my way around her breasts while she panted my name. I lied my ass off, though. Hearing her whispered pleas of my name made me want to kneel between her thighs and give her what we were both desperate for. But I wasn't going to give in. Not yet.

I moved beyond her breasts without giving her what she wanted. When I kissed her belly then raked my teeth over her hipbone, she pushed up and unhooked her bra. She dragged it down her arms and tossed it off the bed. Then she grabbed one of my hands and pulled it to her breast.

I groaned and throbbed at the feel of it in my hand. She squeezed and rubbed her thumb over her nipple. Her hips lifted at the touch, and damn if I wasn't lost to what she wanted. I rolled her nipple between my thumb and finger and groaned when she let out a moan and thrust her hips against me.

"Please, Nico."

I should have known better than to think I might be in charge. Not with her. She had me. I'd give her anything she wanted. I'd abandon everything I knew for her. And she was proving it right there.

I tugged her panties to the side with my free hand and nudged her legs apart with my shoulders. I squeezed her nipple at the same time I sucked on her clit and she lost it.

"Yes," she moaned, long and loud. "Oh, God, yes."

"Off," I growled at her. I pulled my hand back so I could use both to get her panties off. She lifted her hips and helped me shove at them. Once I got them to her feet, I dove back in, licking her wet heat and fondling her breasts while she whimpered and begged.

"Please, Nico. Please." She put her hands over mine and rocked her hips with every move I made. I pulled one hand away and pressed her hips wider before I thrust two fingers into her.

She let go instantly, her moans and screams echoing inside my mind. I wanted to record that sound and play it over and over again. Her breathless pants of my name, her begging me to get inside her. Her whimpers of pleasure. It was the most beautiful thing I'd ever heard.

While she came down, I rolled a condom on and positioned myself between her thighs. She looked up at me with a well sated, drunk expression in her eyes. "That was definitely worth the wait."

I grinned as I teased her entrance. Her eyes slammed shut and she moaned. She shifted her hips to meet me, her body begging me.

"Please, Nico," she said. She quivered with my every move. I rubbed against her, barely able to hold myself back.

One of her moves lined us up perfectly and I pressed hard into her. I groaned as her body sucked me in, pulsing around me while she came once again.

"Nico," she cried. "Don't stop. Please, don't stop."

I withdrew and thrust back in. I watched her face as she fought the pleasure racing through her body. Her mouth fell open on a silent moan, then twisted as the sensations rioted through her. Slowly, I tortured us both, pulling back then pressing in. Giving her a chance to catch her breath while I repeatedly lost mine.

She reached for me, her hands grasping blindly. I took one of her hands and brought it to my lips. I kissed her palm and she sighed. She cupped my cheek and drew me down to her.

"Kiss me," she pleaded.

I supported myself on my elbows and kissed her quickly.

She followed me as I tried to retreat and pulled me back to her. She licked my lips and I groaned, letting her taste herself on my tongue. She moaned and thrust up against me on my next stroke.

We moved together as we kissed, our bodies matching each other's. Slow, deep strokes and slow, deep kisses carried us up and over the edge until we crashed together, moans and whimpers and pleas echoing through the otherwise silent room.

Perfection.

15

LAURA

*E*verything was silent. Deafeningly silent. Our breath slowed to where we weren't making noise. Our conversation and laughter stopped. The entire world felt silent. So silent I could hear the fear racing through my mind.

Was this a one-time thing?

Did he no longer respect me?

Did I respect me? Or him?

Why did I sleep with him so fast?

What did this mean?

It was that last question that kept me from falling asleep as Nico drifted. His hand stayed against my back, his chest rising and falling gently with his every breath. His body was soft and pliable, relaxed. But I was not.

What did this mean?

I'd slept with men on a first or second date before. It didn't phase me a bit. Sex was fun and there was nothing wrong with having as much as a person wanted. But jumping into bed too fast usually resulted in disaster for me.

I didn't want disaster with Nico. I wanted more. Especially after such an amazing date.

He was kind and funny. He was exactly how I hoped he would be. I knew he'd been coached, but I also knew the man I was with was Nico. He didn't have someone in his ear telling him what to do. He took their advice and we had a very good time.

What did this mean?

After our first failed date, I was disappointed. I'd built him up so big in my mind that one and done was more than a little heartbreaking. It meant I was wrong about him, and that he wasn't the man I'd created in my head. But he proved that wrong. He was the man I thought he'd be. But now…was this one and done again? Was he going to wake up and sneak out and we would never talk about this night again?

I tried to tell myself if that happened then he wasn't the man for me. If that was how he was going to treat me, then I knew who he was for real, and I could let go. But I wanted to be wrong.

My mom would have called it borrowing trouble. She would have told me not to worry about things until they happened. But I liked to be prepared, even if it was only mentally. And for someone who always saw the silver lining in a storm, borrowing trouble was not something I liked doing.

Nico stirred and sucked in a breath. I quickly closed my eyes and pretended to be asleep. He eased my arm off of him and slid out of bed. I laid there, listening to him, trying to figure out what he was doing.

The toilet flushed and water ran in my attached bathroom. I kept my eyes closed, straining to hear through the silence of my pounding heart.

"How did I get so lucky?" he whispered.

I fought to keep a straight face.

He eased back into bed, and I rolled over at his movement. I grinned with my back to him, pretending to sleep. He pressed his naked body to my back and kissed my shoulder. His hand slid over my waist and cupped my stomach before tugging my body gently against his. He pressed his nose into my hair and his cock twitched.

Maybe not one and done.

I pretended to sleep for another minute, but his wandering hands made it impossible to hide how much I still wanted him. When he rolled me beneath him, we stared into each other's eyes. Neither of us said a word. We just watched each other. It was the single most erotic experience of my life, reading every emotion, every thought, every bit of pleasure on his face.

When I came, him buried deep inside me and our bodies entangled, he kissed me then followed me over the edge. He rolled off of me and disposed of the condom before returning to my bed and tucking me against his body once more.

Then the silence welcomed me in and told me this was definitely not one and done.

NICO and I turned to each other more than once through the night, and when he finally left my bed early the next morning, he told me he was going and to enjoy my trip to Canada.

Finley picked me up mid-morning with an apology for Karissa that she was finishing up an app and didn't join us. She'd been tentative to come, so it wasn't a surprise, but I was still disappointed.

"How are you? You look exhausted," Finley said. "Do you need to bail?"

I shook my head. "I'm great. A little sore, and definitely exhausted, but great."

"You didn't."

I grinned. "I did. Until he ran out of condoms. Then we got creative."

"Oh, I'm so jealous right now. Good for you. Tell me everything."

I chuckled and spared no detail as I told Finley all about my date with Nico. By the time I was finished, we were stopping and ready to explore a little.

"I love that you two are finally together. I think I'm a little obsessed with romance."

"You have the perfect job for it," I told her. I tied my blonde waves back as we got out. It was a little windy, and the last thing I needed was a mess of knots when we got home.

Finley smiled and tucked her brown hair behind her ear. The four diamond studs she wore daily caught the sunlight and glittered. "Sometimes I wish I thought less about love and relationships. Especially since I'm so single I wonder if I'll ever find someone. My parents have this great relationship and Ian and Blake are crazy in love, the rest of our friends who are paired up are happy. I just want the same thing, but I'm starting to worry I won't find it."

"Says the woman who owns the store about romance and reads books all the time about that exact thing," I said dryly.

Finley chuckled. "I know, but maybe that's it. It always seems easy, but romance has not been easy for me."

"It isn't easy for me either. I don't think it's been easy for a lot of people. We see what people show us, we're looking from the outside, but being outside a relationship means you don't see the pain and frustration that's inside it. My first date with Nico was horrible. I walked away upset that he wasn't the man I thought he was. I was hurt, and I felt stupid for seeing someone who didn't exist."

"Yeah, but you gave him another chance."

I nodded. "I did. Because he apologized. Because he admitted that he messed up and he asked me for another chance. If he'd said he wanted to try again, without asking me if I was willing, I wouldn't have. It was bad. Really bad. But he was willing to tell the guys what happened and accept their advice."

"What do you mean?"

I smiled. "Hudson was being Hudson. He knew I was meeting Nico before Nico showed up and when Nico asked if I was ready to order, I caught Hudson smirking. It was pretty obvious they coached Nico, but he listened to them."

Finley laughed. "It's good to know some men can be taught. I usually think they're either born with the ability to be decent boyfriends or not."

I chuckled. "I'm sure there's some of that in all of them, but you know me. I believe in the fantasy."

She snorted. "You believe that dying to be together is better than living apart. I've never been able to get onboard with Romeo and Juliet."

"It's love. To me, that's the most true way to love some-one. To be willing to die for them and to be unable to live without them. It's what happened to my dad after my mom died. He didn't kill himself, but he died the day she did. It just took his body a few years to catch up. When he died, I was relieved for him because it meant he wasn't in pain anymore. He was with her, and he was happy."

"But that meant you were alone."

I shrugged. "True, but I was their kid, not the love of their lives. I've always hoped to find someone who made me feel like that. Who made me willing to give up everything."

"Do you think Nico could be that person?"

"Maybe, but I have no idea yet. I like him a lot, but it's clear after our dates that there's a lot I don't know about him. But if he's not, I'm not going to stop. I mean, I'll definitely want to, but I'm going to be thirty-nine soon. I've already basically given up on kids, not that I was sure I wanted them anyway. I'm not willing to give up on love. Not yet. Not forever."

"And now that you know he's not dating Veronica, that helps to be open to things with him."

"Yes, that was more than a little embarrassing to admit. He took it in stride, but I felt like such an idiot when he was talking about her."

"I'm thrilled your instincts were right about him."

I chuckled. "Me, too. I hope my instinct to try again is good, too. Last night was amazing."

"I think I might just have great sex for the rest of my life. Not worry about the relationship side of things."

"I definitely see the appeal of that one," I said. "Come on, let's go see what we can find here."

We walked through the open air market together, stopping to check out items from local artists. We found lunch at a cute cafe then wandered some more. On our way back to MacKellar Cove, we stopped for coffee and went through all our purchases.

"That's just gorgeous," Finley told me when I pulled out a sunrise print of the Thousand Islands.

"I thought so, too. No one really knows yet, but Nico is remodeling the upstairs of the clinic to expand. I was thinking of seeing if he wanted to hang this in one of the rooms. Something beautiful for patients to look at."

"That's a great idea." She stared at the print for a long moment. "I'm sorry if I made it sound like I don't think you two should be together."

I shook my head. "You didn't. I'm cautiously optimistic

about things with him right now, but I'm trying really hard to reel in my interest. Romeo and Juliet is my favorite story, but I'm not looking to follow all their leads and marry someone I barely know."

"Or, you know, die, I hope," she said with a laugh.

I nodded in agreement. "That, too."

"I want to find love, and I want the people I care about to find love, but I…it's discouraging after a while. And I hate to say it, but watching everyone else find love and I'm not is hard sometimes."

"You don't have to explain to me. I get it. I was jealous as hell of Peyton and Wyatt getting engaged, even though it wasn't about either of them. And when Blake and Ian got together, and everyone else. Like you said, it seems so easy for other people, but I've known Nico for years and until recently was giving up on him seeing me as more than an employee."

Finley smiled. "I'm glad he finally pulled his head out of his ass and noticed you."

I laughed with her. "Me, too."

I took a short nap when we got home then got ready for girls' night. Sweats and a soft cotton tee were definitely the plan my evening wear. I was still exhausted but looking forward to time with my friends.

I was almost to Book Boyfriends Unlimited when I got a text from Nico. I smiled as I read it.

"What are you smiling about?" Elise asked, surprising me when she appeared next to me on the street.

"Nico," I said.

She chuckled. "Date number two went well?"

I nodded. "Very well."

"Good. I'm rooting for you. Colin said he likes Nico. Reminds him of himself, but you're a lot less crazy than me so hopefully things are easier for you and Nico."

"You're not crazy," I told her. "You're careful. There's nothing wrong with that."

"Thankfully I made a good choice this time," Elise said with a dreamy smile of her own.

"Those smiles can only mean one thing," Trinity said as she met us in front of Book Boyfriends Unlimited.

We knocked on the door and nodded. "Men," Elise provided. "It's still new for me to have someone else who makes me this happy."

"You guys have been together a year. Does it still feel weird?" I asked.

Elise shrugged. "A little, yeah. I was alone for so long and convinced myself I would stay that way. I never saw Colin coming."

"I definitely walked in on the wrong part of that conversation," Finley said as she opened the door for us.

We all laughed and Elise explained while we walked to the back to join the others.

"I wanted to find love but still feel weird with James sometimes," Trinity said. "When I catch him looking at me with a dopey smile I wonder who he's thinking about. It's not easy to go from being someone most men weren't interested in to being the only woman one man is interested in."

"Yeah, but it's such a great feeling," Blake said. "All those years with William I felt invisible, but Ian never makes me feel like I'm anything less than perfect in his eyes."

"I want that," Finley admitted with a smile in my direction. "I feel like I'm getting drunk on love lately. I'm also starting to read more books with anti-heroes or opposites attract. I feel like I need to see that love isn't always easy."

The attached ones of the group groaned and I flashed Finley a smile.

"Love is not easy," Willow said. "Rowan told me this morning that I was a disaster and he would need his own place again if I didn't start cleaning up."

"You are kind of a mess sometimes," Melody told her sister.

"Whose side are you on?"

"Yours. Always. But that means seeing you happy, and that means keeping Rowan in your life. He's going to get over it, especially when he realizes it's temporary that you have these moments. But every relationship takes a little back and forth. Give and get. If anyone knows that, it's me."

Willow smiled and nodded. "You're right. As always."

Melody snorted. "I'm hardly ever right, but I'll take what I can get."

Everyone was quiet for a minute. Piper cut into the lemon merengue pie she brought and handed out pieces. We all groaned when we took our first bites.

"Wow. I'd say this is better than sex, but Colin was extra frisky today," Elise said with a wink.

"Totally agree," half of us said.

"Don't think you can get away with that comment," Piper said to me. "Who are you having better-than-merengue sex with?"

"Dr. Nico," Finley teased.

"What? Are you serious?"

"Good for you!"

"Tell us all about it."

"I gave him a second chance yesterday. Thank you to all your men who advised him on how to be a decent date. He listened. Our date was really good. Really, really good." I smiled.

"Yay! I'm glad it's finally working out," Karissa said.

I smiled at her but didn't say anything.

"She's paranoid," Finley provided for me. "She's built him up so much that she thinks her expectations are too high."

"Aren't they always?" Piper asked. "I don't mean you specifically, I mean in general. We think men are going to be decent. We have these beliefs about people. When they show us who they are, we're shocked and hurt because we never saw the truth. They didn't want us to see the truth."

"That's what I worried about after our first date," I said. "I was hurt because that was not the man I thought I knew. But the second date was. He said most women want to date the doctor."

"Now I feel bad for him," Karissa said. "That sucks."

I nodded. "He's used to pretending for dates, so he was trying to impress me. I didn't want all that, which is why our second date was much better. We went to O'Kelley's and danced and ate and then went back to my place."

"Hey, that was how I kissed Ian the first time." Blake got a dreamy look on her face. "I think Hudson is a master matchmaker."

"You think Hudson has something to do with us getting together with our men?" Elise asked.

"Where did you first meet Colin?"

"His farm."

"And your first night out?"

"Yeah, but I blew him off that night," Elise argued.

"He didn't give up. Hudson," Blake said with a smile. "He talked to Ian, I know he talked to Ramsey. Colin, James, Gavin, and Rowan. He's pulling the strings for all our men."

"He knows how to be a good boyfriend and husband," Finley said. "If Hillary were still here, he would still be a husband."

"Think he'll ever date again?" I asked. I didn't know Hillary, but she was obviously well liked by the way everyone in town talked about her. Hudson rarely mentioned her, but everyone else adored her.

"I don't know. It's been years, but he doesn't seem all that interested in dating," Piper said. "He says he's married to the bar."

"As long as he's happy, being alone isn't the worst thing ever," Karissa said.

"But if he's not happy, that's different," I said.

"Hudson is happy. He's hurt, but I don't know if it's possible to get over losing the love of your life. I think he's as happy as he can be. And if he is matchmaking everyone else in town…he obviously still believes in love," Piper said.

"We should match him. I wonder if he has a Book Boyfriends Wanted account," Finley said.

Karissa snorted. "Uh, no. He doesn't. And you're not creating one for him either."

"You're no fun," Finley said.

Karissa nodded. "I've been told that a time or two. But I'm also not going to let you catfish someone."

"Fine. I just want to see him happy," Finley said.

"We all do. But for now, we need to keep Laura from going all Romeo and Juliet on Nico," Karissa said.

I chuckled and shook my head. "I was just saying the same thing to Finley today. I need all the help I can get."

16

I was still flying high at work on Monday morning. I hadn't spoken to Nico since he left my house early Sunday, but I was in a great mood. The morning was going quickly and even though we hadn't spoken, he kept flashing me flirty looks that made my entire body flush with heat and desire.

The man did all sorts of things to me.

I took a deep breath and smiled when I opened the door to the waiting room and called Damien's name. He looked slightly better than the last time I saw him. He gave me a small smile and said hello as we walked toward an exam room.

"How are you feeling?" I asked him.

He shrugged, his shoulders looking thinner than I remembered. "I'm okay."

"Are you eating? Drinking lots of water?"

"I'm trying."

"Let's get a weight for you."

He groaned and I grinned.

He'd lost five pounds. In two weeks. Not good.

"Are you having trouble with the chemo?" I recorded his weight and circled it so Nico would take note of it.

"Yeah, but that's normal, right?"

"It is normal, but your weight loss concerns me. Are you able to eat anything after treatment?"

He tried to smile but it fell flat. He sighed. "It's hard. Beth…I thought we would be together forever. Better or worse, sickness or health and all that. We weren't married, but we'd been talking about getting married. And now, she's just gone. Packed up, moved out, gone."

I smiled at him and put my hand over his. "I really am sorry. You deserve better than that. You really do. It's a horrible thing for someone to do to a person they care about."

"That's the thing. That's what gets me. You don't do that to someone you care about. You don't treat people like that. If we'd only just met, I could have understood because getting to know someone in this situation is tough, but we've been living together for more than a year. And it was all a lie. All of it. And I just feel so stupid for thinking it was real. For thinking she was a good person."

"You're not stupid, Damien. Some people suck. You deserve so much better. In fact, there's a patient I want you to meet. When we go back for chemo, I'll introduce you."

He shook his head. "I'm not interested in another rela-tionship. I can't. I need to focus on getting better."

"I—"

"Good morning," Dr. Allison said firmly.

Damien and I looked up, but Nico was glaring at me.

"How's everything going in here?"

"Good, Doc. How are you?"

Dr. Allison closed the door behind him and smiled at

Damien. "Well, thank you." He moved toward me, his gaze locked on mine and furious. I wanted to run, but I wasn't going to let him scare me off. I was doing nothing wrong. It was my job to care for my patient, and that included his mental health.

Dr. Allison reached for the tablet I held and glanced at it before handing it back to me. "How are you feeling today, Damien?"

"I'm doing okay, Doc."

"You've lost weight. That concerns me. Are you eating? Drinking enough water? Taking care of yourself?"

"I'm trying, Doc. Life has gotten…tough."

"Is that so?"

Damien nodded. "My girlfriend left me when she found out about the cancer, and I just…" He chuckled. "You wouldn't understand women trouble. I bet you have them lined up."

"Humor me," Dr. Allison said, keeping his focus on Damien.

"I…I feel like I should have seen something that told me who she is. Like I should have known she would do something like this."

Dr. Allison pursed his lips. "What I've learned about women is that they are very good at showing you what they want you to see. If you find a good one, she won't hold back. But you don't always know. And that's hard."

"Yeah, it is," Damien said with a rueful smile. "I'm trying to get into a routine and stuff, but Beth always did the shopping and she always fixed dinner. After chemo, I feel like crap and want to sleep. I usually crash, but then I feel meh for a few days. I haven't really been sick, but I don't have an appetite."

Dr. Allison nodded. "I hear that a lot. We have a list of

some suggested foods. Things other patients have told us they can tolerate after chemo. It's not dietary requirements, just ideas to try. If you can, pay attention to what sounds good the next few days. If you need to, eat that. A lot of patients can only tolerate one or two things for a few days. Even if it's not overly healthy, neither is losing a lot of weight."

Damien nodded. "You're right. I know. I'll pay more attention. And I'll take a look at the list. Thanks, Doc."

Dr. Allison nodded. "Hop up on the table for a quick exam and we'll get you on your way to infusion."

Damien did as he was asked. I took notes as Dr. Allison examined him. Thankfully, everything looked good.

Once Dr. Allison was finished, I walked Damien to the infusion clinic and started on his first dose. Once it was flowing, I said, "I wasn't going to set you up with someone."

"You weren't?" he asked.

I smiled and shook my head. I removed my protective gear and made notes on his chart. "No. I was going to introduce you to another patient, a male patient, who's also single. He has three daughters, and his wife passed away a few years ago. I thought it might be good to have another guy to talk to. Someone who would understand what you're going through."

He chuckled and nodded. "Thank you, Laura. I'm sorry I jumped to conclusions."

I patted his hand. "I understand. I didn't mean to make you uncomfortable. I'm going to get Lucas right now. I'll seat him next to you and introduce you two. No pressure, just someone to talk to."

Damien nodded. "Thanks. I think I could use a friend."

I grinned and went to grab Lucas. On the way back, we chatted about his girls and how he was feeling. He was tolerating chemo well, and since he was in the week before for his appointment with Dr. Allison, we could head straight back to infusion.

I seated Lucas next to Damien and introduced them. As I started Lucas's chemo, I chatted to both men, telling them a little about each other and some things I knew they had in common. By the time Lucas was halfway through his first dose, they were talking easily and laughing. Both men looked better.

"Nurse Kempis," Dr. Allison said. "Can I speak with you?"

I finished my notes and followed him to his office. It was becoming a regular occurrence that I was in there, something that rarely happened before. And definitely not something that was a good thing.

"Please close the door."

I rolled my eyes and did as he asked. He was behind his desk, which meant I was in trouble again. Great.

"Why are you meddling in patients' lives?"

"I'm not meddling."

"It sounded like you were."

"When? What exactly did you hear that made you think I was meddling?"

"You told Damien you wanted to introduce him to someone. I have a hard time thinking that's not meddling. The man just got dumped, and you're inserting yourself into his life. That's not what you're here for."

"Damien is my patient, Dr. Allison. I talk to him. I know what's going on with him. I listen to him. You overheard a few moments of a conversation, and if you hadn't interrupted when you did, you would have learned that I wanted to introduce him to Lucas." I pointed toward the infusion center like he could see the two men through the wall. I sucked and a breath and dropped my hand.

"Lucas? Why?"

"Because I wanted Damien to have a friend. Another man

who knows how hard this is and is also going through it without a significant other."

"Are you bullshitting me?"

I tossed my hands up and groaned. "They're talking right now. I sat them next to each other so they could. I think they're both feeling very alone, and I thought it would be good for them. I'm not matchmaking. I'm trying to help boost the morale of my patients."

Dr. Allison studied me for a long moment. "You're really something, you know that?"

I snorted. "That's not usually a compliment."

"I mean it as one, Laura. I apologize for judging you."

"Do you do that a lot? Judge me, and the other nurses?"

He shrugged. "Probably too much. Especially you. I don't always see the best in situations, or people. I'm always waiting for someone to do something that I don't agree with. I have a tendency to overreact when it comes to you."

"Overreact?"

He sighed. "Fine, get jealous and pissed off."

I tried not to smile, I really did, but I couldn't stop my lips from curling up on the edges.

He chuckled. "Go before I spread you out on this desk."

My body flashed with heat. I bit my lip and glanced at his desk. I could definitely get on board with that. "Another time."

He groaned as I let myself out of his office and went back to my patients.

The rest of the day seemed to go by quickly. Lucas and Damien talked while they were there, and Damien thanked me for introducing them when he left. They exchanged numbers and made plans to meet for dinner over the weekend.

I was good.

Ally asked me about the smile on my face when we were

in the lounge at the end of the day. "I made two patients happy today."

"How did you do that?"

"They both seemed like they could use a friend. I introduced them."

"You know who else could use a friend? Me. What are you doing right now?" Ally asked. She smiled but her eyes pleaded with me.

"Um, nothing. Why?"

"I'm meeting my sister for dinner, and I never know what to say to her. Will you come with me? Please?"

"Your sister?"

Ally groaned and nodded. "We have the same father, but Goldie is a lot older than me. Her mom was married to my dad and then they got divorced and he married my mom. My dad has always tried to get us to get along, but it's awkward. If you come, it'll be so much better."

"Are you sure? She's your sister."

Ally shook her head. "No, I need the help. Please. Usually I make Spencer go with me, but he can't tonight. I never know what to say to Goldie. Please, Laura."

I hesitated. It was totally weird, but I liked Ally. I didn't want to leave her hanging.

"I'll buy dinner."

I chuckled. "You don't have to buy dinner. I'll come with you. Do I have time to go home and change?"

Ally looked at her watch and grimaced.

"Okay, then. I'm going in my scrubs. I hope we aren't going somewhere fancy."

Ally shook her head. "We're meeting at O'Kelley's."

I nodded. It wouldn't be the first time I'd been there in scrubs. Not likely to be the last either.

Ally waited while I got all my stuff and we walked toward the door. Dr. Allison saw us leaving and stopped us.

"Are you going home?" he asked, his eyes bouncing between us.

Ally nodded. "Leaving, but not going home. Laura is going to dinner with me and my sister."

"Oh. I didn't realize."

I tried to read his expression. "Did you need something?"

He shook his head as if realizing someone else was there with us. "No. I…no. Have a good night."

I tried to catch his gaze, but he turned and went back into his office. Ally shuffled me toward the door while she searched for her keys.

"I'm always so nervous around Goldie. She's…perfect. I can never compare to her."

I smiled and kept my mouth shut. I thought Ally was perfect so it would be interesting to meet her perfect sister.

Ally and I drove separately to O'Kelley's. I parked a few blocks over, closer to Catherine Park. Ally was standing in front of O'Kelley's when I walked up. Her shoulders were bunched up and she checked her phone every five seconds. She bounced on her toes and swiped at the imaginary hair on her face.

"Ally. Calm down. It can't be that bad."

She laughed mirthlessly. "You have no idea. Are you ready?"

I nodded and followed her inside. She stopped and scanned the room. I didn't know who I was looking for, but I looked around, too. If any of my friends were there, maybe Ally would want them to join us. A bigger buffer? Maybe big enough that I wasn't the buffer.

"She's here," Ally said under her breath. She took off toward the booths on the right, winding her way through the tables. I followed behind her, trying to see where we were going before Ally stopped.

A blonde woman sat at the table in front of us. Her head

was down, staring at her phone. She wore an expensive suit and a scowl.

"Hi, Goldie," Ally said quietly, barely catching the woman's attention.

"Ally, you're here. And you brought a friend. Hi, I'm Goldie. Ally's sister. It's nice to meet you."

I shook her offered hand. "Hi, Goldie. I'm Laura. Ally and I are friends from work."

"Are you a doctor?"

"No, one of the infusion nurses."

"Wow. The work you guys do is so inspiring. I tell Ally all the time how impressed I am with her job."

"I'm basically an administrative assistant," Ally said.

"And I know how tough of a job that is. I have one, and she's the only reason I'm not always losing my mind. How's Nico?"

I bristled more than I should at Goldie's casual mention of Nico. Maybe he wasn't the only one who got jealous.

"He's doing well. Still at work, of course."

Goldie laughed. "Of course. How are you? How are things going with married life?" She shuddered then smiled at me. "My first marriage was a disaster. I vowed never to get married again. But I'm all for happy marriages like Ally's."

I smiled. I could definitely see why Ally thought her sister was perfect, but I wasn't sure why Ally didn't feel comfortable around her, or why she said she was distant. Goldie was kind and talkative. She hadn't said anything that I thought could make Ally uncomfortable. She seemed to really like Ally. I was confused.

"Married life is good. Spencer had to work tonight."

"That happens. Do you guys want drinks? Since you're here, I can go up to the bar and order for us. Pitcher of something or individual drinks? What sounds good?"

I looked at the sisters and realized neither of them was

going to decide. They were both worried about stepping on each other's toes. Which meant we could sit there all night and not get anything.

"Why don't I get us a pitcher of margaritas?" I suggested. "Hudson makes a really good peach margarita. Does that work for everyone?"

Goldie nodded and flashed me a brilliant smile. Ally nodded, too, but her smile was more grateful than anything else. Until I got up. Then panic filled her gaze as she realized I was about to leave her alone with her sister.

"I'll be right back," I told them.

Ally's eyes went wide but her mouth stayed shut. I walked away, sliding onto a seat at the bar and catching Hudson's attention.

"Are you here alone?" he asked.

I shook my head. "My coworker was meeting her sister and wanted a buffer. Can you make us a pitcher of peach margaritas? I think we need all the help we can get."

Hudson grinned. "Coming right up. You don't have a server?"

I shook my head again. "Not since I sat down."

Hudson rolled his eyes. "Dammit."

"Good help is hard to find."

"That's the damn truth. I'll bring your pitcher over in a minute. Three glasses?"

I nodded.

"Food?"

"Yeah. I know I need food. I'm assuming they will, too."

"Okay. Sorry about the server."

I smiled. "Me, too."

He chuckled and grabbed a blender to make our margaritas. I wove my way back to the table and smiled as I sat down again.

"No drinks?" Ally asked.

"Hudson is making it. He said he'll bring it over in a minute. And take our food order."

"Oh, yes, I'm starving," Goldie said. "Do you come here often?"

I nodded. "Yeah, a couple times a week usually. Hudson is a friend of mine."

"Nice. I don't get out much. I don't even know who Hudson is."

"He owns O'Kelley's. Sorry. I thought everyone knew him," I said.

Goldie nodded. "Makes more sense now. I grew up here, but I went to private school then went away to college and only moved back to the area a few years ago. I'm the tourism director for the area."

"Really? Wow. That's a big job."

Goldie smiled. "It is. I enjoy it, though. I work with local event planners and local businesses to coordinate events that will bring in tourists. This place is beautiful and special and kind of a secret. We haven't always done a great job of telling the world we exist. I want to change that."

"Without changing the beauty of the Thousand Islands," Ally added.

Goldie nodded. "Exactly. It's a delicate balance. But our limited hotel capacity helps with that."

"Would you want to increase hotel capacity?"

Goldie shrugged. "If any, it would be very slight, but I lean toward filling up the hotels we have. None of them are at capacity all the time. Most have plenty of vacancies. I want to help local business owners, not see them go under."

"My friends who own local businesses will love to hear that," I told her.

"I'd love to meet up with anyone you know. See what we can do to work together and make things better," Goldie said.

"I can give you my number to share with them. If you're open to it."

I nodded. "Absolutely. That would be great."

As Goldie keyed her number into my phone, Hudson delivered our pitcher. He took our orders while Ally poured herself a very full glass and drank half of it almost instantly.

Something was not right with this situation.

17

*A*lly kept drinking as Goldie told me about her work and her thoughts about summer activities. Some were new to me and some were the same things that happened every year, but with a new spin.

"Is this your first year in the job?" I asked Goldie.

"It is. I used to work for the events department at Bayside Hotel in A-Bay, but when this job opened up, I had to apply. I've only been on the job a few months."

"That's exciting. Congratulations."

"Thank you. I really love it. And I think with your connections, I can move forward on so many of my plans. I especially love your friend who designs apps. She's going to be my first call."

I smiled at her as Ally snorted next to me. She'd barely said anything since the margaritas arrived. I shot a confused and worried look between them but neither seemed to notice.

"Here we go," Hudson said, delivering our food. "Hopefully everything looks good. Do we need some waters over here? Or something else?"

"Actually," Goldie said, "do you have a minute?"

Hudson looked at me, his brows drawn together. I nodded so he knew it was okay to agree.

"Um, sure. What's up?"

"I'm the tourism director for the area and I'm looking to meet with local business owners about some events I'd like to schedule for the summer. I also want the chance to include events you, and others, host on our website. Would it be possible to talk through some ideas?"

Hudson nodded. He adjusted his baseball hat and shifted his feet. He preferred to stay behind the bar and not have anyone know he was in charge, even though everyone knew. Getting called into the spotlight wasn't his ideal. "I don't really plan events here. At least, not ones that are open to the public. I participate in whatever the town does."

"If you were a sponsor for an event, we could still add your business to the website. A little bit of advertising for you," Goldie said.

"He said no, Goldie," Ally snarled.

Hudson looked between the sisters then to me. I shrugged, letting him know I wasn't sure what was going on either.

"It's fine," Hudson said. "I do fairly well. And when I help out, I don't do it for extra publicity. I do it because it's the right thing to do."

"Of course," Goldie said. "And people like you are exactly the people we need to showcase."

"People like me?"

Goldie nodded. "Absolutely. You're from here, right? And you made this bar into your own. You're very typical for the Thousand Islands. A successful business owner who gives back to the community. That's why this place is so special."

Hudson nodded slowly. "It is special. But the people who live here don't want to change it."

"I don't either," Goldie assured him. "I want to make sure that the people who come here to visit know how amazing it is here. I want them to tell all their friends and to come back for a visit. I want this place to be a destination for people."

"And you think that will benefit the community?"

"Actually, yes. I've been to the community center. The first thing I intend to do is dump some money into it. The parking lot needs to be dug up and completely redone. The building itself could use some work. And the equipment they have is old and not enough. I've been talking to the director about it. She's on board."

"Amelia can definitely use the help," Hudson admitted.

"You know her?" Goldie asked, more than a little surprised.

"Her oldest is a friend of mine. James is a local cop," Hudson said.

Goldie made notes on her phone and grinned widely. "I love this town. Everyone knows everyone. I feel like I missed out on a lot by going to private school."

"Probably," Hudson said. "I need to get back behind the bar, but if you need anything else, let me know."

"Thanks, Hudson," I told him. He winked at me and tapped the table, then walked away.

"He's cute," Goldie said.

Ally snorted.

"He is. And he's a really good guy," I told her.

"Is he single?"

I nodded. "He is, but I'm not sure how open he is to a relationship."

Goldie shrugged. "It's okay. Neither am I. I just don't like to be admiring men who aren't available. It feels wrong."

Ally mumbled something I didn't hear. When I turned to ask what she said, she excused herself and made a beeline for the bathrooms.

I forced a smile at Goldie, wondering if I was supposed to make excuses for Ally or not.

"My mother never made her life easy," Goldie said. "She was jealous and nasty and made things hard for Ally."

"What do you mean?"

"She would insist on my dad being around for holidays with me and she would force him to attend everything I did. She even dropped me off at their house a few times without warning."

"Really?" I blurted.

Goldie nodded and glanced toward the bathrooms. "I don't think she likes me very much, but I try. I love my mom, but I always felt like I didn't really fit in when I was a kid. My dad had this happy family that I wasn't a part of, and when I was there, I was in the middle of everything. It was fun and I enjoyed it, but I was still on the outside. Ally and her brother were a team, and they're a lot younger than me. He moved to Texas after college, so our dad has tried to get Ally and I to be close, but she's not interested."

"I'm sorry. When she invited me, I didn't know what to do."

Goldie smiled. "It's not your fault. Just like it wasn't my fault our parents couldn't figure out how to handle our situation growing up. I was nine when Ally was born. By the time I could interact with her, I was a teenager who was mad at the world for not having both my parents under the same roof. By the time Ally was a teenager, I was living on my own, and shortly after that I got married and had my own kid. Our lives have never been in sync."

"It doesn't sound like it. But you're still sisters," I said.

Goldie's smile was sad. "Blood doesn't make you sisters. Neither does me wanting to know her."

"I can try to talk to her."

Goldie shook her head. "No, I can't ask you to do that. She'll hate you for getting involved."

"She's wanted to introduce us for a while. She keeps telling me you and I should be each other's wingwoman. Don't worry about it."

"She does?" Goldie's lips curled up on the edges. "That's interesting."

I grinned. "Maybe a relationship with her isn't a lost cause."

Goldie nodded. "Maybe not."

ALLY CAME into work the next morning in oversized sunglasses and flats. Her normally bright exterior was dulled and her smile was definitely forced.

"Are you okay?" Bonnie, another nurse, asked.

Ally shook her head, then winced. "Laura got me drunk last night."

"I did not! You did that all on your own."

"It's all Laura's fault," Ally groaned. "She bought a pitcher of margaritas."

"It was supposed to be for all of us, not just you," I countered.

"Yeah, well, my sister was there."

"Oh," Bonnie said, making a quick exit.

"What's the deal with you and Goldie," I asked Ally. I'd been wondering since Ally went to the bathroom and Goldie shared so much with me, but I didn't have a chance to ask Ally anything the night before.

"Goldie is the perfect one. Great job, perfect life, perfect everything. She's the only person I know who walked away from her marriage and came out on top. She could stop working if she wanted to, according to my dad. And her son is some teenage prodigy or something. It's all just…"

The raw emotion in her eyes said there was more going on than she was saying. She was not only jealous of her sister, but she felt like their dad had Goldie on a pedestal and Ally was just there.

"Have you thought that maybe your dad wants you to like Goldie and shares all these things so that you will?"

Ally snorted. "Nope. Why would he tell me all this stuff if it wasn't true?"

"I'm not saying it's not true. Just that I think he wants you to like her. She was telling me—"

"You two are friends now?"

I opened and closed my mouth then shook my head. "No, but she's not my sister so I talked to her last night. She's nice."

Ally nodded slowly. "Good to know she can turn you so quickly."

"Ally, you're the one who wanted me to meet her. You invited me. You've been telling me I should meet her. And now you're mad because I did?"

"I didn't realize you were going to take her side so quickly."

"I'm not taking anyone's sides," I told her calmly. "I want you two to talk or whatever. You might never be friends, but you shouldn't have to drink a pitcher of margaritas by yourself in order to tolerate an evening with her."

Ally winced at the mention of margaritas. "True. And I'm sorry. I put you in a tight spot with zero information. I shouldn't have done that."

"It's fine. I promise."

"Thanks, Laura. I owe you."

I smiled. "Have a meal with Goldie without consuming copious amounts of alcohol and we'll be even."

Ally grimaced. "Are you sure I can't give you my first born instead? Something easier to handle?"

I laughed with her and went to start my day. It was going to be a long one.

I'D JUST SAT down to lunch when a text popped up from Nico.

> Please come see me when you're available.

I looked at my food and shook my head. I was not going to run to him because he asked for me. He'd never texted me at work, so I knew it was personal and not work related.

> Just sat down to lunch. Will you be available in ten?

> Yes.

I sent him a thumbs-up emoji and put my phone down. I was the only one in the break room, which was definitely unusual, but it wasn't unwelcome. My morning was rough and the afternoon was not going to be any better.

I ate my lunch quickly, telling myself I wasn't in a rush to see him even though I was looking forward to it. I was walking out of the break room as Bonnie walked in. She looked as tired as I was and only offered a small smile.

I knocked on Nico's door and he called out for me to come in. I stuck my head around the edge of the door so he could see it was me. "Come in. Close the door, please."

I moved inside and closed the door as he got out of his seat. He came toward me and didn't stop until I was in his arms, my face buried against his chest.

I held him for a long moment, unsure what was going on. "Are you okay?"

He nodded and squeezed me tighter for a moment then let go. "Thank you. I needed that."

"Is everything okay?"

"Yes. This job gets to me at times. It's not always easy."

I breathed a laugh. "It's never easy. Even when it's easy, it's not easy. We're holding people's lives in our hands. We're pumping them full of poison and hoping it kills the right things. It's science fiction, but we do it because there is no alternative."

"Yeah. You're right. There is no alternative. And if we aren't fighting for our patients, no one is. But that's not why I asked you to come here."

"It isn't?"

He shook his head. "No. I wanted to show you the plans for upstairs. I was hoping to catch you yesterday, but Ally beat me to it. Are you free today after work?"

I nodded. "I am."

"Are you open to ordering dinner and walking through everything with me?"

"Is this a work thing or a personal thing?"

He tilted his head. "Does it have to be just one?"

I shrugged. "If it's a work thing, then I'm fine, but if it's personal, I might want to run home and shower."

He grinned. "Can I tell you it's work to keep you here and then make it personal?"

I chuckled. "I'm already sweaty."

"I don't care."

"And gross."

"Still don't care."

"And exhausted."

"Then let me take care of you for a little while tonight."

I raised an eyebrow, to which he only smiled.

"Is that a yes?"

I nodded. "Yes, it's a yes. It was always a yes."

"Good. We can order—I mean, what do you want to order?"

I grinned. "You can always make suggestions, you know."

"I'd like to know what you want."

I shrugged. "I'm open to ideas. I just had a sandwich for lunch, so something different, but I'm easy."

He snickered. "Hardly. What about tacos for dinner?"

"Sounds delicious."

"Okay. I'll see you back here in a few hours."

I smiled and nodded then moved to open the door and go back to work.

"Um, one more thing," he said, moving closer to me again. He took me in his arms and sealed his lips to mine. He licked his way into my mouth and held my body tight to his.

My hands went to his arms and slowly snaked upward. I wrapped them around his neck as he pressed me to the door. His hands splayed wide on my back, holding me to him as he leaned his body against mine.

He teased me with his tongue, alternating between gentle strokes and forceful thrusts, making love to my mouth. I could do nothing more than hold on for the ride and pray it never ended.

He finally pulled back and pressed his forehead to mine. His breath fanned over my face with each pant. His warmth seeped into me, making it nearly impossible for me to make a move to leave.

"Thank you."

I smiled at him. I slid my hand down the side of his face, cupping his jaw. He nuzzled against my palm and kissed it. He pulled me close for a hug then opened the door and released me.

"I'll see you soon," I said softly before I walked out of his office. I nearly tripped over my feet. I could have been floating.

The man truly was intoxicating. I couldn't get enough of him. And the more I had, the more I was sure I was going to need.

WHEN MY DAY FINALLY ENDED, I took a few minutes to myself in the bathroom. I forced myself to take deep breaths and push away all the bad. It was a practice I learned from a counselor years ago, one that had gotten me through all the hard things in my life.

I knew bad shit happened, but I chose to focus on the good things in life. But after days like I just had, the bad was getting overwhelming. Tuesdays were tough days because of the patients who came in. A young single mom who had to schedule her appointments around her son's preschool, a grandfather whose treatment wasn't working well, and a devoted husband and father who cried every time he came. The three of them broke my heart. I listened to them and talked and tried to encourage them, but it was hard. It was all hard.

When my mom died, I decided not to let the bad in. My dad let the bad in and it ended up killing him. I couldn't do that. I had no choice but to force the bad out and focus on the good.

Like my evening with Nico.

I splashed water on my face and freshened up as much as possible then went to the lounge. Everyone else was already gone, so I had the space to myself. I changed into a fresh pair of scrubs, an extra I kept in my locker for emergencies. I applied more deodorant and let my waves fall free. I combed through my hair with my fingers and decided my appearance was as good as it was going to get.

I went to Nico's office to find him but it was empty. His computer was off. Lights were on, but no one was there. I walked around the rest of the downstairs but didn't find him. I thought we were meeting in his office, but I assumed I was wrong and headed up to the second floor.

Nico was standing at the far end of the room when the elevator doors opened. He turned to look at me, the late afternoon sun highlighting him from behind. He looked like he belonged in a commercial.

"Hey. I wondered where you were," I said, walking toward him.

"I thought you left."

I stopped. "You asked me to stay."

"Yes, but you left." He started toward me.

I shook my head. "I got changed."

"I checked the lounge. You weren't in there."

"I was in the bathroom. I needed a few minutes."

"Is everything okay?" He reached for me, grabbing my hand.

I sucked in a breath. "It's better now."

He pulled me into his arms and held me tight. It was definitely better now.

NICO

*L*aura was shaking. Actually shaking. I'd never seen her upset, but she was shaking. "Are you all right?"

She shook her head. "Not really, but I will be. Sometimes things get hard. Today was hard."

I chuckled. "Things are always hard for me."

"You don't seem that way. You're so steady."

I shook my head. "Not really. I hide it. I revert into myself. I go home and I hide out. I don't let anyone see me when I lose it."

"I don't lose it very often," Laura admitted. "Ever since my mom...I know how devastating loss can be. I've seen it first-hand. I watched my dad completely disappear right in front of my eyes. It wasn't on purpose and it wasn't because he didn't love me, but he still vanished. The one person he lived for was gone, and he had nothing else, so he vanished, too. As painful as it was, it helped me to be a better healthcare worker. It helped me be able to let go of things. It doesn't have to be that hard for people. We never know the reason behind loss, but I have to believe there is a reason. I have to believe every loss is to help those of us who are left behind learn something."

"I'm not that evolved," I confessed. "The losses piss me off. I want to save them all, and if I can't, I take it personally."

"And do you change? Do you learn from it? Do you review a case and what went wrong and try to do better for the next one?"

"Of course."

She smiled and shrugged. "Then you learn from them."

I chuckled. "Okay, fine, I learn from them. I'd rather learn a different way."

She nodded. "Yeah."

"What happened today that was so bad?"

She sucked in a breath. "Some patients get to me. When the treatments aren't working well or when they work but take a lot out of them. It's hard to watch. I get emotionally attached, even though I know I shouldn't."

"I think that makes you better. If you care, you don't give up. You keep fighting."

She nodded. "Always." She drew a deep breath and closed her eyes as she exhaled it. I watched as her body relaxed and her face transformed to one of peace.

"You feel better."

She nodded and opened her eyes. "I do. Thank you."

"I've never been able to shake things off like you just did."

"We're all different. I don't take long to grieve. I spent a lot of years doing it and it changed nothing. I choose to focus on the good, on the bright side. I find a silver lining in every-thing, even the awful stuff. And it isn't hard to find the silver lining up here. Tell me about the plans."

I grinned, impressed with her all over again. I walked her through everything I'd discussed with Peter. She nodded and asked questions as we walked through the space. "What do you think?" I asked when I was done.

She smiled. "I think it's perfect. I think it'll be exactly what you want it to be. A combination of relaxing and peaceful with the appropriate medical requirements. When are they getting started?"

"Tomorrow. Even though I signed the contract last week, we were still finalizing all the little things. He had to make some changes to what I wanted to work with building codes and things I know nothing about. They're going to clear everything out tomorrow and start the layout changes. Peter is confident he won't need to change the timeline and will finish in four to six weeks like we talked about originally."

"Wow. That feels fast."

I laughed. "That's what I said, but it's good. The next part is hiring someone new to help out."

"Another doctor?"

I nodded. "Yep. I've been looking, but I haven't gone any further than that."

"This place is changing. I think it's good for you. Maybe another doctor will mean you can take a little more time off."

"Maybe."

She laughed at my expression. "Nope. You have no plans for that."

I grinned. She knew me well.

My phone buzzed with a text from the delivery service. "Dinner is here. I'll be right back."

She nodded and tilted her head back for a kiss as I walked by. One taste of her had me wanting to tell the driver to come back in an hour, but Laura pulled back quickly and grinned.

I got the food from the driver and thanked him then double checked that all the doors were locked and headed back upstairs. Laura was standing at the window looking out at the sunset.

"It really is a beautiful view," she said as I got closer.

I nodded. "Yes, it is." I was not talking about the sunset.

"I picked up some artwork when I went to Canada. One piece that I thought would work in the rooms at the back. If you're interested." She flipped through her phone and finally turned it to me.

I tore my gaze from her and looked at the picture she showed me. Sunset, or sunrise, overlooking the Thousand Islands. "I like it."

"If you don't, it's fine. I can bring it by sometime so you can see it in person."

I nodded. "I don't want to talk about work anymore. This is a date, you know."

"Oh, yeah? I thought this was a business dinner. You wanted to show me the clinic. I don't remember you saying it was a date." The teasing tone of her voice made my lips curl into a grin. She smiled back and licked her lips.

"I'm excellent at multitasking. I already took care of the business part. Now, we're onto the date part."

"Oh, really? And does the date part include dinner?"

I nodded and moved closer to her. The sun caught in her hair and made it glow. The blonde strands were loose around her shoulders. She tilted her head back as I got closer and shook her hair so it would fall behind her. I picked up a piece and wrapped it around my fingers.

"I'm ready for dessert," I told her. "Got anything for me."

"I think I like dirty talk from my boss."

I took a step back. "I'm not your boss right now, Laura. This isn't because I'm your boss."

She smiled and stepped closer. "Does that mean I get to boss you around?"

I chuckled. "I'm not sure about that. I might not be your boss right now, but I definitely prefer to be in charge."

"And you think you're in charge?"

I shook my head. "Not even a little bit. You call the shots."

She grabbed my shirt and hauled me to her, leaning up to let our lips collide. My hands fell to her hips, dragging her body against mine. I groaned as she pressed her tongue to the seam of my lips and eagerly opened for her.

She kept one hand fisted in my shirt and wrapped the other around my neck. She was in control. Sort of. I let her think she was in control while I moved us toward the table off to the side. When her legs hit the edge, she pulled back from me. I lifted her onto the surface and positioned myself between her thighs. The table was just the right height that I could press against her and feel her heat.

"Oh, God," she moaned, dragging me back down to her lips.

Fucking hell the woman did things to me. I'd always considered myself a loner, better off without people close to me, but with Laura...I didn't want to be alone. I wanted all of her. Every inch every second of every day.

Her nails raked down my back. She tugged my shirt free from my pants and tried to rip it apart. She laughed then frowned.

"They make that look so easy in the movies."

I took the edges and yanked, unsure if it would work. When the two sides blistered apart and buttons went flying, the look on her face was well worth the cost of the ruined shirt.

Her eyes went wide. She licked her lips and drew one between her teeth. She splayed her hands over my chest and lingered. Her hands slid up and nudged my shirt off my shoulders. I shrugged it off as she leaned forward and licked one of my nipples.

"Oh, fuck, Laura," I groaned. My breath panted out of me. My cock rose to a painful height. I only had one condom, and I was planning to make good use of it, but dammit, she was making me question whether I could handle only having her once.

"Do you like that?" She looked up at me from beneath her lashes. She wasn't asking to be coy. She was asking because she wanted me to feel good. She had no clue how good she made me feel.

"Yes."

"Tell me what else you like."

"I like tasting you. And I like watching you lose your mind. And I like feeling your body grip me when I'm inside you. But most of all, I like smelling you on me for hours afterward. Knowing I'm the only man who smells like you."

Her smile faltered for a second. Long enough that I hesitated.

"Am I not?" I asked. I needed to know. I had no intention of being with anyone else, but if she wasn't there…

"You are. But I'm not a virgin."

I shook my head. "I never imagined you were. I'm not sleeping with anyone else. Are you?"

She shook her head. There was something in her eyes, but she said, "Just you."

I breathed a sigh of relief and ignored the doubt that tickled my mind. I was telling her the truth, but I knew it wasn't the full truth. The woman I'd been talking to on Book Boyfriends Wanted…I didn't know what I'd say if she wanted to meet up. She wasn't Laura, but she was easy to talk to.

Laura licked my nipple again, and all thoughts of other women fled. She was the one who mattered. She was the one I wanted. She was the woman I'd fantasized about for years.

And she was no longer a dream.

I threaded my hands through her hair and tilted her head back so I could taste her lips again. She groaned and shifted her body to press against mine. Her scrub top kept me from feeling her skin, so we silently removed it.

I pressed her back until she was lying on the table. I covered her body with mine and kissed my way down. At her waistband, I licked her skin. She groaned and lifted her hips, shoving her pants out of the way.

I stood back and helped her remove her pants and panties, leaving her in only a bra on the table. The setting sun streamed through the windows and highlighted her body. She glowed, every inch of her begging for my lips. I wanted them everywhere. I feel everything. To taste her.

"Nico," she whispered. She reached for me.

"What do you need?"

"Everything."

That single word, raw and ripped from her lips, it cost her. She hesitated to say it, but once it was out, I couldn't hold back.

I reached behind her neck to bring her back up to sit. Our lips crashed together at the same moment I pushed a finger deep inside her. She jumped at the sudden intrusion then melted against me and moaned. She eased herself to the edge of the table to give me more room to work and held onto me.

I added a second finger and her body locked around them. I pressed my thumb to her clit and she let go, going rigid for a moment before the tension left her and she released her orgasm.

"Oh, yes," she cried.

I held her up as her body went limp. Her channel pulsed around my fingers. I teased her, sliding in and out slowly. Her soft mewls of pleasure made it impossible for me to stop. I lowered her back to the table and dropped to my knees. I inhaled deep, nearly coming at the beautiful sight of her spread out and ready for me. For me. I never imagined it would actually happen.

My first lick had her arching her back. Her hands dragged over the slick tabletop, searching for purchase. Her legs twitched. I pulsed my fingers inside her and explored her wet heat with my mouth. I wanted to know everything she liked.

She moaned and trembled and gasped. She panted as she inched closer to the edge. And when she finally went over, she cried out my name again, making me feel like the best lover in the world.

"Nico, I need you. Please. Do you have a condom?"

"I do. One."

"Oh, God, please." She whimpered and writhed as she begged me. When I rose to my feet and unbuttoned my pants, she propped herself up on her elbows and watched. Her gaze locked on my erection. She licked her lips.

"You need to stop looking at me like that," I growled.

"I can't help it," she said, not looking away, "you're beauti- ful. I just...I never thought you saw me."

I chuckled. "I always saw you. The way your scrubs stretch across your beautiful breasts. The way your ass looks so inviting when you bend over. The way your head falls back when you laugh. The way you smile at patients and put them at ease. The way you care. I always saw you, Laura."

She licked her lips and bit one gently. She nodded and sniffed like she was holding back tears.

"I still can't believe you're with me, though. I'm still the nerdy guy that no one wanted to be friends with."

She shook her head and stood in front of me. "Everyone who works for you adores you. Your patients adore you. You aren't that guy anymore. You're well respected and everyone wants to know you. Being a nerd is a good thing when you're a doctor."

I chuckled and nodded. "I guess that's true."

"I know it's true. And I really care about you, Nico."

I sucked in a breath. "I care about you, too."

She smiled and pressed her body to mine. We got lost in

our kiss and were panting and groaning before I got the condom on. She wrapped a hand around me and stroked, and I nearly lost it right then and there.

"Fuck, Laura."

"Now, Nico. I need you right now."

I rolled the condom on while she sat on the edge of the table. She smiled as I moved toward her. I sank into her in one hard stroke that had both of us moaning and holding onto each other.

"Oh, God," she whispered.

"Yeah," I agreed. I had to hold myself still so I didn't lose it before I really got started. She was tight and warm and wet. Perfection.

I eased out and stroked in again, holding her close to me and using only my hips. She shivered as her orgasm built slowly inside her. When she dropped back to her elbows, I lost all sense of control and slammed hard into her.

"Nico," she begged.

I was gone, lost, desperate to get us over the edge. Her head fell back and her body flushed. I stared at her, her breasts bouncing with every stroke of our bodies, her hair a waterfall, her curves quaking with the tension fighting inside her.

Then she fell. Her mouth opened on her moan. She dropped back to the table and scratched her nails over it. Her legs tightened around me. And her channel pulsed with her release, dragging me with her like a tidal wave.

The suddenness shocked me. I slammed hard into her, sweat pouring from my body as I flashed hot and cold. I erupted into her, pouring all of me out. She owned me. She owned all of me. Every last drop of what made me who I was belonged to her.

I knew I was gone before, but in that moment, I knew there was no coming back. Laura was it for me. She was the only woman I wanted for the rest of my life. She was perfection, and for me to even consider being with anyone was preposterous. She was it.

My head finally cleared after a minute and she was watching me with a sleepy smile on her face.

"What?"

"I enjoy watching you," she admitted. "You look…"

"Pleased?"

She chuckled. "Yes, that, too. But it's more than that. You look like this is the only place you ever want to be."

I breathed a laugh. I couldn't tell her. Not yet. Not when it was so new. She wouldn't understand. So I just nodded. "How could I ever want to be anywhere other than right here, with you?"

She smiled. "Me, too."

I leaned down to kiss her and my stomach growled loudly. She laughed.

"Maybe we should eat dinner. Since our tacos are probably cold by now."

I nodded. "Probably a good idea. Then dessert."

She laughed. "You already had dessert."

"Life's too short to only eat dessert once."

She sucked in a shaky breath and clamped her lip between her teeth. Her body flushed again. "I wouldn't mind some dessert."

Fucking hell. So much for recovery time. And dinner.

19

LAURA

The tacos were cold and mushy by the time we took a break from each other to eat them. They still tasted good, but I'm sure they would have been better warm.

Nico and I watched the sunset from the upstairs windows, sitting together on a blanket he grabbed from the clinic downstairs. It wasn't the softest thing ever, but it was clean, which was the most important thing.

We lazily enjoyed each other's bodies until the sun went down, then admitted we needed some sleep before morning came. I considered asking if he wanted to stay at my place, but I held back. Things were moving fast. Very fast. And I hadn't told him about my match yet. It felt wrong.

I was still thinking about that the next night when I met Elise and Sofia at O'Kelley's. Sofia was at a table and talking to Piper when I arrived.

"Hey," I said as I sat down.

"Hi! How are you?" Piper asked.

I shrugged. "I'm good, I guess."

"That's not very convincing," Sofia said. She leaned forward.

"What's going on?" Piper asked.

"I just…things are going well with Nico. Really well. It's weird how well they're going."

"But?" Piper asked.

"But I was matched with someone right before Nico and I started…whatever we're doing. My match is smart and funny and I enjoy talking to him."

"Okay," Sofia said, her tone adding a question.

"I haven't told Nico," I admitted.

"Haven't told Nico what?" Elise asked as she sat down. "And hi. Sorry I'm late."

"Hi, and you're not late," I told her. "And I haven't told Nico about my match."

"Colin was my match. We knew before we started sleeping together," Elise said. "No awkward conversations. Why do you need to tell Nico about your match?"

I shrugged. "I feel like I should. We talked last night about only sleeping with each other, which I am, but this other guy…"

"You're waiting for things to blow up with Nico," Sofia said.

I breathed a laugh and nodded. "Yeah. I am."

Sofia offered me a sympathetic smile that only made me feel worse somehow. "I'm not the one to talk you out of that, unfortunately. I know I would be the same way."

"I totally waited for everything to blow up with Colin. Then I made sure it did," Elise said. "I'm horrible with relationships. I pushed him away every chance I got. And he almost walked. He should have. But I got lucky."

"Things with Gavin weren't easy either. He did walk. He actually left. Things got too close, and he left. But then he came back," Piper said.

"Relationships are always going to be hard," Sofia said.

"Are you really afraid of things going bad, or is it something else?"

I shrugged and blew out a breath. They stared at me and waited, not giving me any excuse to not say exactly what I was feeling. "I've never had a relationship that worked out well. And the example of love I had growing up was debilitating. My dad loved my mom so much that he couldn't live without her. Actually couldn't. He died a few years after her. I've lived my life trying to help people avoid that kind of pain, but avoiding that pain means…"

"Means avoiding that kind of love," Elise finished for me. She smiled and nodded. "I get that. It's why I stayed away from relationships for a long time. Love brought pain. But that wasn't love. Love makes you better. Love makes you stronger. Love makes you everything you never thought you could be. Being with Colin is…it's everything to me. The thought of losing him makes me wonder if I'll survive it, but it also makes me happy I have him right now. If all we get is a few years together, I want those years."

"Me, too," Piper said. "None of us know when our time is going to be up. I know you face it a lot more than the rest of us. You see it all the time, and you grew up with it, but not everyone has a tragic loss. You need to live with no regrets like you say you do."

I chuckled at her. I nodded slowly. "You're right. Both of you. I tell my patients they should enjoy every minute and life their lives to the fullest, but I hold back on my own."

"So stop holding back," Sofia said. "I grew up the opposite, with a parent who went full force into everything. It was reckless and terrifying, and it's made me overly cautious about everything in life. I'll make you a deal."

I raised an eyebrow at Sofia. "What deal is that?"

"If you go all in with Nico, tell him about your match and

really give things with him a shot, I'll do something that scares me."

"Like what?" Elise asked. She smiled, her amber eyes sparkling with excitement.

"I'll sign up for Book Boyfriends Wanted," Sofia said.

I looked at Piper to see how big of a deal that was. Most of us were signed up and had been for a while. I assumed Sofia was, too, but the look on Piper's face said she never thought it would happen.

"Sof, are you sure?" Piper asked.

Sofia nodded. "I am. It scares me to put myself out there, but I'm willing to do it for Laura."

Sofia met my gaze. "I know you don't get it, but this is huge."

"Why don't you just go out with Sebastian instead of signing up for online dating?" Elise asked.

Sofia chuckled and shook her head. "Because Sebastian and I are not like that. And because dating scares me, but I don't want to be alone forever either."

"Wouldn't life be so much easier if we could meet the person we're meant to be with forever and not have to guess? Just boom, there you go, soulmates," Elise said.

We all nodded.

"Then you and Sebastian wouldn't have to date other people," Elise added.

Sofia laughed and shook her head. "One day you'll see that you're wrong. Sebastian is like a brother to me, honestly. He's never been someone I think of like that. At all."

"They work really well together," Piper added, "but they fight like siblings. It's funny because some of the conversations Gavin and Zoey have are so similar to the conversations that Sebastian and Sofia have. They really are like siblings."

Elise scowled.

"I need to get back to work. My break's over. I'll bring you guys some drinks and take your order in a minute," Piper said.

We nodded as she moved to the next table and asked if they needed anything.

"I'll do it," I told Sofia. "I'll tell him."

She forced a smile and drew in a shaky breath. "Good. Now I'm terrified, but good."

"Do you want help setting up your profile?" Elise asked with a gleeful smile. "I'm really good at that."

Sofia chuckled and shook her head at Elise's wicked grin and villainous hand rubbing. "I think I better keep you far away from my profile."

"Smart move," I told her.

Elise stuck her tongue out at me.

I laughed. I was lucky to have friends like them.

I MANAGED to avoid Nico the next morning since I was working in infusion and he was seeing patients, but it was my afternoon to spend with him. I knew I had to tell him about my match, and the sooner I did it the better, but that didn't mean I was happy about it.

I was also anxious about telling Dictator about Nico. I liked him, and ending things was going to be hard, but I had to do it. Online dating meant a lot of people dated multiple people, but I'd never felt comfortable doing that. It didn't matter to me if Dictator was seeing someone else or not, but I wasn't going to juggle two men.

I took my lunch break after my last morning patient was done and on his way home to rest. My food sank into my stomach like a lead balloon. I dreaded my afternoon.

My phone buzzed with an alert, and I opened Book Boyfriends Wanted. Dictator had sent me a message.

DICTATOR

Do you have a minute?

NOREGRETS

Yeah, sure. Is everything okay?

DICTATOR

Yes and no.

NOREGRETS

Um, cool. Sounds good.

DICTATOR

LOL. Sorry. Not trying to be cryptic. Listen, I've been seeing someone. We started dating after you and I started speaking, but it feels wrong to continue this when I'm involved with her.

I sucked in a breath and smiled. I was a little jealous, if I was being honest, but I knew it was for the best. And I hoped it worked out for him.

NOREGRETS

Totally understand. I was going to reach out later today for the same reason. It's hard, though, because I really enjoy talking to you.

DICTATOR

I feel the same. I hope things go well for you.

NOREGRETS

Thank you. Same.

He signed out of the app. I closed my eyes and smiled. It was a good thing. I was still going to tell Nico, but it was good.

I finished what I could of my lunch and used the bathroom before heading up front to get the first patient of the afternoon.

I took vitals and talked to each patient before Nico joined us for his exam and a review of any test results. For the most part, my patients were responding well to treatment. It was always a good day when things were going well. Unlike Monday.

By the time my last patient left, I had almost forgotten about talking to Nico. Almost. As soon as work was done and I could find him, the anxiety that had been simmering below the surface returned.

"Are you ready?" Ally asked when she saw me in the lounge.

I shook my head. "I need to stay for a few minutes. I'll see you tomorrow."

She nodded and waved and headed for the door. I wanted to run and ignore the conversation I needed to have. I hoped it went well, but it was just as likely Nico was going to end things. I told him just a few days earlier that I wasn't involved with anyone else, and now I was going to admit I'd been speaking to someone I'd never met.

I grabbed my stuff and slung my purse over my shoulder so I could leave after speaking to him. I didn't want to stick around any longer than I had to, especially if the conversation went the way I thought it would.

He was sitting at his desk when I knocked on his door. He was staring off like he was in a different world.

"Dr. Allison?" I said, snapping his attention to me.

"Uh, hey. Dr. Allison?"

I shrugged. "I need to speak to you about something."

He leaned back and sucked in a breath. He sat up straight in his chair, his hands resting on the surface of his desk. A muscle ticked in his jaw. "What can I do for you?"

"Um, well, I…I've been talking to another man," I blurted, forcing the words out before I could clamp my lips shut and hold them in.

He froze for a second, his entire body perfectly still. His eyes narrowed at me, then he tilted his head. "What?"

I took a breath and closed my eyes. I opened them and met his gaze, unwilling to hide from him. If we were going to be together, really be together, I had to tell him the truth. It could mean the end, but I didn't feel right about continuing our relationship without letting him know. Even though things were over with Dictator, Nico should know about him.

"I've been talking to another man. Texting, more like. There's this dating app, Book Boyfriends Wanted. I have a profile there, and I've been talking to one of the men I was matched with. Usually I talk to them for a few weeks or a month and then meet up and decide if we want to keep talking. I've been talking to this guy since just before you and I… anyway, we haven't met in person or anything, and he ended things today because he's seeing someone in real life, but I was going to end things with him because of you. But I thought you should know because we talked the other day about only being with each other and I meant it, but I liked this man. And it didn't feel right continuing things with us without you knowing about him." The word vomit was everywhere, spread all around the office between us. I couldn't clean it up if I tried.

"What was his name?" Nico asked. He hadn't moved. Again, he was still.

"His name?"

He nodded. "What was his name? The name of the man you've been speaking to."

I shook my head. "I don't…I don't know. We never exchanged actual names."

"What was his screen name?"

"Why?"

"Please tell me."

"It was Dictator."

He chuckled.

"Why are you laughing at me?"

He shook his head and pushed his chair back. He stood and moved around the desk to me. He handed over his phone.

"Why...?"

"Read it," he said.

I read the screen, confused. "Why do you have my conversation on your phone?"

"Because I broke up with you earlier because I felt bad about sleeping with you and talking to you."

"What?"

"I'm Dictator, Laura."

"Are you..." I scrolled through the conversations and breathed a laugh. "Wow, so we were...yeah."

He laughed and took his phone back. "I guess I can't be mad at you, and you can't be mad at me."

"Pretty much," I said. I laughed again. "Wow. When did you figure it out?"

"Right now when you were telling me. I had no idea, I promise you." His eyes begged me to believe him.

I cupped him jaw and smiled. "Neither did I, but I'm happy about it. You...wait a minute, you told me that horrible story about the woman who died!"

He waggled his eyebrows. "And you were a phone sex operator in college."

My cheeks heated at the low timbre of his voice. "I...I wouldn't have told you that if I'd known it was you."

"Why not?" he asked. He tucked an errant strand of hair behind my ear.

I shrugged. "It's kind of embarrassing. I don't tell a lot of people. Not that I'm ashamed of it because it wasn't a bad job, but it's not something I talk about."

"I think it's sexy," he whispered in my ear. He licked the side of my neck. "I think you should tell me all about it."

I moaned softly as he kissed his way up my neck and nibbled on my earlobe.

"I think you should tell me what you want me to do to you. There's no one here, Laura. Just you and me."

He wrapped an arm around my back and dragged his teeth down my throat. He licked my collarbone. I held onto him, enjoying the feel of him against me. "I want you, Nico."

"I want you, too. No regrets, right?"

I smiled and nodded. "I'm not so sure about Dictator, though."

"You're the one who gave me that name," he said with a smile against my neck. "I joined that app with you on my mind. I knew you were on there, but I never thought you were the woman I was talking to. The sexy, dirty talking woman who made me laugh."

He walked us toward his desk and pulled back when my thighs hit the edge. He raised a dark eyebrow.

"I want you to spread me out on this desk, Nico."

"Tell me exactly what you want."

"I want to watch you take off all your clothes," I said.

He hurried to follow my instructions.

"Now take mine off."

He yanked my scrub top over my head and licked and kissed his way across my breasts. He unhooked my bra and added it to the pile of discarded clothing. Then he dropped to his knees and took my pants and panties down with him. He looked up at me from the floor, his eyes dark and dangerous.

"I like giving you orders," I admitted.

He grinned and gripped my hips. He licked below my belly button. "Enjoy it while it lasts."

I smiled.

"Get on the desk," he ordered.

I didn't hesitate to follow his instructions.

"Spread your thighs wide."

I put my feet on the desktop. He groaned and pressed my hips wider with his large hands. Goosebumps spread across my flesh at his tender touch.

"What do you want me to do, Laura?"

"Lick me," I said. "Make me come on your tongue."

He dove in, lapping at my clit relentlessly. It wasn't long before I was dropping to my back on his desk, grateful he kept it clear while I gave in to the pleasure.

Nico groaned and pushed a thick finger inside as he sucked hard on my clit. I shattered, every inch of me letting go. I surrendered completely to him, my body, my soul, even my heart in that moment. I always told myself I loved him, but until that moment, spread out on his desk after sharing my most private secrets and knowing the two men I wanted were one, I knew Nico was it for me.

I just hoped I didn't lose myself in him.

He nudged at my entrance and I blindly reached for him. He grabbed my hand, and I pried my eyes open to see him. The depth and darkness in his eyes said he was as lost as I was. I was not alone.

He brought my palm to his lips and kissed it as he pressed inside me. Our gazes locked. I wrapped my legs around his hips, holding him close. He panted as he stroked in and out of me, his body tensing. Staring at him, seeing everything inside him, sent me spinning up and up until I couldn't hold back from another release.

I cried out, his name a prayer on my lips. He grunted and thrust harder, the heavy desk shifting with his movements.

He slammed into me one final time, staring at me and letting me see him, really see him.

"Nico," I breathed.

He shook as he scooped my body off the desk and pressed us together. He was still breathing heavily when he kissed my neck and said, "Yeah, Laura. Me, too."

20

NICO

"Wait, you said 'me, too' when she just said your name?" Veronica asked. Screeched really.

I winced. "It just came out."

Veronica sighed and sank back in her seat. She shook her head and stared somewhere off camera.

"I don't do well with people, especially women. I never have."

"Don't give me that, Nico. I know you better than anyone else on the planet. You are not that nerdy kid who gets beat up anymore. You're a highly sought after oncologist with a successful track record. You're asked to speak at conferences and give lectures. You're amazing."

"Not with women. I've never been good with women."

"No," she said with a sigh. "You haven't. Except me, but I know you don't think of me as a woman. I'm just Veronica."

I opened my mouth to say something but she held up her hand.

"I don't mean that as a bad thing. I understand. You're my best friend in the world. And you see me the same way. There was never any awkwardness between us because we were always the same. But with Laura, and all the other women you've dated, you put them in a different category. One that required a level of vulnerability that you struggle with."

"Yeah," I agreed.

"What we need to do is figure out a way for you to be vulnerable. I've been trying, but when most of our conversations are focused on grieving the loss of patients, vulnerability got shoved to the back. If you want to hold on to Laura, you need to show her who you really are. Invite her to the island."

"What?" Veronica knew what my island meant to me. It was my sanctuary. My home. It was the only place I felt like I could truly be myself. I opened one bedroom up and converted it into a library when I moved in so I didn't have to worry about never having something to read. I kept my bedroom exactly how I wanted it. Everything was how I wanted it.

I tried, once, to let a woman into my world. Not here, but before I moved to the Thousand Islands. I was dating a woman, Amber, and invited her to move in with me. It was…

"This isn't like Amber," Veronica insisted. "Amber was a horrible woman. She only wanted one thing from you. From everything you've said, Laura isn't that way."

Amber targeted me. She put herself in my path enough that I noticed her. When we started dating, she was shy and sweet. She made me think she was someone who understood me. She was a master manipulator. She was playing me from the start, but I didn't figure it out until she stole from me. And lied about it.

"I didn't see who Amber was. What if I'm missing something about Laura?"

Veronica sat back and let me stew on the question. It was my greatest fear. No, that wasn't true. My greatest fear was—

"You didn't love Amber," Veronica said after a moment. "You wanted to, but you didn't. You loved your mother, and her loss was…impossible. I remember when you told me. I don't know if you remember, but you were nearly catatonic for weeks. Losing someone you love takes a piece of you. Your patients have hurt you, and you've felt their losses, but you recovered from them in a few days, if not sooner. Your mother is a loss you'll feel forever. But Amber? You never loved her."

I drew a deep breath and blew it out slowly.

"I believe you do love Laura, and I think that scares you more than anything else because love is fragile. Not all love ends with pain, though, Nico. There's so much more to it than that."

"What if she doesn't feel the same way?"

Veronica smiled sadly at me. "Then you know she isn't the right one for you. But knowing is always better than guessing. Knowing means you can begin to heal and move on or decide if you're willing to wait until she shares your feelings. We don't all work at the same pace. You've always been ahead of everyone else. In school, and in life, you were always the one who raced to the front. You were smarter and better than everyone else in med school. And now, you fell in love hard. If Laura isn't there, don't take that as a sign she never will be. But only you can decide if you're willing to wait and see if she catches up to you."

"What if she never does? What if I waste my time waiting and she doesn't get there?"

"Loving another person is never a waste. It's a blessing."

"Even alone?"

She smiled. "Even alone. But if you let her in, really let her in, you might find out you're not alone."

I nodded. It sounded good. I wasn't sure she was right, but it sounded good.

VERONICA'S ADVICE bounced around in my head over the next few weeks. Laura and I fell into something of a routine, but every so often there was a separation between us. A tension that I wasn't sure about.

"Dr. Allison," she said, walking into my office one afternoon. She kept things very professional at work, and I'd stopped worrying about what she was going to say when she called me that. Well, I'd mostly stopped.

"Yes?"

"Marie Kaufman is having some trouble today. Could you fit her in for an appointment?"

"Marie's here?" I saw Marie the week before. She wasn't supposed to be on the schedule. "Is she here for infusion?"

Laura shook her head. "She's supposed to come on Fridays for infusion. She just showed up. She's in the waiting room. Tina just called me."

I nodded and glanced at my schedule. "Bring her to an exam room. Do you have time to see her with me?"

Laura nodded. "I have a few minutes. Would you like me to get her now?"

"Please. Thank you."

Laura nodded and left my office. Marie had been a difficult case from the beginning. She was one that I knew could take a turn at any moment. I was following protocols and keeping a close eye on her, but her case made me pay attention.

So did Marie. She reminded me so much of my mother, and not just because they shared a diagnosis. They were both strong and independent. My mother knew she was sick for a long time, but she was dismissed by so many doctors that she believed everything was fine. By the time they figured out what was wrong, there was very little they could do. Marie wasn't as far gone as my mother, but her chances were still smaller than if she'd come in when her symptoms first appeared.

I went to the exam room and found Marie talking to Laura. Marie looked as though it was a struggle for her to sit on the exam chair. Her friend from before was with her again.

"Hi, Dr. Allison," Marie said weakly.

"What's going on, Marie? How are you feeling?"

"I'm—"

"She can barely get out of bed," her friend said. "She's not eating much. She complains that her stomach hurts a lot of the time. She keeps trying to tell me this is normal, but none of this seems normal."

I examined Marie while her friend detailed her symptoms. None of it was unexpected, but that didn't mean it was normal. Her body was fighting itself. It had grown accustomed to the deadly thing inside her. It had welcomed it, even as the cancer slowly killed her. Now we were fighting back. We were telling the cancer it needed to leave. And the cancer didn't like that.

"When is it the worst?" I asked the friend. Marie wouldn't tell me the truth, but her friend would.

"The day after chemo is always the hardest on her. She barely gets out of bed. It slowly gets better, but this week has been the worst. She's losing weight, Dr. Allison. She's not okay."

Laura handed me the tablet with all of Marie's latest labs and scans. She was due for another scan, but not for a few more weeks. We could do one, but there was more going on. And if I was right, she needed more help than I could give her.

"Marie, I think it's time we try something else," I told her.

"What do you mean?" Her voice was raspy and weak. Her

clothes hung off her shoulders. Nothing about the way she sat there looked natural. She was in pain, just sitting there, she was in pain. It took everything in me to not react. I recognized the slump. My mother had it.

"I'm going to make some calls, but I'd like to admit you. I have privileges at East Syracuse Hospital. I know it's a drive, but it's where I always recommend people go. If you two can make it down there, I'd like you to go right now."

"Now?" the friend looked scared for the first time. She'd been tough, the fierce one, but my words took the fight out of her.

Marie, on the other hand, looked relieved.

I nodded. "Yes. If you can't take her, we can arrange for a medical flight, but it's an expensive trip. If possible, I always recommend driving. In Marie's case, driving is okay. If you're able."

"Call my mom," Marie said, reaching for her friend's hand. "My parents can come get me. You've done too much."

"No," her friend said. "I'll drive you. I'll call your parents and have them meet us there. What else do we need to do, Dr. Allison?"

"Laura can give you copies of all of Marie's paperwork, but the hospital has all our records, too. We will have them ready for you when you get there. Marie will have to sign some admission forms, but I'll have one of my colleagues meet you at the hospital. I want new scans and a full workup done. We need to find out what is going on, Marie. We will find out."

Her friend sucked back a sob. Laura patted her hand. "I know, Janice."

Janice. I hated that I couldn't remember her name. Laura was good with things like that. With patients. It was one more thing I loved about her.

I caught her gaze and smiled at her. She offered me a sad

smile back. We both knew it wasn't good for Marie, but we refused to give up hope.

I told them I'd be in touch soon and would be down to check on Marie as soon as I could be. Janice pushed Marie out in a wheelchair Laura got for them. I waited until they turned a corner.

I kept staring, even though they were gone.

"Dr. Allison?" Bonnie asked.

I snapped back to attention and focused on her. She had a tablet in her hands. Another patient. Another life that needed saving. It never stopped.

MARIE'S SCANS showed the original tumor on her pancreas had shrunk slightly, but the ones on her other organs had not. A new one on her liver was causing her pain since it was pressing into her stomach, and the growth in such a short time while undergoing treatment forced me to change her treatment plan. I was still reviewing it when Laura walked into my office after everyone else had left for the day.

"Any updates?"

"Treatment isn't working. We're going to try something else."

Laura didn't reply. I wasn't sure if she was still there until I looked up and found her watching me.

"What?"

"I've never noticed this side of you."

"What side?"

She shrugged. "The side that cares so much you're ignoring your own health."

"My health can recover. Marie's might not."

"True, but if you work yourself to death, there are a lot of other people who won't survive. Have you found another oncologist? The second floor will be done in what? A week or two?"

I nodded. "Yeah. And no. I haven't had time to look for someone else yet."

"Have you eaten dinner?" she asked after another long moment.

I sighed. "No. I have some frozen meals under my desk. I'll probably eat one of those."

"Nico," she sighed, her tone imploring me to stop and look up.

Her head tilted to the side, her blonde hair a curtain over her shoulder. The blue scrubs she wore were wrinkled but still clean. She had her weight on one foot. One eyebrow was raised.

"I'm sorry. I get wrapped up and…I should be paying you attention."

She snorted. "That isn't even on my mind. I'm worried about you."

"And I'm worried about Marie."

"I know. Why don't you come home with me tonight? I'll fix dinner while you obsess over her case. We can relax and watch Weird Science or something."

I couldn't help but smile.

"Tomorrow will be a better day."

Her smile challenged me. Not because she intended it, but because she could put work aside. I'd never been able to do the same. A case was a problem, and I had to solve it. But she was right, and I also had to eat. And actual home cooking was something I didn't enjoy often.

"Okay," I finally agreed.

Laura smiled and waited patiently while I packed up half my office. I was sure I wouldn't be able to sleep so I grabbed everything I thought I might want or need so I had plenty of work to do.

Laura offered to drive to her place and leave my SUV at the office. I debated but agreed when she said I could read emails or look through notes while she drove.

A part of me was surprised she wasn't giving me an attitude when I parked at her kitchen table and spread out everything I brought with me. Instead, she worked her way around the kitchen as though I wasn't there. She sang along with the soft music playing through a speaker I couldn't find and she cooked something that all of a sudden hit me and reminded me of how hungry I was.

"Are you at a place where you can take a break?" she asked.

I nodded and stretched. "I am. Sorry I'm not paying attention to you."

"I didn't ask you here so you could pay attention to me. I promise. My best friend is a powerful woman. She works constantly and gets into her head. She focuses so much that the entire world disappears, including her husband and kids. She told me, before she met Wyatt, that she never thought she'd find a man who understood how she felt. The singular way her mind would zero in on one thing and the rest of the world would disappear."

"Does he?"

Laura chuckled and nodded. "He does. So much so that he quit his job as the town's mayor so he could be a full-time stay at home dad. He wanted her to have the opportunity to focus on work and not have to feel like she couldn't do her job because she also has a family. It works for them, and I know it wouldn't work for everyone, but I just want you to understand that I get it."

"Thank you," I said. I pulled her close and pressed a kiss to her lips. One kiss wasn't enough and led to more. I groaned and licked my way inside her mouth, forgetting all about the dinner she fixed so I could have her instead.

She pushed me back slightly. "You need to eat. We both do. I know you're worried about Marie, so I need to know you've eaten something."

"Can't I just eat later?"

She chuckled. "Nope. Food now. Because if we have sex now, you're going to skip dinner and get right back into your research. Eat something. It'll help you."

I scowled at her, but she only laughed. I knew she was right. I wasn't going to admit it, but I knew she was right.

Dinner tasted as good as it smelled. I didn't realize how hungry I was until I had the first bite. Before I knew it, I'd cleared my plate and was going back for more.

When I finally leaned back in my seat and closed my eyes, Laura said, "Feel better?"

I nodded. "Yes. Thank you. I shouldn't have argued with you."

She laughed. "You're not going to argue? Not happening. I've known you too long to think you might agree without trying to tell me all the ways your opinion is right."

"Am I really that bad?"

She smiled. "It's not bad. It's who you are. You think through things. You form an opinion when you believe you need one and once you decide something, nothing can change your mind. You aren't swayed no matter how convincing the other side is because you've thought through every option. More times than not, I end up understanding your thought process and agreeing with you before you finish an argument."

"Wow, I really do sound like a dictator."

Laura chuckled. "You have your moments."

I nodded. My gaze drifted back to my computer.

"Want to talk through anything with Marie? I know I haven't done nearly as much research as you, but I can be a good sounding board if nothing else."

I considered it and nodded. "That's probably a good idea. This case definitely has me off guard. I don't know if it's because of what kind of cancer it is or if it's because it's being extra tricky, but it's not an easy case for me."

"Pancreatic cancer is not straightforward. I know it's extra hard for you because of your mother. All the cases I've read have talked about how tough it is. It sucks, but you always make the best decision possible for your patients. I know you will this time, too. And if not, you'll learn and make it better for the next one and the next one. There's always going to be another one."

I nodded. She was right. I was emotionally involved because it wasn't just Marie I was fighting for. It was my mother. I couldn't separate the two and see Marie as any other patient. She was different, and I didn't want to fail. I couldn't fail. But I didn't know how to win.

21

I stretched and yawned. I felt…well rested, which was highly unusual for me. A hand slid up my chest and I smiled. "Good morning."

"Good morning," Laura said. "Want some breakfast?"

I grabbed her hand and pulled her on top of me. She took care of me the night before, making sure I ate and giving me space to think. I'd never been with a woman who was understanding of the way I worked, but Laura was. She wasn't trying to pretend so I wouldn't end things. She really got it.

"I want something."

She smiled as we moved toward each other. Our lips brushed as my hands caressed her back. She spread her thighs and moaned softly when my erection lined up with her center.

"You won't get a fight from me," she whispered.

We hurried to get naked. I rolled on a condom and had Laura back on top of me in under a minute. She sat up and positioned herself to take me in, one incredible inch at a time.

Watching her face as our bodies came together was an

erotic experience all on its own. Her eyes closed, leaving me to study the curve of her lips and the flush of her skin. She eased up before sinking down again, taking me in deeper. Her body sagged with the movement. Mine pulsed in anticipation.

I held her hips until she was ready to move. She took everything she needed and wanted from me with no complaints from me. Watching her lose herself was better than any fantasy I could have ever dreamed up. She was stunning. Her breasts bounced with her rhythm, her mouth twisting in pleasure. Her hands splayed on my chest, using me for leverage. And when she sank down, she squeezed her channel and nearly sent me over the edge every time.

She came with a whimper and a loud moan that spurred me on. I stroked up into her and let go, bursting inside her. She collapsed onto me, still without a word, and we laid there, our bodies linked.

"Better than breakfast," I whispered in her ear.

She huffed a laugh and sighed. "Thank you for that. I didn't mean to lose myself."

"It was perfect," I told her honestly. "Everything about you is perfect."

She chuckled but didn't say anything else. She climbed off the bed and went to the bathroom. When I heard the shower turn on, I wondered if she would mind if I joined her.

After our shower, we hurried through breakfast and I packed up all my stuff. I had an extra suit in the office so we left early so I had time to change before everyone else arrived.

The day seemed to fly by. I barely had time to eat my lunch let alone check in on Marie while I saw my other patients.

Dr. Elliott left me a message about Marie saying she seemed to be improving. It was too early to tell if the new treatment was helping, so she recommended keeping Marie a few days, maybe as long as a week to monitor her.

"What is your plan for tonight?" Laura asked from my doorway.

I shook my head. What I wanted to do was drive to Syracuse and check in on Marie. See with my own eyes that she was doing better. But she wasn't my only patient. Leaving meant missing appointments the next day.

"Are you going to go see Marie?"

"I don't know," I answered. "I can't get there and back tonight. And driving back early enough tomorrow is a challenge."

"What appointments do you have in the morning? Is it anything you can miss? Or anything someone else can handle for you?"

I shook my head. I couldn't ever miss appointments. I was the only oncologist. It wouldn't be responsible for me to not show up.

"I know you don't want to," Laura said, "but I also know every other patient would understand and would feel comforted to know you are this dedicated to them all. If it will make you feel better to see Marie, then you should go."

"I just…"

"Look at your schedule, Nico," Laura urged.

I pulled up the schedule for the next day and found it was lighter than I'd expected. My first appointment was at eleven, and before that, I had time blocked out for…Veronica and office work.

"I don't remember this."

"What's wrong?"

"Did you rearrange my schedule?"

Laura shook her head. "No. I would never."

"Ally," I said with a laugh. "She thinks she knows what's best for me."

Laura grinned. "It looks like she does. Now you have no reason not to go. Maybe you can stay with Veronica tonight. That way you have a little extra time tomorrow with Marie."

I nodded and starting packing up my office. "Good idea. I need to run home and get some things. Then I'll head out. Thank you."

She smiled. "You're an amazing doctor, Nico. We're all lucky to have you."

I stopped what I was doing and stalked over to her. I didn't stop until she was in my arms and her lips were on mine. I kissed her like a soldier going off to war, like I might never see her again. I needed her to know how I felt, even if I still couldn't say the words.

When I finally pulled back, her cheeks were flushed and she was breathless. I wanted to drag her back in and never come up for air, but I had a job to do. I had a life to save. And for the first time in my life, I believed she understood that and supported it.

"I'll see you tomorrow," Laura said when we stopped at her car. "Drive safe. And if you have a chance, let me know how Marie is doing when you get there."

"I will. Thank you. Have a good night."

She smiled and got into her car. I watched her drive away then focused on what I needed to do.

East Syracuse Hospital was quiet when I made it to Marie's floor. The staff was taking excellent care of her, and she was resting. I looked at her chart then went to see Marie. She looked better than when she ended up in my office, but her color was still off and she had clearly lost weight.

"Dr. Allison," Marie said with a weak smile. "I didn't know you were coming here tonight."

I nodded and moved closer to her. I smiled at the woman sitting in the chair next to her and knew it had to be her mother. "I wanted to see how you're doing, Marie. Are you feeling better?"

She nodded. "I think so. Dr. Elliott started the new treatment today. She thinks it's a better option at this point."

"Yes, we spoke about it. I agreed with her."

"Why wasn't that what you started with?" Mrs. Kaufman asked.

"Mom," Marie hissed. "I'm sorry, Dr. Allison."

I shook my head. "No reason to be sorry. It's a valid question." I turned to her mother. "Your daughter's cancer is aggressive. When it was found, it was already at a point where we knew it would be difficult to treat. The course of treatment I chose is the standard of care. It is what has been the most effective with the fewest side effects for the majority of patients. Unfortunately, not all patients respond the same way to treatments. In Marie's case, the treatment was only partially effective, but the side effects were numerous. Changing the course of treatment is the best choice, but this treatment can be much harder on the body. The side effects will be worse. She will need more care to function. She will be weak and she will struggle to do normal activities. Starting with this treatment is not common because of how hard it is on patients. We go into every case hoping to disrupt a patient's life as little as possible, but it isn't always an option."

Mrs. Kaufman swallowed roughly and turned to Marie. She took her daughter's hand as tears slid down her cheeks. "This is all my fault. I should have taken a leave of absence so I could stay with you."

"Mom..."

"This is the cancer's fault," I told her firmly. "The cancer is to blame. There was no way of knowing the original treatment wouldn't be enough until we tried it. Even if Marie had someone living with her, we would have started with the treatment we did. Please do not blame yourself."

Mrs. Kaufman nodded but it was obvious she still doubted herself. She wiped away a tear and forced a smile.

Marie's eyes were drifting closed and it was already late. I said good night and told them I'd be back in the morning before I headed back to MacKellar Cove then drove to Veronica's.

Veronica and Jeff lived in an attached home in downtown Syracuse. The neighborhood had been through a revival over the last decade, and they'd bought in at the right time to ride the wave up. Their home was cozy and comfortable but was also suited for an elaborate dinner party if the need was there. Jeff loved to cook and had a chef's kitchen as the centerpiece of the home.

"You look like hell," Veronica said when she opened the door for me. She still wore a button down and pencil skirt, but her feet were in fuzzy blue slippers and her hair was tied up into a ponytail.

"It's good to see you, too," I replied.

"Long drive?"

I shook my head. "It wasn't bad."

"The patient?"

I nodded.

"Jeff is already cooking and has a drink ready for you. Come on."

I followed her up the half-stairs to the first floor. The living room had picture windows overlooking the tree-lined street. It flowed into the kitchen with the dining room at the back of the house. The first floor also had a half bath for guests and Veronica's office since she mostly worked from home.

"Nico, good to see you. Are you hungry?" Jeff asked. He

looked like he hadn't been home long with his dress pants and button-down shirt still on. His sleeves were rolled up to expose the tattoos on his forearms.

I nodded and took a seat at the island. He pulled a pitcher of something out of the fridge and poured me a very full glass. I lifted it in appreciation and took a long drink.

"Whoa, slow down. There are like four kinds of liquor in there," Jeff said with a chuckle. He put the pitcher back in the fridge and shook his head.

"I told him he should have used five so we would know not to drink so fast," Veronica said.

"Thirsty Teddy's," we said at the same time.

"You two and your med school stories." Jeff laughed. He'd gotten used to our stories over the years and heard them so much it almost seemed like he was there for them.

"If you want people to drink slow," Veronica said.

"You have two choices," I continued.

"Cheap liquor or lots of it," we finished together.

Teddy owned a dive bar near our apartment. We went in there to study many nights because he also had the best mac and cheese in the city, which was always Veronica's favorite food. We got to know him and he shared his secret with us. He always used expensive drinks and made them taste so good, people wanted more. They would keep drinking, and he'd keep making money. The local cab drivers waited outside Thirty Teddy's to make sure everyone got home safe.

That was where I got my taste for sweet drinks. They got me through med school.

Jeff laughed at Veronica and I as we caught up on life. When the conversation turned to Laura, Jeff was more than a little interested in what was going on.

"I didn't know you were seeing someone," Jeff said.

I looked at Veronica. "You didn't tell him?"

"You told me about her during a session. I'm not going to share that. Even if I thought you might not mind."

I rolled my eyes at her. "You could have told him. Anyway, yes. Laura is one of my nurses. She's worked for me for years, but it wasn't until recently that—"

"He pulled his head out of his ass and told her how much he wanted her," Veronica provided.

"She's my employee," I said firmly.

Veronica opened her mouth to argue, but Jeff interrupted her. "No, I get that. If you asked her out, she might feel like she had to say yes or risk losing her job. And at a place like yours where there's no HR, it's an enormous risk. It sucks, but you were protecting her."

"Exactly."

"I think he could have said something without it being an issue. And she's as into him as he is into her, so obviously it would have been fine. Except that he has no game at all."

"Nico? No way," Jeff said.

"Not even a little. He got all flashy with their first date and almost ruined everything. She's real. She doesn't like that. But he got lucky and found some friends who gave him excellent advice and he got a second chance."

"Oh, are you that friend?" Jeff teased.

Veronica laughed. "No. But I am the smart one who told him to reach out to those friends. He needs people. He only has us, and until I can talk you into moving to the middle of nowhere, he needs more people."

"You're moving?" I asked, more than a little hopeful.

"No," Jeff barked with a glare at his wife.

Veronica beamed at him and shook her head. "No, we're not. But I like to tease my amazing husband about it. Maybe a summer home."

Jeff rolled his eyes. "Dinner is ready, but I'm not sure I'm going to let you have any."

Veronica smiled and sashayed her way to her husband. She distracted him with a kiss and had no issue at all stealing a plate from behind him.

He just laughed at her.

We sat and talked and caught up on work. Jeff was dealing with a major crisis and getting frustrated with it. Veronica said nothing new was happening with her, but she was going to be interviewed for a local segment. I told them about work and the progress on the expansion.

We talked and drank and let the hours pass without a thought beyond the evening. When Jeff announced he had to be up early and was going to bed, Veronica said she'd be up soon. He kissed her on the way past and said goodnight to me before heading up the stairs to the master bedroom on the upper floor.

"Are you really doing okay with this one?" Veronica asked.

She'd been there for me on the fifth anniversary of my mother's death. The ones before hadn't hit me, but being in med school and studying all the things that go wrong, it sank in that my mother's death could have been prevented if she'd been taken seriously. Not a guarantee, but it was possible.

"I don't know. Marie reminds me of my mom, but it's hard no matter who it is. I watch her and wonder if my mother's doctors were trying all the things I'm trying. I know cancer happens, but…"

"You want to stop as much of it as possible. How's Laura with it?"

I shrugged. "She's fine. She lost her mom, too, but she also lost her dad and said she doesn't want anyone to experience the pain he went through, so she chooses to be happy. To see the good side of everything."

"Wow. That's very…"

"Insane?"

Veronica chuckled. "I was going to say rare. Or impressive. Most of us get dragged down into the depths of despair. Even when the pain isn't ours. For her to be able to see the silver lining, she might be just what you need in your life."

I snorted. "As long as I don't mess it up."

"Have you let her in yet? Like I told you to?"

I shook my head. "All this happened and…"

"When you get back, invite her to your island for the weekend. You both could use some time away from everything by the sound of it."

"Yeah, maybe."

"Are you staying here this weekend?"

I looked up at her. "I should."

Veronica shook her head and stood. "No, actually, you shouldn't. Most doctors don't sit by the bed of their patients when they are in the hospital. You need to live your life, too, and people understand that." She sighed heavily. "I know you think you're an island, Nico, but you shouldn't be. You have people who care about you. Your island is amazing, but it shouldn't be a fortress for you to hide out so you don't have to face the things you don't want to see."

"What does that mean?" I asked.

She smiled and said, "It means I love you and I worry about you. It means I want to see you happy, and I think Laura makes you happy, but I don't want you to mess it up because you're holding back from her. Women need to feel connected. We need to know the person we're with is in the same place we are. If she's giving more to the relationship than you are, she's going to think it's one sided. You have to be willing to let her in."

"I will. I just need to get through this case."

Veronica scowled. "There will always be another case, Nico. There will always be another patient, another treatment, another conference. You tell me all the time that cancer and mental health are the same. It's a constant battle to succeed. If you put off letting Laura in, or some other woman if things don't work out with Laura, then you'll lose her. I'm just trying to help."

She walked away before I could formulate a response, leaving me alone in the brightly lit living room. She was right. If I wanted Laura in my life, I couldn't hide myself from her. I owed her that much. I owed us both.

> Do you have plans this weekend?

No. Is everything okay? Do you need me to come to Syracuse?

> Marie is fine. I need you to come home with me over the weekend. I want to show you my island.

Thank you.

22

***

LAURA

In the four years I'd lived in MacKellar Cove, I'd never once been to one of the private islands. It felt ostentatious to be going to a private island, but it was Nico's island. Doc Rock. It was…

I tried not to think about all the things I hoped it meant. Nico was not the kind of man who let people in, but he invited me to his home. I knew he had a place in town, but I also knew his island was the place he felt most comfortable.

Which was part of why I was so damn nervous.

I packed a bag for the weekend and left it in my car in case he wanted to leave straight from work. I didn't know how long it would take to get to his island, so I tried to be prepared for anything.

I hadn't seen much of Nico all day. He got to work around lunchtime and saw patients all afternoon while I administered chemo. He was in his office when I went looking at him at the end of the day, staring at his computer with his mouth set into a scowl.

I knocked on the doorframe and waited for him to look up. He waved me in and pushed the computer away, sitting back in his chair and reaching for me as I walked closer. He tugged on my hand and pulled me down into his lap and held me tightly.

I stroked his hair and held on to him, needing the connection as much as it appeared he did. He kissed my shoulder and turned my face so he could kiss my lips. A soft, quick kiss.

"Are you okay?" I asked.

He nodded. "I'm better now."

"The trip?"

He nodded again. "Marie is doing better, but it's hard for me."

"I know. Lucas has lung cancer like my mother, and it gets to me sometimes. If he wasn't doing as well as he is, it would be harder. But a lot of progress has been made in lung cancer treatments. Pancreatic cancer is different, even now."

He smiled up at me and nodded.

"If you need time this weekend, we don't have to…I mean, I don't have to go with you."

He shook his head. "I want you there. I want you in my house and in my bed and with me all weekend. If you're still willing."

Heat rushed through me as I nodded. His voice was rough with not enough sleep and too much emotion, and the jagged edges of it scraped over all my nerve endings and left me wanting to fix him in the only way I knew how.

"Do you need to go home?" he asked.

I shook my head. "I packed some stuff just in case you wanted to leave from here."

"Thank you. That would be great. I need to run upstairs and check on the progress of the clinic, but otherwise, I'm ready."

"Can I come with you?"

He breathed a laugh. "I'd hoped you would."

Nico held my hand on the ride up in the elevator. There were a few people still working when we got upstairs, but mostly the place was deserted.

"Wow," I breathed. It had truly transformed since I was last there. The rooms in the back had been sectioned off and were closed off except for missing doors. The walls had been painted a soft blue color. Lights hung from the ceiling. Wires poked up from the floor where each station would be set. It no longer looked like the office space it once was. It looked peaceful and calming. A good place to curl up with a book.

"Peter," Nico said, dragging me across the room toward the other man. "Everything looks great."

Peter nodded. "They're doing a good job. Is it your vision?"

Nico shook his head. "No, it's definitely better. Thank you."

"You're welcome. We should be finished by the end of next week at the latest. We might be done mid-week, but I don't want to commit to that just yet."

"That's still early," Nico said. "It's amazing."

I looked back toward the elevator to take in the entire space from our view by the window and saw the large sign over the elevator. "Nico."

He looked at me then followed my gaze. He squeezed my hand when he saw the sign. "That's…"

"It came in earlier this week. Eddie ordered it for you. A buddy of mine did it. Is it okay?"

Nico smiled and nodded, unable to form words at seeing his mother's name on the wall.

"It's perfect, Peter. Thank you. And thank you to Eddie, too."

Peter nodded and finally understood. He clapped Nico on the arm and moved away to speak to one of his guys. Nico kept staring.

"She's going to be okay."

"Who is?" I asked.

"Marie. I have to trust that. My mother is going to make sure she's okay."

I smiled even as I wondered if she would make sure Marie was okay on earth or in heaven.

"Let's go. Let these guys finish up. We can head out."

I nodded and said goodbye to Peter then followed Nico out of the building and to his SUV. We left my car at the clinic and drove the short distance to the marina where his boat was parked. He grabbed my bag and his and took my hand again on our walk to his boat.

The ride out to his island was quiet. I took in the views and marveled at how peaceful it was out on the water. A gentle breeze whipped my hair around but I let the strands sting my cheeks as I sucked in the fresh air and enjoyed the ride. I understood completely why someone would want to live there.

Nico pulled up to a dock on the west side of a small rocky island. He tied the boat up and tossed our bags onto the dock before reaching for me and helping me steady myself to get out. He grabbed our bags again and moved toward the sliding glass door on the large deck.

"This place is beautiful, Nico."

He nodded. "I love it out here. It's…it's home."

I smiled at him and waited while he unlocked the door and let us in. He turned off an alarm then pushed the sliders wide open and flipped on lights as he moved through his home. I took my time, soaking in everything I could about the man.

His kitchen was elaborate but looked like it was barely used. Cabinets lined one wall and curved around to create an L in one corner of the house. The living room was open to the kitchen with an island separating them. Three couches formed a U in the living room, all focused on a fireplace and a large TV that sat dark on the wall. The other side of the open room was a library with floor to ceiling bookshelves. The shelves were mostly full of colorful spines of books that were well worn and creased in many cases. A chaise lounge sat in the corner of the room with a lamp for the perfect reading nook.

Nico walked back out of a room on the far side of the house and stopped. He looked at me. He glanced around his home and waited.

"I love…it here. It's beautiful," I said.

"I love you, Laura," he replied. He sucked in a breath, almost like he didn't mean to say the words. "I…maybe I shouldn't be saying that to you already, but I've never invited a woman here. I've never wanted a woman here. But seeing you standing there…I couldn't keep it in any longer."

I moved toward him slowly. He watched me, not retreating but not meeting me in the middle either. He'd already exposed himself to me, though. I had to meet him. "I love you, Nico. I've wanted to tell you for a while, but—"

He pulled me into his arms and pressed his entire body to mine. I could barely draw a breath with him holding me so tight, perfectly. He turned and walked us back to the room he'd come out of. His bedroom.

A large bed dominated the space. Wide windows on the wall opposite the bed showcased a stunning view of MacKellar Cove and the coastline. But the town was the last thing on my mind with the man I loved looking at me like I was the most beautiful thing in his paradise.

"Laura," he groaned.

I drew in a breath and understood what he was asking. He needed me as much as I needed him. Our gazes locked and held as we quickly removed all our clothes and met on his bed. He pressed my thighs wide and drove me crazy with his hands and his tongue before he finally sank into me, repeating *I love you* until we both came apart and crashed naked with the soft glow of the fading sunlight dancing across our skin.

When I woke up, the room was dark and the bed was empty. I heard Nico moving around the kitchen. I found his shirt and pulled it on, smiling to myself when it covered my butt and was loose on me.

Nico was wearing a pair of gray sweats low on his hips, his chest exposed. Music played softly from the TV and through speakers I couldn't see. It sounded like it was coming from outside.

"Hey," he said when he saw me walking toward him. "I was trying not to wake you."

"You didn't," I told him. I walked over and stepped into his arms, letting him hold me. "What are you doing?"

He chuckled. "I was going to make some dinner. I don't cook much, but I like to grill. Are you okay with steak?"

I nodded. "I love steak. Is there anything I can do to help you?"

He shook his head. "Nope. I was going to head out to the deck if you want to join me."

"Of course."

I helped him carry things to the deck and sat in a chair looking out at the water. Lights blinked in the distance. A glow surrounded his island, and I realized the glow was from lights that helped ships know where the islands were.

Nico grilled steaks and vegetables and sipped the drink he emptied from a pouch in the freezer. I enjoyed my drink and smiled to myself. I'd never known him to be so relaxed.

When dinner was ready, we sat on the lounge chairs and ate. I asked Nico about living on an island.

"I have a place in town, too. It's where I lived first, but I had trouble turning off Dr. Allison. I would see patients in town and I would run into families and it...I had to be Dr. Allison. Out here, I'm just Nico."

I smiled. "I think both are amazing men. When I first found your clinic, I was impressed with the way you operated. I didn't know much about oncology, but what I did know, I could tell you were different. You talked about treating the entire patient, not just the cancer. I've seen that from you. It's made me love you."

"Do you ever feel guilty?" he asked.

"Guilty for what?"

He shrugged and looked out at the water. "Veronica told me I needed to let you in. She was the one who encouraged me to invite you out here. I wanted to, so I don't want you to feel like she forced me, but I was afraid. Our first date...I wondered if you would feel the same way as you did then."

I shook my head. "That was different. That was keeping me away. This is...not."

"No, it's not," he said. He got up from his lounge chair and moved to me. He stretched out next to me, pushing me over and making us both laugh as we tried to fit on the chair together.

"I'm not sure we can fit."

"We'll make it work," he insisted. He turned to his back and pulled me next to him so I was on my side. He wrapped his arm around me and held me close. I put my leg over his and nuzzled against his chest. "See?"

"I'm glad Veronica suggested this."

He chuckled. "She's going to be thrilled you said that."

I smiled and smoothed my hand over his chest. "What do you feel guilty about?"

He sucked in a quick, sharp breath and let it out slowly. "Every day we see people who are sick. People who are dying. People who have to focus on the most basic of things in order to live. I own two homes because of those people. I met you because of those people. I have things so many people don't have, and not just people with cancer, but people in general. It just…"

"I don't think we can go through life thinking it's a zero-sum game. There will always be people who have more and always be people who have less. I believe in doing everything I can to help, whether that's with my money and financial donations or my time or my job. But money isn't the only thing that matters in the world. I've been without my parents for a very long time. I've never had a serious relationship or been married. I've never had kids. I have debt, although not as much as some people. We all live our own lives, and there are people who don't have the same opportunities as I've had. I worked through school, but I had the chance to go. My parents are both dead, but I had them when I was growing up. I always lived in places where I felt safe. I know I have privileges that so many other people don't have. I can't fix that on my own, but I'm aware of it and try to do what I can to change it. It shouldn't be that way, and yes, I do feel guilty that I have opportunities that should be available to everyone. I will always feel guilty about that. But I can't feel guilty for loving you today because someone else is losing the love of their lives. It will happen to everyone some day. And it will always be horrible, but I'd never want someone else to choose to be unhappy because they felt guilty that I was."

He hugged me tighter to his side and kissed the top of my head. "I forget that you see the bright side of everything. I struggle to let that light in. To accept that being unhappy one day doesn't mean a person is unhappy every day. We see people on their worst days. I give them the worst news of their lives. And even when I can tell them everything is going well, I know nothing is ever normal for them. They come back to me year after year, waiting for the other shoe to drop. It's hard for me to think about the good things in their lives in between."

"Especially if you keep yourself closed off from others," I said softly. "I know my friends help me to remember there are always good things. My mom was a positive person, and it crushed my dad, but I tried to hold on to her. For him, there was nothing good left on the earth without her here. For me, I looked for good. Some days it was a flower growing through a sidewalk crack. Some days it was a smile from a stranger. Some days it was a penny in a parking lot. Good is everywhere, but we have to be willing to see it. Being around others always helps me to see the good."

"Do you think I should sell my island?" Nico asked quietly.

"No. This place is a part of you. It is you. Why would you sell it?"

"You just said I'm closed off."

"That doesn't mean sell your home. It means invite people out here. It means make friends with Ian and the other guys. It means open up to people so they know who you are. Be Nico when you're in town, and let people see you aren't just Dr. Allison. Because Dr. Allison is great, but Nico…I like Nico a lot more."

I pushed myself up and crawled onto his lap. He scooted over in the chair so I could straddle his hips. He slid his hands up my thighs and groaned when he realized I had nothing on beneath his shirt.

"Fucking hell, Laura."

He lengthened beneath me, pressing against my core, his sweatpants the only barrier between us. "Any chance you brought a condom out here?"

He smiled and pulled one out of his pocket before drawing me down to kiss him. He thrust up against me, making me moan. He slid his hand between my thighs and pressed a finger deep inside me.

"You're wet," he said with a groan. "You feel so good."

"You make me feel good." I pulsed around his fingers and let the sensations roll through me. He added a second finger then stroked his thumb over my clit and made me scream. "Someone's going to hear me."

"I don't care. I'm claiming my happy right here and right now. With the woman I love on my own fucking island."

I chuckled and moaned when he stroked over my clit again. My hips rocked and my entire body tensed then I let go, coming hard in his arms.

He kissed and licked my neck and tapped my thigh for me to move to the side. He shoved his sweats down and rolled on the condom, then positioned me over him again.

"Nico," I sighed as I sank onto him.

"I love you, Laura," he said. He brushed the hair back from my face and held my gaze as we moved together. Every stroke inside sent me higher and higher. He clenched his jaw and tightened his muscles, waiting for me. "Laura."

"I love you," I said, letting go of all my fears and letting my orgasm and my heart take over. I belonged to him. I had for a long time, but I wasn't going to fight it for another minute. I was his, and he was mine, and we were going to get our happy ending.

23

NICO

I couldn't remember the last time I felt as good as I did. The last time I laughed and smiled so much. Having Laura in my home was like opening a door that had been locked forever and finding everything I'd been missing inside.

We went for a ride on Saturday, but otherwise, we stayed on my island the entire weekend. We cooked and drank and made love and I told her I loved her over and over again. She repeated the words back to me. I chuckled as we packed up Sunday afternoon for our return trip. I didn't know life could be like this.

"I feel like I'm missing a pair of panties," Laura said. She was standing in the middle of the library and looking around the room. "I swore I was wearing them before we came in here."

I walked over and wrapped my arm around her waist. She smiled and broke from her search to melt into me.

"Hi," she said with a smile.

"Hi."

"Do you know where my panties are?"

I shook my head. "You can get them next time if you did leave them here."

"Next time? You sound like you're going to invite me back."

I nodded. "I want you here any time you want to be here."

She smiled and rested her head on my chest. We stood there, just holding each other, for the longest time. The idea of leaving was not one I wanted to think about. I wanted to stay here with Laura, hold on tight to her, and forget that a world existed off my island.

"How long do you think we could survive without leaving here?" Laura asked.

I chuckled. "I was just wondering something similar."

"I'm not ready to burst the bubble yet."

"The bubble?"

Laura nodded. "Yeah, you know. When a relationship starts and you're in this little bubble where nothing can touch you and it feels like nothing can go wrong. We've been here, cut off from the outside world, for two days. We had our own little bubble. But as soon as we get back to MacKellar Cove, you're my boss again and we have other responsibilities besides orgasms."

I laughed and squeezed her tighter. "I could quit my job and just give you orgasms forever."

She sucked in a breath and froze, just for a second. I realized what I said and considered backtracking, but I didn't want to. I would give up everything for Laura.

"I love you, Laura. Nothing is going to change when we get back."

She nodded. "I love you, Nico."

I kissed her softly, keeping my desire in check and just letting her feel my emotions. What we had was not just about sex. It was about love. I didn't want her to ever doubt that.

We packed up the rest of our things silently and locked up

the house. She never found the panties she thought she was missing. I promised her we could lose more of her panties next time.

We were just about to start the boat when my phone rang. The answering service. My gut sank. It always did when I got a call from them. "This is Dr. Allison."

"Hi, Dr. Allison. We have a message for you from East Syracuse Hospital about a patient, Marie Kaufman. The message says her situation is critical and she might not make it through the night. They are doing everything they can."

I sank down onto a seat and dropped my head. "Thank you. Is there anything else?"

"No. That's the only message. I'm sorry, sir."

"Thanks."

I hung up the phone and sat there. Marie. She was supposed to be my do-over. She was supposed to be the one I saved. She was supposed to be my success story, the one that proved if I'd been able, I could have saved my mother.

But she was dying.

"Nico?" Laura said, putting her hand on my arm.

I jumped. I'd forgotten she was there. Witnessing me falling apart. Causing this pain. If I hadn't gotten so wrapped up in her, maybe I would have saved Marie. Maybe everything would have ended differently.

But no, I selfishly decided it was time for me to have some happiness.

"We need to go," I said roughly, not looking at her. I grabbed the last bag from the dock and untied the boat. I started it up and took off, going at a much faster speed than I would usually travel, the water and wind slapping me relentlessly. Punishing me.

We arrived at the marina in record time. My head raced with thoughts about Marie and how I'd let her down as I tied up the boat. I never should have left Syracuse on Thursday. I should have stayed there for the weekend to watch her myself. I knew nurses were overworked and an on-call doctor wouldn't always know what to look for. They were good, but they were never a substitute for me.

"Nico, tell me what happened," Laura said. She put her hand on my arm. I shook it off.

"Marie's going to die."

"Oh, Nico, I'm so sorry."

"Sorry? Really?"

"Yes, I'm sorry. I know she meant a lot to you. And I'm sorry for her family."

"You don't feel anything more than that?"

She shrugged and studied me carefully. "We both know her cancer was aggressive and had a low success rate. We knew it was likely this would still be the outcome. I know it isn't what we want, but we can learn from it. Maybe Marie's death will help someone else to live one day."

I huffed a laugh. "Is that what you think? Really? Are you going to tell her mother than it's all good that her daughter is dead because one day we might be able to save someone else's daughter thanks to Marie dying? Do you think that will bring her comfort?"

Laura shook her head. "I would never say that to a patient's family. It would be callous and cruel. But you know we have to move on. You know we have more patients to save. We can't let one end the fight."

"Do you want to know what I think?"

Laura nodded. "Of course."

"I think this was a mistake. Us. This weekend. If we weren't together, I would have been with Marie. I would have been able to save her. But instead, I was with you. And a young woman is going to die because of it."

Laura opened and closed her mouth. She kept it closed

and glared up at me. She nodded once then turned and walked away.

And I let her go because being with her only brought pain.

BY THE TIME I made it to Syracuse, Marie was barely hanging on. Her mother saw me and rushed over to me.

"Thank you for coming, Dr. Allison. I know you have a life, but my daughter is my life. She's the only child I've ever had and I can't stand here and watch her die. Thank you. I know you'll save her."

"I…I'll do my best, Mrs. Kaufman. I promise you."

I found the head nurse and she got the doctor on-call for me. Dr. Elliott wasn't available so the on-call doctor had been making all the decisions for Marie through the weekend. He didn't know what he was doing. He followed protocol, but protocol constantly changed with cancer patients.

As they walked me through everything they'd done in the last forty-eight hours, I knew they made all the right choices. I wanted to find fault with them, but without being there to see things myself, I couldn't know if I'd have seen or done something different.

"Thank you," I told them both. I took the tablet from the nurse so I could review everything about Marie's case and asked her to show me to an unused office.

I sat there for hours, pouring over everything. My records, Marie's hospital records, case studies, everything. I told myself there had to be an answer, but I couldn't find one. I looked through everything, but there was not a solution.

"Fuck!" I threw a file across the room. It opened and papers went everywhere. I stared at the mess, watching the papers float and settle on the table and the floor and against the wall.

It wasn't fair. None of it was fair. Marie was supposed to be okay. She was young and healthy before this. Her family doctor ignored her complaints. Or didn't understand them. It was so late when she came to me.

But I should have been able to save her.

I picked up everything that scattered around the room and stuffed it all back into the file while hating myself. I never should have listened to Veronica. I never should have let Laura into my life. I should have stayed as an island. I should have kept everyone else away because I was at my best when I was alone.

My emotions didn't matter there, so I shoved them down and stuffed all the paperwork into my bag and left the room. I wanted to talk to Marie's mom. Try to help her. If nothing else, be there for her, because she would need someone to blame.

Marie was smiling when I walked in, but it was a dreamy smile, one that people had when they teetered between life and death. She was seeing things the rest of us couldn't see. Things that weren't of our world.

"Where have you been?" Mrs. Kaufman asked when I walked in. "I thought you were going to help her."

I drew a breath and nodded. "Unfortunately, we've done everything that can be done for Marie."

"What? No. You can't be serious. You haven't even been here. She's been in this bed for days and you came by for ten minutes. You can't be giving up on her. She said you knew what you were doing."

I nodded and took in her words. I needed them. I wanted them. I deserved them. "I am sorry, Mrs. Kaufman. I should have been here for Marie. I should not have left on Friday."

"No, you shouldn't have. My daughter is dying because

you were selfish. I hope whatever you had to do this weekend was important enough to kill my daughter because that's what you did. You killed her!"

A man rushed into the room and looked at us. He looked at Marie, smiling at nothing, then to Mrs. Kaufman. He went to her side and pulled her close. "I think you should go," he said to me.

"He killed our little girl," Mrs. Kaufman cried. "He killed her. He should have been here, and now it's too late."

The man, obviously her husband, turned to her and held her. I slowly left the room, knowing every word she said was right.

I went back to the abandoned office and sat down. I stared at the wall and waited. There was nothing else I could do but wait. I wanted to be in the room with Marie, but I didn't deserve to be. I deserved to be alone. And I was.

MARIE DIED at four-oh-three the next morning. Her parents were with her. I was not.

A nurse found me and told me about Marie. She asked if I wanted to see her or the family before her body was taken away. I told her no and asked if Marie's parents were still there.

"Yes, they are. We're bringing in a counselor to speak to them. They need someone to help them understand this."

"Will you ask the counselor to come find me before they see them?"

"Of course."

The nurse left me alone again. It wasn't long before there was a knock on the door and Veronica was sticking her head in.

"What are you doing here?"

"I'm the counselor on call. I didn't know you were here."

"The family is Marie's."

Veronica's brows went up. "Your patient you came to see Thursday? The one with—"

"Yeah. I wanted to talk to the counselor to fill them in on everything, but I guess you already know. You shouldn't talk to them, though."

"Why not?"

"Because you're partly to blame for Marie's death."

Veronica leaned back as though I slapped her. "Excuse me?"

"I would have been here if you hadn't told me to go. I would have been by her side watching everything and making changes as soon as they needed to be made. Instead, I left her in the hands of people who only checked in every few hours."

"Nico," she sighed.

"No. You know I'm right. You know she should have survived. I could have saved her. I should have saved her."

"They can't all be saved."

"This one could have."

Veronica drew in a breath. "It's easy to blame ourselves when we feel as though we fell short. When we put our happiness above others. But we can not let the darkness of the world overtake the bright. We have to let the light in. We have to find joy."

I huffed a laugh. "Why? Joy is fleeting. Joy is useless. Joy can't bring Marie back from the dead."

"No, but joy is what makes the pain happen. We lost joy. You need to find it again. Did you see Laura over the weekend?"

I scowled at her.

"Is that why you're being like this? You took what you wanted for once?"

"A woman died, Veronica. A young, healthy, kind woman is dead. And she'd dead because I was too busy fucking my nurse for either of us to pay attention to her. It's my fault."

"Nico—"

"No. Just…Stop, Veronica."

Her phone buzzed in her purse and she pulled it out. "I need to go. Stay here, Nico. Let's talk after I see Marie's parents. Please."

I stood and shook my head. "I need to go. I need to get the hell out of here. I can't be here another minute. I just…I need to go."

I threw the door open and stalked away, ignoring her calls for me to stop. Veronica had a job to do, and I knew she would do it and not chase after me, so I was able to leave. Leave the hospital. Leave Syracuse. Leave everything.

I sent Ally a message that I was taking the rest of the week off and would be unavailable. I told her I would check in on labs and scans, but otherwise, I wouldn't be into the office and wouldn't be taking calls. I also told her things with Laura were over just in case Laura asked Ally anything.

I parked the boat next to my dock and tied it up. I looked up at my home, at what used to be my sanctuary, and saw Laura. I never should have invited her there. We could have spent time together in town, at my other place or hers. I could have let her in without giving her access to every inch of me.

But I couldn't turn back time. I had to accept that Laura had been there.

I opened the sliders and swore I heard her laughter. I shook my head and went inside. Her scent lingered in the air. She was a living, breathing thing in my home.

The first thing I did was strip the sheets off the bed and replace them with clean ones that didn't smell like her. The second thing I did was make myself a large drink. It didn't matter that it wasn't even lunchtime yet. I needed a drink.

I opened all the windows in the house to air the place out. I needed to get rid of her scent. The chairs outside would eventually smell like the water instead of Laura, so I just had to avoid sitting there and remembering the way she crawled on top of me and let go.

I forced memories of Laura to the side and focused on Marie. I let her down, and I let her family down. I told them to trust me and promised I would do everything in my power to help her. Instead, I let her die.

Just like my mother's doctors did with her.

Sunlight streamed into all the open doors and windows and made my home seem bright and cheery. There was nothing bright and cheery about the day. It was a day of loss.

The library was the one place that wasn't bright. The one place where windows that showcased the view didn't dominate. Maybe I could get lost in a book.

I shook my head knowing I wouldn't. I needed to process. Every other loss hurt, but this one...I needed to process this one. To find a way to move on and remember Marie.

I sank onto the chaise in the library. A flash of bright blue caught my eye. I dug between the arm and the cushion and pulled it out.

Blue panties. Laura's panties. The ones she swore she lost.

The memory of taking them off of her when she lounged in the chair assaulted me. The smile on her face and the way she moaned when she came on my tongue.

I brought the panties to my nose and inhaled deep, then I threw them across the room and screamed.

I hated myself for still wanting her, but I did.

Laura.

24

LAURA

*D*ays passed with no word from Nico. Ally said he was fine and that he was taking a few days off, but she had a look in her eyes that said she knew something else, something she couldn't, or wouldn't, tell me.

I called him and messaged him and waited, but it was radio silence in response. He was ghosting me. My boyfriend, my boss, was ghosting me.

The selfish side of me wondered if it meant I was going to lose my job. The human side of me wondered if Marie's family was okay. The emotional, squishy, in love side of me wondered if Nico would recover from this one.

That first day Marie came in, I knew her case was going to be hard. The young, otherwise healthy ones always were. I searched back through my memories and tried to recall another time Nico vanished like he had and knew this one was different than the others. This one hurt him more. I wasn't sure if it was because it was the same cancer as his mother or if it was something else.

He obviously blamed me for Marie's death, too. We'd never been close when we'd lost a patient, but I thought he would lean on me. Call me. Let me be there for him. Instead, I was forced to suffer in silence, wondering how he was.

I forced a smile and called Damien back for his appointment. His chart was marked approved for treatment, so I went ahead with everything, chatting with him as I got things started.

"Is Lucas coming in today?" Damien asked me.

I nodded. "He'll be here shortly."

"Thank you again for introducing us. He's really helped me to get over everything with Beth."

"Of course. Happy to help. This is tough enough with support. Without it's…" My voice trailed off as I thought about Marie. Damien could have ended up the same. Different cancer, similar situation. Alone. Defeated.

"Are you okay?"

I smiled again. "Yeah. We lost a patient over the weekend. It's always tough."

"Wow, I'm sorry. Was it one of yours?"

"Yeah, she was. Twenties, which is always harder for some reason."

"Ouch. Whenever someone dies, it's hard, but there seems to be a line somewhere that says too young and old enough. There isn't because we're all going to go at some point, and no one knows when it'll be their time, but it feels different. I'm sorry."

"Thanks. I'm glad I knew her for a little while, and hopefully what we learned from her treatment will help us with others like her, but it's tough to know we failed."

Damien squeezed my hand. "You didn't fail. I hope you know that. If I don't survive this, I wouldn't blame you or Dr. Allison or anyone else who's tried to save me. When it's our time, it's our time."

"Thanks, Damien. I can usually remember that, but it's been tough this time."

"Is that why Dr. Allison isn't here?"

My chest hurt with the sharp intake of my breath. I told myself I just sucked in too much, but even I could admit that was a lie. It was the mention of Nico. Casually, like it was no big deal he hadn't spoken to me in days. Since he got the call that Marie was worse off and he was needed.

"I assume so. He…it was hard."

"Sorry. I could tell you two are close. He'll come around."

I forced another smile, my face so tight it ached. My cheeks were sore from pretending everything was okay. And the rest of me…I was a horrible human being. A woman was dead, and I was more worried about the state of my relationship.

Maybe it would be best if I did lose my job. I deserved it.

I went through the motions for the rest of my day, smiling and talking to patients like my heart wasn't overflowing like a lava cake. I survived. Barely, but I survived.

I sank onto a chair in the lounge and just sat there for a minute. I needed a minute. Maybe more, but a minute was all I was going to give myself. I had to pull it together. The man I loved had dumped me. It was over. Done. And it hurt like fucking hell, but I knew. I knew what it was like to be loved by him, to love him. To go through the rest of my life without that would be painful, but I could not, would not, regret the time we had.

"You have a phone call."

I looked up and found Ally in front of me. She was watching me like she'd been standing there longer than a few seconds. Her brows were pinched together and her eyes confessed all the things she couldn't say out loud.

"You know what's going on with us, don't you?"

She shuffled her feet and nodded. "He told me a month ago."

"Wow. Okay."

"I was harassed in my previous job, and…it was bad. He knew, and he wanted to make sure everything was documented…to protect you. He's a good man. He's just in pain right now and him ending things with you—"

"He told you that?"

She chewed on the inside of her lip, which told me all I needed to know. I didn't want to believe it was over, even after what he said, but I couldn't bury my head in the sand any longer.

It hurt.

"I'm sorry," Ally said.

"It's fine. I'll take the call."

I pushed off the chair and followed Ally down the hallway. She turned at the end toward her office instead of leading me to the reception area.

"I'll give you some privacy," Ally said softly. She nodded to the phone on her desk then backed out and closed the door.

I stared at the phone like it was a snake ready to strike. I knew he was on the other end. I was tempted to hang up on him. I didn't want to hear whatever he had to say because if he was calling me through Ally it meant he was wimping out. Firing me without an explanation.

I drew a breath and steeled my spine. I was good at my job, but I didn't want to be here if he didn't want me here, so I'd accept the termination and demand a glowing review. Or maybe I'd just call Peyton and ask if I could work for her again. Run back to Winterville and lick my wounds far away from Nico Allison.

I cleared my throat and lifted the phone. "Hello?"

"Laura Kempis?"

"Um, yes?" I did not expect a woman's voice.

"My name is Veronica Charles. I'm—"

"The therapist," I blurted.

She paused, the silence stretching out between us even though I was sure it only lasted seconds.

"Yes, and his friend."

"Sorry, yes. I know that, too. Um, he's not here."

"I know. That's why I'm calling you. I've been trying to reach him for days. He won't return my calls. Ally said he's reviewing patient files and responding via email so I know he's alive, but he's holed up on his damn island and not talking."

I nodded even though I knew she couldn't see me.

"I need your help, Laura."

"I'm…I'm not sure what I can do."

"I know about your relationship. He told me. He also told me he blames himself for Marie's death. I was the counselor for her family after her death, so I'm aware of the situation. Nico…Do you know about his mom?"

"Yes."

"Okay, good. You know this hit him hard. I need you to go talk to him. Force him to see this wasn't his fault. Patients die. Things happen. It sucks, but it's never going to change."

"I'm sorry, but he doesn't want to see me. He hasn't responded to any of my messages and he told Ally things are over between us."

"Nico believes love can be taken from him. He sees it as a privilege, not a right. He thinks he can be a good doctor or he can have love in his life. He's never tried to have both, until you. And he thinks loving you caused Marie's death."

"Then I'm the last person he's going to want to see."

"I think it's the opposite. I think you're the only one who'll be able to get through to him. The only one he'll listen to. You've lost patients before. You both lost your mothers. People die every day. And none of them died because someone else lived. It doesn't work like that. But Nico feels like he let everyone down. Especially Marie and her family."

"Veronica, I just…"

"Laura, listen. You don't know me. I feel like I know you because Nico has been talking about you for years. At first, it was small things. He would mention your name and smile. He would tell me something you did in passing, like it was just a part of his day. But over the last year or so, he's talked about you more and more. He's in love with you. He has been for a long time. I love Nico very much. He's been my best friend for many years. I've never known him to be like this. I'm asking a lot of you, but I wouldn't be asking if I didn't think I knew what his reaction would be. He needs you, Laura. He needs to know he isn't alone right now. He pushes everyone away, and if you stop pushing back, he tells himself it's because you never really cared in the first place."

"I love him," I blurted, the words erupting out of me like a juice box in the hands of a toddler.

"I figured you did. Don't let him push you away. Push back."

I opened my mouth to say something else, but she was gone. I closed my eyes and felt the painful way my lungs expanded. Everything hurt. Everything had hurt for days. He'd been pushing me away, just like Veronica said, and I'd let him.

I was done.

I thanked Ally for letting me use her office and went back to the lounge. I changed while I sent a text and felt better when I got a reply. Nico Allison was done hiding from me.

THE BOAT IAN loaned me was fast. It skipped across the river, sending water behind me as I flew toward Nico's island. The sunlight was fading, but I wasn't worried. For the first time in days, I knew exactly what I was doing and I wasn't worried at all.

Okay, fine. I was terrified, but I wasn't going to focus on that part. I was going to trust Veronica and believe that Nico would be happy to see me.

I pulled up to his dock and parked the boat. It wasn't something I'd done often, so it took me a few tries to get it right. By the time I reached to tie the boat to the dock, he was standing above me.

"What are you doing here?" he demanded. His voice skittered down my spine and settled in all the exposed parts.

"I came to see you." I kept my voice light like it was normal for me to borrow a boat and drop by his private island like I'd been in the neighborhood.

"I didn't ask you to come."

"I came anyway." I finished tying up the boat the way Ian showed me and climbed out. Nico blocked my way to his house. His arms were crossed, his feet wide. The scowl on his face would have sent me running back to shore if it weren't for Veronica's encouragement that he needed me.

I faltered for a moment. Was she wrong?

I shook my head and stiffened my spine. I was not backing down. Not now. The shadows in his eyes and the tightness across his face told me he wasn't okay.

"Why are you here, Laura?"

"Because I love you. And you might hate me right now, and you might hate me forever, but I love you. I've loved you for a long time, and loving you has never cost me a patient. Loving you has been a blessing to me. It's been frustrating at times because you're stubborn and a pain in the ass, but it's all been worth it for the time I had when you loved me back."

"Loving you cost Marie her life."

His words slashed through me. His anger dug deep. It was

going to be a fight to get him to see love wasn't to blame for Marie's death.

"Cancer cost Marie her life. Just like it cost your mother and my mother and countless others."

"I should have been with Marie."

"You aren't ever there around the clock for patients. It's not practical."

"I should have been! Marie should not have died."

"I'm not going to argue that point with you. I'm not going to tell you she deserved it, because she didn't. She shouldn't have died. What we do every day is hard. We will never save them all. It sucks, but it's true. And if we can't find a way to move on, why are we doing this?"

"To save as many as we can," he spat.

I leaned back and crossed my arms. I knew he would hear it in a second. I waited.

"Marie should not have died," he breathed.

I nodded. "I know. But you and I both know she needed more support. It's not her parents' fault or her friends' fault or Marie's fault. She was very sick when she came to us. If we had started her treatment a year ago…"

"We need to educate primary care doctors to see these signs sooner," Nico said.

"Yes, we do."

"So we can save more people."

"I agree."

He sighed. "She still shouldn't have died."

"I know."

"I blame myself."

"You can't. We have an office full of patients who need you. Who need your help. One of them told me today that if he didn't survive, he knows it's his time and not our fault."

"Is that why you came here? To tell me that?"

I shook my head and stepped closer to him. My breasts

rested on his arms, tempting him to uncross them. He drew in a breath. "I came here to tell you I love you. And to tell you I'm not going anywhere. Except home because technically I'm trespassing and you could have me arrested. But I'm going to be here for you, whenever you need me."

"Laura…"

"And if you don't need me, and you need someone else, I'll move out of the way. I want you to be happy, Nico. You deserve to be happy. If I don't make you happy, I'll live with that, but loving you has made me happy."

"You're the only thing that makes me happy." His voice was guttural, pained, like admitting that took everything out of him. I stared up at him, half expecting him to collapse. "I hate that I love you so much because it means you could destroy me. If you walked away—"

"I'm not going anywhere. I already told you that. You can push me away all you want, but I'm not going anywhere. I've tried for years to stop loving you. It hasn't worked yet. It's not going to work. I'm done. I love you. Only you. And I just have to get over the fact that you're it for me."

He growled and finally dropped his arms, only to wrap them around me. "You're it for me, too. I've never wanted another woman the way I want you. You've gotten past everything I've thrown in our way. You…You make me want to stop hiding."

"Then stop hiding. Stop blaming yourself. Stop beating yourself up for something out of your control. And let's make things better."

"You really are an optimist, aren't you?"

I smiled. "No. I just have a lot of faith in the people I love."

"People?"

"My friends and coworkers."

"Which am I?"

I shook my head. "Neither. You're something else entirely. You're the man I love. The only man I've ever loved."

"I don't know how I got so lucky."

"You were smart enough to hire me. That's how."

He chuckled. "Thank God for that."

I smiled and stepped back. "Okay, so, now that that's all settled, I'll see you tomorrow." I moved to get back on Ian's boat.

Nico caught me around the waist. "Where do you think you're going?"

I shrugged. "You haven't invited me to stay yet. I figured before you call the cops on me, I should leave."

"You're not ever leaving my side. You're mine, Laura. And I'm yours."

"Does that mean you want me to stay?"

"If you'll have me."

I smiled and turned in his arms. "Like you even need to ask."

He smiled as he lowered his head to mine. Our lips brushed and all the pain from the week melted into the water around us. There would always be loss in our lives, but together we would find a way to make that loss mean something.

For now, we were going to celebrate life. Naked.

EPILOGUE

SEBASTIAN

Ilifted my bottle with the others and said, "To Ms. Georgia." Everyone moved around the group, tapping bottles and glasses together. I joined in, pretending I was a part of the crowd since I was there.

I'd known Ms. Georgia before she died, like everyone else in town, but I wasn't a part of the celebration in the past. I stuck to the lighthouse where I belonged, away from the hustle and bustle of the crowd.

I laughed to myself. Hustle and bustle were not words that described MacKellar Cove. We barely boasted two thousand full-time residents. But leaving the solitude of my lighthouse and cabin and being in O'Kelley's with a few hundred people felt like hustle and bustle to me.

"Oh, hey, I have good news," Gavin said.

He got the attention of the rest of the crowd. The ring he bought months ago was burning a hole in his pocket, so I was sure he was going to tell us he finally got up the nerve to ask Piper to marry him.

"My sister is moving up here for the summer!"

Fuck. Shit. Damn. If it weren't for the roar of the crowd, I would have sworn I dropped dead right then and there. But no such luck. I was still kicking.

Fuck. Shit. Damn.

Gavin's sister was Zoey Holbrook, the first and only woman I ever loved. She was everything to me once upon a time. Even when I knew she was off limits, she fueled my desires. I tried to forget her, fucking hell I tried, but she wasn't the kind of woman you got over in a lifetime or two.

When she came back for Christmas last year, I wanted to hate her. I wanted to be happy her marriage imploded and left her as a single mother. I wanted to celebrate that she was wounded and alone like I'd been for so many years.

Until I saw her.

Then I wanted to claim her as my own once again.

A few weeks for Christmas was one thing. It was temporary. I stayed away from her as much as I could. But the summer?

"Is she just coming for the summer?" Blake asked. Blake and Zoey had a connection. Not that it surprised me. Everyone connected with Zoey. She was…Zoey.

"For now. It took a lot of convincing to get her to come up for the summer. I'm hoping when she's here we can talk her into staying," Gavin said. He was watching me, judging my expression. I had nothing for him. I could pretend it didn't bother me, but that wouldn't serve anyone. I was pissed. Not at Gavin or Piper. Not even at Zoey. I was pissed at her husband. The fucktard who had the nerve to fall for her, promise her the moon, and sign away her life when he was done with her.

Fuck. Shit. Damn.

I wanted to kill the guy. He had no idea what he had. He let her go. And now she wasn't just free from him, she was leaving and taking his kids away. He didn't just reject her, he rejected his children. His flesh and blood. People he should have given his life to protect. But that stick dick got to love Zoey and those kids and then peaced the fuck out when he was done.

Death was too kind for him. Not that I was actually going to kill him, but I wouldn't shed a tear if a building fell on him or something.

The room swelled around me and the need for fresh air pinned me like a Sumo wrestler sat on my chest. I needed to get out. Now.

I set my beer on the table and forced my feet to carry me outside. The air was like soup, too thick to pull into my lungs. I started walking, leaning against the buildings for support as I left the scene of the crime.

"Sebastian!"

The word was muffled, like I was underwater.

I closed my eyes and waited for her.

"What are you doing?" Sofia asked.

"I had to get out of there."

"Are you okay?"

"Not even a little bit."

"Shit. I'm sorry. Want a ride home?"

I nodded and followed Sofia to her truck. She side-eyed me the entire time she drove, but I just leaned against the window, praying the door would pop open and I would roll out and not have to think about this day any longer.

Sofia parked outside my house and turned off the engine. "Need help getting inside?"

I drew a breath and leaned back in the seat. "I don't know if I can do it."

"I know. If I'd known..."

"Thanks, Sof. I don't think I would have survived these last few months without you."

She laughed. "That's what friends are for."

Friends. She made the word sound so simple, but Sofia

wasn't just a friend. She was more. Like a part of me I'd never known was missing. She'd become my closest friend in the world. I told her things I'd never admitted to anyone else. And she kept my confidence. I owed her.

"Are you sure—?"

"If you ask me if I'm sure you can talk to me about Zoey one more time, I might lock these doors and push the truck into the water. I told you I don't care. It's no different than Piper talking to me about Gavin." She rolled her eyes and shook her head.

"I guess I'm still getting used to the whole friends-with-a-woman thing."

Sofia chuckled. We'd talked many times about our mutual friends assuming there was more happening between us than friendship. We also both agreed they were crazy. "I know this summer is going to be hard."

"You don't know the half of it," I admitted through gritted teeth.

"What do you mean?" Sofia turned toward me in her seat, her brows drawn together.

"Gina cornered me yesterday. She has a special project she wants me to work on."

"What project?"

"She wants me to fix the garden."

"Um, okay?"

"That garden…it's where Zoey and I…"

"Oh. Do you think she knows?"

"Have you met her? Gina knows everything."

"Well, shit."

Yep, that pretty much summed it up.

THANK **you** for reading Laura and Nico's story! I wanted to tell this story for a long time, and I knew it was going to be a hard one for me. My own battle with cancer was difficult but very, very easy compared to that of a lot of people, and I hope this story helps to honor the ones who never give up and never stop fighting to save lives.

The next book in the series is Zoey and Sebastian's book. She fell for him when she was barely old enough to under-stand love, but she walked away before giving it a real chance. Now, she's back in MacKellar Cove with her two kids and a shattered confidence she might never repair. Zoey and Sebastian fight their attraction, but when two people are meant to be together, nothing will stop love from conquering all. Read His Curvy Ex today!

WANT MORE from Laura and Nico? They still have to celebrate the opening of the Margaret Allison Memorial Clinic! Bonus epilogue only available to subscribers. Sign up now!

MACK MEETS his match when Scarlett walks back into his life. Their chemistry is off the charts hot, and for Hawaiian nights, that's saying something! Read Mainland vs. Island today!

ABOUT THE AUTHOR

USA TODAY Bestselling Author Mary E Thompson spent most of her childhood wishing she had a few less curves. She hid in the pages of books because her favorite characters never cared what size her clothes were. Now, neither does Mary, and she writes stories that celebrate women like her. Real women who have curves, chase dreams, and find love, because we should all be happy, no matter our dress size.

Mary spends her non-writing time with her husband and two kids, watching too much TV, cheering for her hometown football team (Go Bills!), and hiding chocolate from her family.

Visit https://MaryEThompson.com/ to sign up for Mary's newsletter, **Romancing the Curves**. Subscribers get free ebooks and other fun stuff, like exclusive, members only content and giveaways, plus are the first to know about new releases and sales!